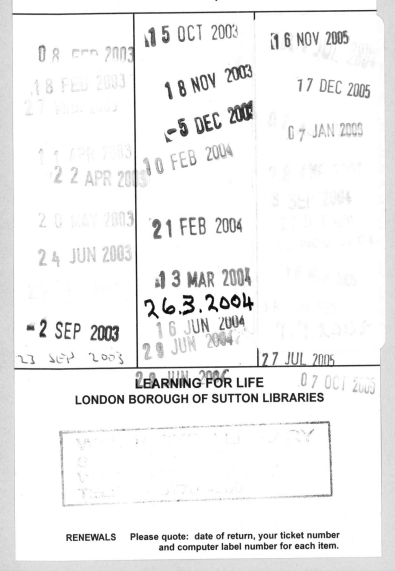

LOSING IT

Also by Jane Asher

The Longing
The Question

JANE ASHER

Losing It

HarperCollins*Publishers*

This novel is entirely a work of fiction.
The names, characters and incidents portrayed in it are
the work of the author's imagination. Any resemblance to
actual persons, living or dead, events or localities is
entirely coincidental.

HarperCollins*Publishers*
77–85 Fulham Palace Road,
Hammersmith, London w6 8jb

www.**fire**and**water**.com

Published by HarperCollins*Publishers* 2002
1 3 5 7 9 8 6 4 2

A catalogue record for this book
is available from the British Library

ISBN 00 225902 8

Typeset in Monotype Spectrum by
Palimpsest Book Production Limited,
Polmont, Stirlingshire

Printed and bound in Great Britain by
Clays Ltd, St Ives plc

For Rory

Acknowledgements

I am extremely grateful to all those who spoke to me so openly of their feelings and experiences while I was researching this book — I know you would rather remain anonymous.

My thanks, too, to Rachel Hore, Julie Davies, Carole Blake, Lynne Drew, Jane Barringer and Marina Allen for all their help and support.

As ever, I must express my love and gratitude to my family for their enthusiasm and forbearance.

Now

Judy

I couldn't move. That was the problem.

I wanted to be quick so I'd decided to take the direct route, rather than going by the back streets. It's quite a bit longer by the back way, of course, but it does mean I avoid passing − what shall I call it − the scene of the crime? Hardly.

As soon as I saw that neon sign shining out across the wet pavement I knew I'd been crazy to attempt it and I stopped dead in sudden misery. I'd done it before in daylight, forcing myself to look away to the other side of the road as I approached the dreaded place-I-can't-name. I even enjoyed the test sometimes: seeing just how much or how little it took to trigger me into going back over it all; watching myself almost disinterestedly for signs of hysteria, regret or anger.

But this was different. I hadn't realised how strongly it would make its presence felt once darkness had fallen. I turned away quickly as the old panic began to churn in my stomach, and I looked back towards the way I had come and took deep breaths in an attempt to calm myself down enough to be able to walk on again.

I was outside the post office, and, as usual, there was a pitiful little huddle of swaddled figures in the doorway beside me. Poor things, they looked more like heaps of old clothes than ever. I pulled off a glove and fumbled in my bag for some change, grateful for the excuse to stand still a little longer. I found a fifty-pence piece and threw it into the battered box they'd put out on the pavement; if they used it for Special Brew or whatever then good luck to them. I felt desperately in need of a drink myself.

I didn't get a thank you of any kind, mind you. Not even a grunt this time. I tried not to feel irritated: the joy is in the giving, and all that. But it did make me hesitate for a moment – whether because I was seriously considering admonishing them or because it was still part of my effort to delay moving on again I really can't say. I'm prepared to find my subconscious capable of plotting just about anything these days: it's taken me by surprise so many times over the last year or so while it's been dealing with the unthinkable. Giving me an excuse to avoid facing the painful reminder just a few yards ahead of me would be simple – only sensible, in fact: no point in giving my poor old brain the opportunity for another sand papering unless it had to.

I did move on, though. The moment of panic had passed and the cold wind and thoughts of the as yet uncooked casserole were enough of a spur to encourage me to walk on towards Dixons.

As I came nearer to passing the – how can I describe it? – supermarket sounds too cosy and everyday for the place that can still make my heart beat faster in remembered anxiety. Anyway, as I came closer I felt braver, and, without any intention of going in (that would be one test too many, even for my reconstructed self), I stopped outside. I tortured myself for a few moments as I looked through the large plate-glass window and searched quickly for what I half-dreaded and half-wanted to see. Funny, I thought, that here I am, looking with the same eyes, standing on the same legs, wearing – and I glanced down at myself – yes, even wearing the same coat as I did over a year ago, before it all started. So which bits of me have changed? I vaguely wondered. What makes me so utterly different from the woman I used to be, who walked into this wretched place so many times over so many years to do the shopping? Awareness, of course. Memory. Knowledge. Knowing what he did — what the two of them did. Knowing that, even as I pretend to carry on my life as if it still has a point, everything has changed for ever. That, once I've completed my pathetic little outing, bought my packet of floppy disks from Dixons and gone home again, he won't be there. That he never will be again.

Then

Judy

He was at home the evening that started it all. If he hadn't been there, then perhaps – no, I won't let myself go through all those ifs again. Not any more: that's over. I know I can't stop myself replaying it all like an old film, but I do surely have enough strength now to recognise that it can't be changed.

I can still picture him that evening. Or can I? Perhaps I'm imagining it. Maybe it's another sign of this bloody crafty subconscious of mine inventing the bits that have got lost. I could be conjuring up an image from any one of the thousands of evenings of our marriage. It wasn't unusual for Charlie to be home first, and that day didn't feel any different from hundreds of others before it. Why should it? Nothing signalled that it was to be the start of the end. In fact all that strikes me now about that evening was just how extraordinarily ordinary it was: the way I remember it, it was a masterpiece of uneventful domesticity hiding the horrors to come.

He was sitting reading the paper in the sitting room. And, no, it's not my imagination: I can see it clearly. He was in the large green armchair on the far side of the fire and I saw his profile silhouetted against the striped wallpaper just before he noticed I was there. He'd already put on his old burgundy cardigan, and he'd loosened his tie and pulled it away from the collar of his blue shirt. (God, it's fascinating how much I do remember: I suppose, as well as being the opening scene of the impending terrible drama, it was also the last scene of my other life.) He looked up as I came in, and put the paper down in a rustling heap on his lap.

'Hi,' he said, then, after a pause, 'What?'

'How do you mean?' I answered, knowing, of course, exactly what he meant. I was quite aware of the hint of weary resignation that I'd allowed to settle onto my features as he greeted me. Although I've no idea now which school I'd been inspecting, I do remember I'd had a particularly frustrating and tiring day, but I don't think there was any other excuse for taking it out on him. It wasn't as if he didn't work just as hard as I did – more so, probably.

'You look tired. Or something.' Oh, how subtle is the language of the long married! How many layers of subtext lurked dangerously under the innocent words! Why didn't you say it, Charlie? You, of all people, who were always so good with words in court; how clearly and succinctly you could have put it. 'You look fed up and resentful. You clearly disapprove of the fact that I am happily relaxing in this chair when you have only just come in from working all day,' might have been near the mark. But the habit of years allowed us to speak without acknowledging a fraction of what was really being said. What a waste.

'No, just tired. You're right. I am. Exhausted.' And I turned and walked out of the sitting room, and the hairline crack, which might just have opened up into a discussion of how we really felt, was safely papered over – again.

I put my briefcase down at the foot of the stairs while I hung up my coat, and called out over my shoulder to him as I moved into the kitchen, 'I haven't shopped yet – I just couldn't face it.'

'Hang on – I can't hear you. I'll come.'

I heard him grunting as he pulled himself up out of his

armchair, and felt a tiny stab of satisfaction at the fact that I'd got him to move. He stood in the kitchen doorway leaning against the frame, the newspaper still in one hand.

'What did you say, darling?'

'Oh, you shouldn't have moved – it's not important. Just that we're out of everything and I haven't shopped yet, that's all. I'll go in a minute. I'm having a cup of tea first. Do you want one?'

I looked up and smiled at him as I switched on the kettle. He'd pushed his half-moon glasses up on top of his head, and looked, even more than he usually did, like an eccentric professor. Or how one should look. His eyebrows were tufts of permanent surprise, swooping up at the outer edges in a sort of wild abandon above his ridiculously bright blue eyes. (His habit of twisting and curling the brows upwards with his fingertips while he studied a brief or read the paper used to irritate me, but so many things used to irritate me then.) The arms of his glasses had pushed some of his still thick, greying hair into ruffled wings on either side of his face, and I noticed his cardigan was wrongly buttoned. I smiled at him again, feeling a familiar echo of what I took at the time to be sentimental fondness. Now I know it for what it really was – love, of course.

'Darling, come over here,' I said. 'You're done up all wrong. Here, let me do it. Honestly, you're worse than a child.'

I remember I reached a hand up to his face and stroked his hair, trying in vain to smooth it back tidily behind his ears. It was a habit I had, and my fingers miss the feel of it as much as my ears miss the sound of his voice, and my body misses touching his in our large double bed. Such an attractive, confident man he was then – or so I thought. And as for me – so much I took for granted: all of it, at the time.

'The whole point of half-glasses,' I went on smugly, 'is that you don't have to take them off or shove them on top of your head when you're not using them. You're meant to peer over them. You look like a startled koala when you push them up like that, you silly old thing.'

'Nonsense.' Charlie laughed. Yes, he did; he laughed, I'm sure of it. He used to laugh a lot, and it was often at something I'd said; I can't have made that up, can I? And that's the most important part of a successful relationship, they're always telling us. A sense of humour. The couple that laughs together stays together. Make your man laugh. Well, yes. But not enough, apparently, in my case.

'Anyway,' he went on, 'I can't bear peering over them at the world. It makes me feel like I'm playing the old fogey. The dull, dusty barrister.'

And I didn't answer, did I? I just raised my eyebrows and threw him one of those knowing looks of mine that I used to think were so clever, as I finished buttoning up his cardigan and then gave him a dismissive pat on the belly. A subtle reminder in a look and a gesture that he was older, fatter and greyer than I was, and that his career was, indeed, a little dusty. At the same time, it was quick reassurance for me of my own relatively good shape and tactfully tinted hair. Oh yes, it was – don't deny it. At least I can be honest with myself now, one of the few comforts I have left.

Charlie sighed and went to walk out of the kitchen, then stopped and turned in the doorway, pulling the glasses back onto his nose and looking at me over the top of them. 'And I know I could indeed be considered an old has-been but I'm not quite ready to agree to it. Not just yet.' And, although he was joking, the acknowledgement of my casual put-down wasn't lost on me.

'Of course not, darling,' I said. 'You're in your prime. As

is your wife.' I walked over to the fridge and put a hand on one hip as I opened it and scanned the contents. 'Not too exciting, is it? I'll go in a minute.'

'Hmm?'

'I'll go in a minute,' I repeated. 'Shopping.'

'Oh, haven't you been?'

'Oh, for God's sake, Charlie: no, I haven't been. I said. I told you when I first came in − I do wish you'd listen, it'd make life so much simpler if I didn't have to repeat myself all the time.'

'Sorry, I expect I was thinking about something else.'

There was a short pause, but, although he was still looking at me, he didn't go on.

'What − work?'

'Hmm?'

'Were you thinking about work, do you mean?'

'No. Just life. You know.' He smiled as he said it, but I felt the tiniest hint of something chilly and − sinister settling into the silence that followed. Neither of us acknowledged it. 'I'll go, if you like,' Charlie went on. 'You look far more tired than I feel. What shall I get?'

'No, it's all right. I don't know what I was going to get, I hadn't decided. I'll go. I can't be bothered to go all the way to Sainsbury's − I'll pop round to SavaMart and get a bit of mince and do a shepherd's pie, OK? Even the ghastly SavaMart doesn't get mince too wrong.'

(There. I've said it. Named it. Not exactly out loud, but at least in my thoughts. SavaMart: what a drearily unattractive word to be the cause of such pain as I form its ugly syllables in my head.)

'No, I insist. I'll go. How much do I get? Is it just us?'

'Oh, darling, are you sure? I really don't mind, you know.'

Charlie put the newspaper down on the corner of the kitchen dresser and felt in his trouser pocket.

'No, it's all settled. Just tell me how much mince and – that's fine, look, I've got twenty pounds; that should cover it, shouldn't it?'

'Good God, I should hope so. It's us and Ben – Sally's out. Get about a pound and a half of mince and – oh, damn, it won't say that any more. Just get a couple of those ready packs and a large bag of potatoes. I've got onions. Oh, and some bread and a small milk.'

'Right. Put your feet up and drink your tea and I'll be back in a flash. I'm far quicker at shopping than you are.'

And I did. I'm sure of it. As he went out into the evening and made his way towards that place where it all began, towards the start of the nightmare – I made myself a cup of tea.

Stacey

My feet hurt and I'm shattered. He ain't looked at me today – not even one fucking glance. It really pisses me off. I ain't never rung my bell once – not like Sheila, who rings it every five minutes. She takes the bar codes off – I swear she does – just so's she can ring her bell. Then if Mrs Peters comes over, suddenly she don't need nothing. Mrs Peters is stood there, waiting, and suddenly Sheila don't have a problem. But if *he* comes over it's all, 'Oh, I'm sorry to ring again, Mr Chipstead, but there's no price on this.' She leans forward and lets him look down her overall at her little pushed-up tits. They don't exist, her tits. They're just little bumps pushed up on all that Wonderbra padding. If you had X-ray eyes you'd

14

see there's half a tit there, sitting on a shelf of wadding.

My bum hurts too. There's a new sore patch on it. I'll have to rub it later and it'll hurt more: it's just like when Auntie Madge spent all that time in bed with her leg and got them awful raw bits on her hip 'cos she couldn't turn enough. Disgusting.

There's a picture in *Hello!* this week of Dawn French and she looks really pretty. If I could just get my hair like hers I could – no, it's her eyes. She's got beautiful eyes. My mum says I have too, and even Sheila once said she wished she had eyes like mine – topaz or some crap, she called them – but I don't think mine are all smiley like Dawn's. And why do her clothes always look good? My top always seems to catch and get stuck in those folds round my waist – then it sticks right out at the back until someone tells me. Hers never do that.

Because you're three times her size, you stupid fucker, that's why. She's normal – she's big, but she ain't gross like you. You're disgusting. Of course Mr C don't look at you – why should he? You're revolting.

My mum gave me that new diet sheet that came with the paper yesterday. Try it yourself, I said. If you're so clever at telling me how to do it, try it your fucking self. She had a laugh when I said that – she's got a good sense of humour, my mum, I'll give her that. But I've had a look at it, anyway: it don't sound so bad. All protein again. No skin. No carbohydrates. It ain't that different from the one Crystal told me about in her letter last week that all the stars are doing over there. She says Oprah lost half her body weight in three days. Or was it six weeks? Anyway, it must be good if people like her are doing it. They can afford all them personal trainers and that, so if they choose the diet instead it must be really easy. All lean protein, that's the idea. I told Ma to get a pack of them chicken breasts when she's down at Iceland tomorrow. No skin – a pack of them skinless ones. 'You got to be joking, Stacey,' she says. 'I'll get a pack of sausages – that's half the price. That's meat,' she says. I says, 'Don't be daft, Mum, that's not lean protein; that's bread and stuff. That's no good. Get the chicken breasts and we'll do without the biscuits. And no bread, all right? Don't get no bread and no biscuits.'

So I'll start the lean protein tomorrow. We're having pie and chips for tea tonight so I'll just eat the meat and the chips and leave off the pastry. That'll ease me in.

Charlie

I loathe SavaMart but I couldn't face telling Judy I'd rather walk to the car and drive to Sainsbury's. I knew it would start the whole boring discussion all over again and it just wasn't worth it: there's only so much time I'm prepared to donate to questions of mince and potatoes and the quota had been well and truly fulfilled already. A brisk outing in the crisp November air would do me good, in any case, and, once out of the house and round the corner, it would only take me a couple of minutes to walk down Palace Street and into Victoria Street itself. With luck I could be back within fifteen minutes or so and thus gain a bit of kudos for doing the shopping quickly into the bargain. Always helps the atmosphere at home. Especially on days like today when she has her 'it's all very well for you to lounge about in that chair' look when she comes in. I also thought it might help to shake off the unpleasant feeling of ennui that had been stalking me again since lunch time. However much I

16

try to talk myself down from these moods – mentally listing all the pros in my life like in some puerile magazine self-help quiz – nothing but brisk physical action has much effect. There seems to be something immensely helpful in the mere act of walking away from the house, or from Judy or from whatever has triggered the mood: as if I can persuade my mind to distance itself as easily as I can my body.

The shop was unpleasantly full, and I picked up a basket instead of trying to negotiate the packed aisles with a trolley. I'm extremely organised in my shopping, and, unlike Judy, I would leave the supermarket with only the items I intended to buy, so the basket would be fine. A quick plan of strategy – I'd been often enough to know pretty much where to find the five items I needed – and I launched into the heart of the store, confident that I could make my way round the various sections without too much retracing of steps.

There was a delicious and strangely comforting smell of warm bread wafting about, contrasting oddly with the packaged, mass-produced look of the food on the shelves on either side. I knew it simply meant, of course, that the ready-made loaves had just come out of being finished off in the oven, but for a second or two I imagined I was somewhere in France, strolling to a small café in the early morning to drink a café au lait and pick up a couple of recently baked croissants and a baguette. It reminded me of the last holiday Judy, the children and I took together a couple of years ago in a rented house in Provence, when my favourite part of each day was my solo walk into the village. I've never been the best companion on holiday, but that one pointed up even more sharply than usual just how much our little family unit is changing, and how far our interests have diverged over the last few years. None of us liked to admit it, but I think we all felt a sense of relief once back home and away from the obligatory closeness of a family holiday.

The cooking smell gave enough hint of good food to be seductive, anyway — no doubt fully intended — and I picked up a loaf in its Cellophane packet, still warm. I resisted the temptation to break off the crusty tip on the spot and eat it, and continued on quickly round the shop, picking up mince, potatoes and milk as I went. Congratulating myself on the speed of the venture, I looked over to the checkouts and was depressed to see how busy they were. This is another thing I'm proud of: my ability to pick the quickest queue at the beastly checkout. I sized them up smartly and found one that was distinctly shorter than the others and — and this is a crucial point in the fine judgement of queues, of course — the trolleys in it didn't appear to be particularly full. I made a beeline for it, brushing past an elderly lady who tutted at me as I did so.

'Sorry,' I said, 'just trying to —'

'I can see what you're doing,' she interrupted, 'it's the way you're doing it that is unnecessary.'

Very precise, I thought. You sound like one of my juniors.

'Sorry,' I said again, attempting a regretful smile. 'Do you want to go ahead of me?'

'No, no, you go ahead if you're in such a rush.'

Wonderfully full of put-upon self-sacrifice, that reply was. Almost up to the standard of my mother on one of her better days, or Judy on one of her worse. I gave her what I hoped was another of my most charming smiles and joined the queue ahead of her, giving in to temptation and pulling the tip off the still-warm baguette to nibble as I prepared to wait my turn.

There were three people ahead of me. The young man

in the process of stacking his goods onto the moving belt had lank hair falling forward out of a hooded anorak and sniffed as he unloaded his basket. I could see a tin of beans, two packets of sliced bread, four yoghurts strapped together under a brightly coloured foil topping and two large bottles of Coke. As they neared the till they were picked up by the extremely chunky-looking arm of the checkout girl, and then swept briskly in front of the beeping eye of the scanner.

I leant forward to get a better view. That arm was more than chunky. It really did look extraordinarily big. And the fingers on its end were — sausages. The cliché description had leapt into my head and was the perfect word for them, suiting their shiny pink roundness to a T and seeming particularly apt in the surroundings. I felt as if I could stretch across, lean forward and gather them up in a full, squashy handful and pop them in my basket for Judy to use in one of her toad-in-the-holes.

I shuffled forward as the young man finished packing his goods into a carrier bag and reached into his pocket to pay, but the elderly woman two in front of me moved in the way just as I tried to take a look at the owner of the sausage fingers, and I could see no more than the arm and hand I'd already studied. I looked down again at the latest load of shopping to make its way along the belt. Dog food; packets of sauce mix; frozen peas. I pictured the grey-haired woman at a dining table sitting next to a large dog, the two of them tucking into huge piles of peas and Pal respectively. Meanwhile, the sausage fingers waved to and fro as the goods were picked up one by one and passed across the magic eye, the huge hand moving heavily and slowly, pausing every now and then when the beep took an extra repetition or two to encourage it to respond.

Chips, loo paper, tomatoes. All glided silently along the belt until grasped by the chipolatas. No − not chipolatas: the big ones. Bangers. As the arm moved, relentlessly and rhythmically, and the shopper shifted to the side of the till to reach over for a carrier, I lifted my eyes and for a moment felt confused between what I saw and the images of the food still passing across the bottom of my field of vision. Why was the vast packet of pink marshmallows wearing glasses? And why was it moving: squidging and undulating in sticky, sweaty ripples? When the eyes behind the glasses looked up into mine it shocked me, breaking the moment and forcing me to recognise what I'd been staring at unthinkingly. I dropped my gaze quickly from the face but I was even more unnerved at the sight of the shiny pink folds of flesh continuing downwards in vast Michelin-like coils towards the open neck of a green-checked overall.

And that was just the beginning. I went on working my way down the overall in disbelieving fascination. From where the material began at the collar everything was tension: trussed, straining dollops of flesh, battling to burst free of the huge swathes of green-checked cotton encasing them, pulling at the poppers and oozing from the spaces in between in pale-pink polyester-covered bubbles. The entire human parcel was jammed into the space behind the counter, spilling over the edges in pleats of green-checked fat, as if the unfortunate girl had been crammed in there as forcefully as an ugly sister's foot into the glass slipper.

As I shifted forward towards the end of the belt, with just one young woman remaining in front of me, I glanced back up at the girl's face. She was still looking at me while she continued her relentless scanning, and I realised − with a sudden jolt of guilt − that she was aware of me studying her, had probably been aware of it the whole time. I looked away quickly and began to unpack my shopping onto the belt, stopping to reach over and grab the plastic divider with NEXT SHOPPER on it and placing it hastily between my sliding packs of depressed-looking mince and the large box of Persil belonging to the woman in front of me. I arranged and rearranged my five rather pathetic items as they were carried towards the giant fingers, placing the baguette diagonally across the other things, carefully avoiding glancing up, and assuming what I hoped was a look of casual introspection. I removed the plastic divider as the Persil woman got out her purse, and placed it neatly behind my little assortment of goodies, separating them from the rest of the as yet empty belt. Out of the corner of my eye I could see the pink bangers reaching towards my baguette.

'Bog off!'

I was quite startled by the volume and confidence of her voice. There was such a ring of command in the tone of the incomprehensible words that I started guiltily, assuming I was being given some sort of large person's reprimand, that she had seen me watching her and was giving me a justified insult in return.

'I beg your pardon?'

'Did you know it was a bogoff?' she went on, looking straight at me through the slightly smeared lenses of her glasses

I didn't know how to answer this. While being more than a little relieved to discover that she had not, after all, been retaliating with a mysterious term of abuse for my uncharitable thoughts on her size, I was still at a loss as to the main drift of her communication. I hadn't, in other words, the faintest idea what she was talking about, and, before I could decide if I knew it was a bogoff, it was clear I would have to establish not only to which object the 'it' in question referred, but also what exactly was the meaning of the term 'bogoff'.

'What was a – I'm sorry,' I ventured, 'I still don't quite –'

'It's a Buy One Get One Free – did you know? The baguette. We have to ask.'

The resignation in her voice told me that I was probably not alone in my ignorance, and that she had had to translate the simple acronym many times before. I was glad to find myself alone at the checkout, unembarrassed by any smirking housewives behind me (the elderly woman I had supposedly pushed in front of having given up the wait and moved to another till).

'Oh, I see!' I smiled at her. 'Sorry, I'm with you. Buy One Get One – yes, yes I see. Bogof! I had no idea. I mean I had no idea that bogof meant two for the price of thingummy and I had no idea that baguettes were – um – bogofs.'

'Well?'

She looked bored, but not impatient, I thought, and her eyes – a startlingly cat-like shade of yellowy brown – seemed surprisingly young behind the up-tilted spectacles amid the puffy cushioning of the cheeks around them.

'Oh, I see. Well, yes, of course, I'd be a fool not to have the free one, wouldn't I? Thanks for telling me – I'll just pop over and get one.'

I walked quickly back to the large cardboard stand that held the baguettes, grabbed one and brought it back to the till. As the girl grasped it in a large, sweaty hand, I was pleased to see that the fingers touched only the Cellophane.

'Six pounds thirty.'

As I handed over a twenty-pound note, I couldn't help having another good look at this dumpling of a girl in front of me. Her hair was shoulder length, mousey and

lank except for the ends, where it frizzed out into curls that
seemed to have a life of their own and bear little relationship
to the rest of the head. On her forehead, in particular, the
tightly curled fringe looked completely out of place, as if
it had been separately attached to her somewhere near the
dead-straight, white parting that crossed her head in a scurfy
furrow. I can never quite make out how women's hairdos
go, in any case. Judy winds hers up and clasps it back in one
of those bulldog clip things with teeth – a croc, I think she
calls it – in the most extraordinary, gravity-defying ways.
But it does at least always look as if it belongs to her. This
girl just didn't come together physically in any rational sort
of way: even the bright-pink lipstick that she wore, instead
of emphasising her mouth – presumably the intention –
just seemed to accentuate its lack of size against the huge
background of her face. Her nose, too, was delicate and
small, looking almost comically out of proportion to the
rest of her. I guessed her to be in her early twenties –
perhaps even younger. While she opened her till I quickly
scanned the four checkouts behind her: the other assistants
were of normal proportions. This mammoth young girl was
one of a kind.

The open drawer of the till was pressed into her abdomen
and I wondered if it hurt. She took out my change with one
hand and with the other burrowed into the soft folds of her
body to find the edge of the drawer so she could push it
shut, then passed the money into my hand. As she did
so, she glanced up at me, and for a split second I found
myself looking straight into those oddly mesmeric amber
eyes. I think I must have been frowning slightly: I know
I was wondering just how this poor creature coped with
the physical difficulties she must surely face at every stage
of her day.

'Is there a problem?' she asked half-heartedly, in the same tone of dreary boredom that her voice had had all along. It would be hard to imagine anyone sounding less as if they had the tiniest speck of interest in knowing if I had a problem. In an attempt to elicit some sort of response I briefly considered telling her that my leg had fallen off or that a man with a bloody axe was standing immediately behind her, but decided not to bother.

'Is there a problem with your change?'

'Oh, I see. No, no, not at all. It's fine. Thank you. Good night.' If I'd had a hat on, I think I'd have tipped it. That's just the way it felt, somehow. The benevolent old gentleman being charming to the young unattractive pleb. How did I come to cast myself in that role? Why did I sound to my own ears so patronisingly middle-class?

But she'd already turned away and was sitting with her hands now resting on the top of the till drawer. There was still no one waiting at her checkout and she slumped back a little in her chair and began to scratch her nose with one fingertip.

When I reached the exit with my plastic carrier I turned and watched her for a moment. She sat unmoving, not scratching now, looking like a huge, unwanted soft toy stuffed into an open drawer. She seemed to have caved in on herself since I'd left the checkout, and her head was barely visible above the magazine rack. I wondered if she needed help to get out at the end of her shift, and for a second I was reluctant to leave. Now that the thought had occurred to me that the poor creature might need a hand to extract her from her packed-in position behind the till, I felt oddly responsible: she didn't look the type to find help easily.

A woman pushed briskly past me as she made her way into the store, and her busy purposefulness brought me back to thoughts of Judy, home and the waiting frying pan. I turned and headed out into a chilly Victoria Street.

Judy

Charlie was longer than I expected doing the shopping. I even began to feel a tiny hint of unease – he's usually the fastest shopper of us all, and if he says he'll be less than twenty minutes he always is. Ben tends to get waylaid by the magazines and the sweets, and Sally's just like me – she gets diverted and remembers a hundred other things we need – or spots something we didn't know we needed but now that she sees it she knows that we patently do, if you see what I mean. I may be the one to handle all the finances in this family, but I have to admit that Charlie is by far the most economical of us when it comes to shopping: he sticks to a list and is seldom tempted by special offers and new products. I go for the magnetic school of purchasing: things just seem to be drawn to me as I move about the shop, even in a down-market little shop like SavaMart. Charlie says I come back encrusted, like a barnacled ship. More than a hint of truth in that.

So, after twenty-five minutes or so had passed I started glancing at the clock. I couldn't identify my hovering worry: I didn't picture road accidents or muggings, and I knew it was ridiculous that I should be disturbed by his marginally extended absence. I can only describe it as an irritating shadow in the background. When he reappeared, I felt not relief but annoyance that I should have taken the time to be concerned, and his perfectly reasonable explanation of having to queue at a slow till underlined to me my own stupidity.

I took out my mild irritation on him, irrationally blaming him for having caused me to feel uneasy. It makes me quite melancholy sometimes when I think about our conversations: most of them have become a matter of scoring invisible points, and I sometimes wonder when and how we reached the stage where simple pleasure in each other's company was no longer enough. I couldn't leave it alone, even once he'd explained what he'd been doing.

'Why on earth did you go for a long queue? They must have had them all open at this time of the evening, surely?'

'I obviously wouldn't have done so intentionally, would I, Judy? In fact it looked shorter than the others — it was just that the girl herself was unbelievably slow. She's huge — I mean really extraordinarily fat — have you seen her? Do you know the one I mean? I felt quite sorry for the poor kid — there must be something wrong — she's vast. And so young.'

'Oh, *her* — yes, I know exactly the one you mean. She's hopeless. Very young: not much more than Sally's age, I should think. I do feel a bit sorry for her sometimes, although I'm sure she could make more of an effort if she really minded. And she always seems perfectly happy, even if a bit abstracted. Very unfriendly, though. Lucky to have the job, if you ask me. I can't believe she was that size when she first went or she'd never have got it.'

'She didn't seem to make any mistakes, though. In fact she quite clearly pointed out my rights as a customer. Two baguettes for the price of one.'

'Is that why you got two? I did wonder. We'll never get through all that before it starts to dry out.'

'Well, as it cost us nothing I don't think that's anything to worry about, do you?'

I didn't answer, and he came up behind me and put his arms around my waist. 'I should think three of you would fit into that giant overall of hers. There's nothing of you. I remember the days when you were all rounded and – soft. There's something to be said for a bit of flesh to get hold of, you know.'

'Out of my way, Charlie, come on. I haven't got time for all that nonsense. I want to get supper over and cleared up so I can finish my report.'

'I don't know why we bother to have meals, really. You'd be happier just taking the plates out of the cupboard and stacking them straight into the dishwasher. It'd make life much simpler. Or not even bother with that: just open the cupboard door, have a good look at them, imagine you've used them and shut it again.'

'Brilliant idea. I've far more important things to do than cook and eat this revolting-looking mince. Let alone clear it up afterwards.'

'We should have gone out.'

'Nonsense. Ridiculous waste of money. And I haven't got time, anyway.'

'No, nor have I really. I've got to write up my notes.'

'What are you on?'

Charlie leant back against the worktop and crossed his arms in front of his chest as he looked down and frowned. 'Particularly unpleasant one. Two children involved, and the mother's remarried a bloody difficult Spanish chap. Lot of machismo involved. And the physical distance, of course. Seems perfectly plain that the father's not a bad sort of customer – bit short-tempered and quick to take offence but basically a good egg. But the mother's tricky: quite prepared to whisk the kids off to the Costa del Sol or whatever and keep the father out of their lives for ever.

Unfortunately she's good-looking and speaks well. So it's not cut and dried, by any means. Even the simplest access could be complicated – if you see what I mean. Makes me feel quite depressed, I have to say. I never used to let these things get to me, but – well, the thought of those wretched children being bartered over like goods, and whisked to and fro so that the parents can get their quota – I don't know, I just sometimes wonder what the hell I'm doing. Whether it's really for the good.'

'Well, someone's got to sort it out, after all. And you're very good at it, you know. I'm sure you'll do the best for them that you can.'

'Of course I will, or at least I'll do the best I can for my client – but whether that's best for the family as a whole is an entirely different matter. I just –'

'Oh, Charlie, do we have to get into all this now? Sorry, sweetheart, but I've had a pretty foul day myself and I'm bloody exhausted. Shall we just have supper and watch a quick bit of rubbish on telly and talk about this tomorrow? We've both got work to do, after all, and it'd do us good to have a break from it for a while. Don't you think?'

I walked over to the sink with the frying pan, tipped it sideways and drained off the fatty greyish liquid from round the pale-grey worm casts left in the pan. 'This meat looks awful: I'm really not sure it's worth using SavaMart for this sort of thing. We should have gone for pasta or something.'

'You did ask about the case, Judy,' Charlie said quietly. 'I've no desire to bore you with my work, I can assure you. And no doubt you'll remember that going round the corner to shop was your idea. I don't particularly like shepherd's pie anyway.'

'Yes, you do! Why on earth didn't you say you didn't

feel like it? It's not as if I wanted it. I'm not doing it for me, you know. I'd be just as happy with a sandwich or a salad – happier. I just can't bear it when Ben puts on that deprived expression when there's no meat for supper. And you do too, you know you do.'

'Don't make such a thing of it. Now, do you want me to peel some potatoes or –'

'No, I don't. I'm fine. But you choose what we eat tomorrow, OK?'

Charlie sighed and walked out of the kitchen, picking up his briefcase from the hall as he called back to me, 'Give me a shout if you need me – I'm going to do a bit of work till it's ready.'

I could feel martyrdom welling up inside and let myself wallow in it as I began to peel a large, lumpy potato. A bit of a mutter into the sink always helps when I'm feeling sorry for myself, even when I know I'm being totally unreasonable. 'Oh, fine – that's absolutely fine,' I grumbled quietly, 'you just carry on with your important work – never mind about my report, that can wait till I've served up your meal. Just because I'm exhausted, that's no reason to eat something cold for once. No, of course not – that would be too much to ask, wouldn't it? Barristers come far higher in the pecking order than tired old Ofsted inspectors. You have a good relax in that chair again, like you were when I came in. Haven't seen me relaxing in a chair since I came in from work, have you? Just time to put down my case and make myself a quick cup of tea and then it's straight out to the shops and –' But then I remembered, rather spoiling my flow: 'Oh, Charlie went tonight, didn't he? I'd forgotten. Oh well, he doesn't usually.'

The door slammed, interrupting my enjoyable self-pity, and Ben's voice, which still surprises me, every time, with its depth, called out a loud 'Hi!' from the hall. I plopped the peeled potato into a saucepan of water, and picked up a tea towel.

'Hi, darling!' I called back, drying my hands as I walked to the kitchen doorway and leant against it. I watched Ben's tall figure struggling to close the front door. His brown hair flopped over one eye and his long neck was bent forward like an inquisitive bird's. He looked too long for his clothes, awkward and gangly in the tangle of coat, bag and arms that flailed around in a vague attempt to shut the door.

'Take your coat off first, darling,' I laughed. 'And drop the bag off your shoulder. It's swinging all over the place. You can't hope to close the door with all that in the way. Here – let me take it.'

'Thanks, Mum.'

'My God, that's heavy!' I said, as I lifted the enormous black canvas bag off his shoulder. 'You'll get some dreadful malformation if you weigh yourself down with all that. I keep saying, I just don't believe you have to cart all those books to school and back again every day – it doesn't make sense.'

'Oh, for God's sake, Mum, don't start all that as soon as I walk in –'

'No, really, it's just not feasible that you could need all these – it's crazy. You do all of twenty minutes' work in the evenings, if that, and most of these just go straight back again. Why don't you clear it out, for heaven's sake? It's such a waste of energy. If I lugged everything around all day without going through it before I left in the mornings I'd be taking the whole of my desk with me.'

Ben said nothing, but looked straight at me for a moment. I noticed how sharply his brown eyes stood out against his pale, mottled skin with its sprinkling of crimson teenage spots, and I saw something else, which made me want to look quickly away. It wasn't the first time I'd seen it, either – that quick flash of dislike that passed across his face whenever we argued, or when I said something he considered stupid or embarrassing. Ben shook his coat free of his arms, swept it up in one hand and grabbed the bag off me with the other. He pulled the strap back onto one shoulder and sighed as he headed for the stairs.

'I've had a long day, I'm exhausted and fed up and you have a go at me as soon as I walk in the door. Just lay off, Ma.'

'I didn't have a go, Ben, don't be so touchy and childish. Supper's about twenty minutes, by the way.'

I turned and walked back towards the kitchen.

'What is it?' Ben asked, without any apparent interest, as he made his way up the stairs.

'Mince.'

'Great.'

'Are you being sarcastic, Ben? Because just don't, that's all. If you want something else, you cook it. And buy it, for that matter. I've had a long day, too, you know.'

'For Christ's sake, what is the matter with you? No, I'm not being sarcastic. Mince is fine – what do you expect? Applause?'

'Don't be so bloody cheeky, Ben.'

I walked back into the kitchen and slammed the door behind me. For a moment I stood still, frowning, then I moved over to the sink and picked up another potato. Why do I always do that? Why do I always lay into him? He's only sixteen; he's only a child. He's going to hate me if I go on like this. I reached forward and switched on the small portable radio that stood next to the sink, but the sweet, swooping sound of Delius only made me feel worse, and I quickly changed to Radio 4, hoping that the crisp tones of a newsreader or the laughter of a studio audience would distract me. *The Archers* was on, and I listened with one ear as I tried to dismiss the picture of Ben's resentful gaze from my mind.

I knew that to let myself sink too deeply into the thoughts that were bound to come next was far too dangerous. Ben and Sally growing up, Ben starting to loathe me. Sally off with her friends all the time and Charlie and I skittering about on the surface of our lives, tired and irritable. What does it leave me to look forward to, I thought sadly: my work?

Hardly. I'd known for some time that there was no realistic hope of actually changing anything, in spite of all the good intentions I'd had originally. I soon abandoned the simplistic ideals I started out with on those first few inspections once I was faced with the reality of just how far wrong the system had gone. I suppose hard grind took over and wore me out. How could I possibly hope to improve even the basic standards of literacy, when I could see that the majority of the teachers' time was spent in keeping the peace and preventing outright physical damage to children, staff and property? If I closed my eyes I could still picture my latest inspection, and I shuddered as I recalled the scenes in the playground: the huge figures of teenage girls, made more menacing by their giant Puffa jackets and stacked shoes, towering over and threatening any teacher brave enough to interfere in the constant fighting and bullying.

I decided to put my mind firmly onto the problems of *The Archers* while I finished off the pie, and, once it was in the oven, I went upstairs, intending to give myself a quick tidy in the bedroom, but stopped on the landing outside Ben's room. I knocked loudly, hoping the sharpness of the sound would work its way into his consciousness through the relentless, rhythmic tones of the rap music, but after a couple of seconds I opened the door without waiting to find out. He turned to look at me from where he sat at the desk, and I felt a little stab of remorse as I took in the school books laid out in front of him.

'Hi!' I said, trying to sound interested but not too concerned.

'Yes?'

'Nothing, darling, Just wanted to say I'm sorry I got ratty again. Didn't mean to.'

'That's all right. What do you want?'

There was something in his tone that didn't sound right, and I noticed he avoided looking at me and instead turned quickly away again and studied the notepad in front of him intently. He picked up a pencil and began to doodle on it as he waited for me to answer.

'No – nothing. I told you. Just to say sorry, that's all. How's it going?'

'OK, thanks.'

'Really?'

'Yes, really. I'm just finding it a bit hard to – to get down to it, that's all.'

'Anything I can do?'

'No, thanks.'

I walked over to him at the desk, then bent forward to kiss him briefly on the cheek.

'Supper about fifteen minutes, all right?'

But he wasn't listening. He was tapping his pencil unthinkingly in time with the music as he stared at the books in front of him. I watched him for a second, then turned to go.

'Mum?'

'Yes?'

'Nothing. It's OK.'

I nodded briefly, and left him alone. I started to walk towards the stairs but paused outside my bedroom. I didn't feel good – the brittle exchanges with Charlie and the worry of seeing Ben so abstracted and isolated had unsettled me. If I went into the bedroom now, using the excuse of a quick brush of my hair, I knew it wouldn't stop there, that I would give in to temptation and indulge myself. I took a deep breath, then turned away from the door and went back downstairs.

I peered round the sitting-room door on my way to the kitchen and was about to call out to Charlie when the sight of the back of his head bent over the small desk stopped me short. I could hear his quiet, steady breathing as he concentrated on the papers in front of him and I leant against the edge of the open door for a moment and watched him. He was concentrating so hard that I felt excluded, and I had a pang of some terrible, nostalgic need for the Charlie of old who had loved me so much and so irreplaceably. Why do I always find it so difficult now to tell him how much I need him? If I ever try, my words become twisted into something ironic and jokey, as if I've lost the ability to convey any genuine emotion without being embarrassed.

I stood there quietly a little longer, then spoke gently to the back of Charlie's bent head.

'Charlie. Supper's almost there.'

He turned to me and smiled.

'Good – I'm starving.'

Maybe the warmth of his smile stayed with me. In any case, I felt more at ease, I remember, as I walked back to the kitchen, and the feeling of contentment persisted as I opened the oven to check my pie.

So it wasn't all bad before it happened. It would be tempting to think I saw it coming, that the signs were obvious, that our life as it was then was untenable. But it wasn't − not at all − and it's not as if I didn't appreciate the good things we had. I did − I'm not imagining it. I used to think that people who have terrible tragedies or who lose everything must look back and wish they'd known just what they had at the time. But I did − I did know just what I'd got. And it still didn't stop it going, did it?

Stacey

He thought I didn't know he was watching me. But I always know, don't I? And it's not as if I dunno why, is it? Like that time at school. Just bend your leg up on this bench, Kylie said. Just bend it up. What for? I said. Just do it, she says. Why? I says. I want to show you something, she says. So I bend it up and she calls the others over and they all start laughing. 'It's gross' − that's what Steph said. 'Oh my God, it's so gross!' Just 'cos she'd heard that on TV. She never said gross before that. No, she never.

It did look gross. They was right. I had my gym shorts on and the way she'd made me put my foot up on the bench and then bend my knee it made all my leg go wide. It was gi-normous; even I could see that. Even then. That's what I can't stand. They think I don't see it just as well as what they do. I'm not stupid. I may be fat, but I'm not stupid.

35

So this idiot guy today thought I didn't see him looking at me while I was serving the customers in front of him. He was staring at my hands and all like anything and thought I didn't know. Fuck me, he's the one that's stupid. I had to say everything over to him. Bleeding stupid – and trying to be clever. Like little Andy in the back stores: he's so dim he don't know a fishfinger from a packet of Persil.

I had another letter from Crystal today. I knew it was her straight I saw the pink envelope. And the writing. All loopy and sideways. I always know it's her. Not just the stamps – there's a few of them write to me from America. I had loads of replies when I put that ad in the slimming mag, and they come from all over. That was my mum's idea. She saw it on *Kilroy* or something: a problem shared is a problem thingummied. It's true, in fact – Crystal knows the way I am better than anyone and I don't feel embarrassed at telling her stuff. Anyway, in today's letter she'd put glitter in again: angel dust, she calls it. With little red shiny hearts mixed in. It went all over the table and bits went in the cornflakes. I hate that. She really does believe in them, though. The angels. Weird. Says she has her own angel watching her. Well, he couldn't miss her really, could he? She says she's even bigger than what I am now: not a bad job for an angel if you've got to watch someone, I suppose. At least Crystal makes it easy.

And she'd wrote LYLMS on the back of the envelope. God knows what that means. I like her letters but I can't be arsed to work out all that stupid writing on the back. It was OK when she stuck to LOL for Lots of Love, but now they've got so long and complicated I can't be fucked. And all those stickers with little hearts and teddies and 'May the Lord be your whatever-it-is. Helper – no, Guide'. Something like that. They're quite cute, in fact, the stickers, but she uses too many of them.

She's going over to the other side soon, Crystal. That's what they call it over there. Anyone who's done it is 'on the other side'. 'The Lord will welcome you, too, Stacey, when you come over to the other side.' That's what she said at the end of today's letter. Some chance. It's all very well for her: it's easy to get it over there. No one will listen to me here. So I'm stuck. On this side.

That old guy today wouldn't have looked at me like that if I was on the other side, would he?

Charlie

I knew I'd go back to SavaMart, of course. Judy's attitude to the giant girl behind the checkout had inspired me to take another look at the poor creature, and I still felt an odd shadow of the impulse to help her. Catch my wife unawares on her home ground and some of the old reactionary background seeps out – not that she's the only one, of course. I know I can be just as guilty of it. And it makes me as patronising as if I were being outright prejudiced, I suppose, even if the effect on both of us is to make us more tolerant than we would otherwise be. Positive discrimination taken to such lengths that we end up bending over so far backwards that we topple over. Wrecking the entire attempt at whatever it was and making an idiot of oneself into the bargain. Class, race, size, whatever – you name it – and there's a little store of bias hiding in our every gene. Hers and mine. I should have said more to defend the checkout girl really; I despair sometimes at how undynamic I'm becoming, but it just never seems worth it at the time. I know Judy doesn't mean any harm – she's the most generous and compassionate of women when you reach her from the right angle, so to speak, and she'd be horrified if it were ever suggested to her that she has an in-built snobbism that can come out as patronising in the extreme. But she can be maddening at times. Particularly about anything domestic, of course. She really does believe that she's the only one who ever shops or cooks or tidies up or makes the beds; those little glances that she gives when anyone else tries to help – as if no one can ever know the vast amounts of hardship she endures to look after us all. She works too hard, that's half the problem; since she's been doing this Ofsted stuff I can see how tired she gets. She's always nipping up to her room to lie down with one of her headaches. I must get her out for the odd meal again.

So, in any case, on to my trip back to the supermarket and to the banned checkout – no, not banned: the checkout that no one who's in the know ever uses. A sort of perversity on my part, a challenge to prove Judy wrong. Maybe we should have a bet on it? That the huge creature might just prove herself to be the zippiest, snappiest checkout girl of the lot. Untried for so long; not given a chance; growing ever more bored and less practised without the stimulus of chatty, interesting customers such as myself. What hidden depths of wit, charm and skill might not be buried under those mounds of cushioning flesh. Judy's always chastising me for not doing my bit for all those good works she promotes: is my charitable role perhaps to be Higgins to this generously endowed Eliza?

The day hadn't gone too badly. Most of the time I wonder what the hell I'm doing in my work – God knows what happened to all my early ideals and ambitions: I look in despair at this run-of-the-mill, middlingly successful person I've become. But my questioning of the father today did just what I wanted: showed him up to be the loving kind of bloke he obviously is. An entirely good influence in my opinion: the two kids will be far better off with some time with him than disappearing to Malaga or wherever. If I can get the judge to agree to his educating them over here as he wants to then it might just be possible to keep everyone happy. Pity the mother's so good in the box. More than a touch of the 'all women together' angle going on, if you ask me. The judge is clearly a bit partial to having her femininity appealed to, specially by someone pretty. Probably because she's such an old boot herself she's cheered to find that another female can still identify her as the same gender, let alone treat her as one of the girls. Still, it didn't go badly at all. And I was in the mood to brave SavaMart again, do my bit for mankind by bringing a little joy into the fat girl's day and then make a little magic in the kitchen. In any case, I wanted to give Jude a break: the tension in the house when she writes her reports is left strung around like trip wire – the kids and I creep about for fear of falling over it. So I could kill two birds with one stone: give myself the fun of the checkout challenge and set up a peaceful, relaxed evening at home.

I phoned Judy on her mobile and caught her in the car, sounding distinctly weary and defensive – in exactly the right mood to be seduced by the thought of not having to cook. If I'm honest, I have to admit that when she sounds like that there's a bit of me wishes I didn't have to go home and face her: I sometimes indulge the fantasy that I could disappear and live quietly round the corner without her ever knowing. Still, it never lasts long. I've no doubt she entertains the same kinds of thoughts about me from time to time.

'I'm going to pick up some bits of chicken and do one of my specials. I know this report's taking it out of you and you must be exhausted. Go straight home and make yourself a cup of tea.'

'Charlie, that sounds great. But how was your day? What sort of —'

'Not bad at all. Not a bad day. I managed to —'

'Pick up a decent bottle of red, will you, darling? We've only got disgusting plonk left and I need something a bit more cheering.'

She was there. Squeezed into the space behind her cash register as tightly as before; as large as I'd remembered. It was a bit disappointing to see she had a small queue at her checkout; not as long as the others, but still a respectable number of people. I had rather hoped to be her only customer: a lone experimenter braving the empty wastes of her conveyor belt and discovering the gem of sensitivity and wit buried under the muffling pounds of surplus fat. Kilos of fat, I should say.

I did my shopping quickly and joined the queue, uncomfortably aware that it appeared to be unchanged since I had entered the store. The same five people were lined up with their trolleys and baskets, although the shopper at the till was even now tidying her change and receipt away in her purse. The line shifted forward a little and I watched my marshmallow girl intently. She sat impassively with her hands neatly folded on the rubber surface of the belt, watching the customer slowly pick up her shopping and turn to go, then reaching forward for a plastic-wrapped loaf of bread and mechanically passing it in front of the scanner. The elderly woman she now served lifted a worn shopping bag off her arm and laid it at the end of the belt, not glancing at the girl in front of her, who appeared equally uninterested. Each seemed totally unaware of the other's presence, as if a mutual pact had been made to get through the next few minutes with the least possible amount of human contact. Only when the small selection of goods was packed into the bag did the girl mutter a barely decipherable couple of words vaguely in the direction of her customer and money changed hands and some sort of minimal communication took place.

My original idea of trying a joke was looking more and more risky as my turn approached and I began to feel slightly nervous. My sense of humour is not altogether unappreciated in the courtroom, albeit a bit too old-fashioned and well rehearsed to be as funny as I imagine when I'm lying in bed planning it. But it generally lightens things up a little, if nothing more. It does require, though, that the recipient takes enough interest to be able to listen to several words at a time. Or, at the very least, allows a little eye contact so that the principle of one party attempting to amuse the other can be established, even if the words themselves are not appreciated or understood. It's tricky to be even faintly funny if the audience is looking in the opposite direction wearing an expression of utter indifference and boredom. I was horribly shy as a child, and the memory of that excruciating feeling of something being expected of me that I just couldn't produce still surfaces from time to time. Judy's always telling me I'm like a different person in company, and she's right: I clam up. I'm far happier in the circle I know, unless I'm dressed up in my armour of gown and wig and well prepared for what appear to be off-the-cuff remarks in court.

So, as I approached the checkout, I trimmed my sails somewhat. I abandoned any attempt at an anecdote or at telling one of the children's cleaner jokes and decided to join her on her own ground, so to speak, and to be amusing about an aspect of her world. At the same time I thought it a good opportunity to offer a small reminder of our first meeting, perhaps to reassure her that I was up for a little unthreatening conversation, and that here was a chap who didn't mind laughing at himself. If all that could be achieved I might just open the tiniest chink of the gate to communication, and begin the process of revealing the hidden glories behind it.

As the last customer in front of me moved away I began to unload my shopping and glanced up at her. It's fascinating how quickly one's parameters adjust to the unusual: although she was clearly enormously overweight, on this second viewing it no longer seemed to be her dominating characteristic. I was more aware of those pretty eyes, and the fleshiness of the girl was this time less grotesque, more – pleasantly Rubenesque.

Her gaze was still unfocused, but the head was at least facing the right direction. I picked up a packet of butter from my basket and waved it about in front of her, forcing her to pay it attention.

'Is it a bogof?' I smiled.

A faint frown rippled the heavy folds between her eyebrows. She stopped moving my shopping and looked directly at the yellow pack of Anchor that I was holding directly in front of her nose.

'Only you may remember I missed a bogof when I was here the other day. You kindly pointed it out to me. And I didn't know what you meant – do you remember? I even thought you were using some sort of offensive term, or something!'

The frown remained.

'When you said "bogof", I mean,' I floundered on. 'I thought you were – oh never mind.'

'No, it's not.'

'Right.'

'And I do remember,' she went on, taking the butter from my hand and scanning it. 'I'm not stupid, you know. I remember all the customers.'

'Do you really?' I asked, genuinely interested in whether this were true. It seemed unlikely that she could really recall this very ordinary man in whose direction she had hardly glanced for more than a couple of seconds at most, let alone the hundreds of others who must pass in front of her till each week. 'How extremely clever of you.'

'MR CHIPSTEAD!'

Her shout made me jump.

'What? What's the problem?'

'Mr Chipstead's my manager. I'm calling him, aren't I?'

'Yes, but –' I had a horrible vision of being dragged by the collar from the store, accused by Mr Chipstead of overfamiliarity with the checkout girl. 'Is there a –'

'No bar code.'

She held the packet of chicken breasts towards me.

'Ah, no. I see. Won't beep, eh? I can't remember how much they are, I'm afraid. I think they were about –'

'Don't matter. I need the stock code.'

'Of course, yes. The stock code.'

'MR CHIPSTEAD!' she shouted again, and then looked back at me. 'Bell's gone.'

'Sorry?'

'My bell's gone. That's why I'm shouting.'

'I see. Well, I'm sure he won't be long.'

I suppose I deserved the withering look she gave me in return, my remark having been based as it was on a

43

complete lack of evidence of any kind. In a second's glance she managed to imply that my pronouncement on the timing of Mr Chipstead's arrival was so entirely awry as to be laughable. I wondered if perhaps his slowness of movement about the store was legendary. His non-appearance surely couldn't be blamed on a lack of awareness: the volume of the girl's shouts had been phenomenal, and there could be few customers or staff ignorant of the fact that his presence was required.

'Couldn't we carry on with the other things while we wait?'

But the girl had disappeared behind her glasses, and, with one hand still grasping the uncoded chicken, her body seemed to settle down into itself like a collapsing balloon, her head sinking a good two inches lower than before and telescoping onto the rolls of fat at her neck. She floated, as if on a rubber ring in a calm sea, suspended only by the neck, drifting gently out of sight. I felt challenged to bring her back to the conscious world and wondered if the forceful use of her name would return her to shore.

I decided to be bold, and took a quick look at the badge on her chest, semi-buried in the depths of the green-checked bosom. I could just make out the first few words of cheery greeting: 'Hi – Happy to Help You! I'm St—' but beyond that it was tucked out of sight. I couldn't immediately think of many names that would fit – she didn't look like a Stephanie, which was the only one that leapt to mind – but a second later she shifted in her chair and the remaining letters were revealed.

I leant forward and said, quite firmly, 'Stacey.'

The reaction was, surprisingly, instant. 'Yeah?'

'Um – why don't we carry on with the other things, meanwhile?'

'If you want.'

She put the chicken down on the metal side of the till and reached forward for a large iceberg lettuce, grunting as she untelescoped herself and made the effort to negotiate the distance imposed by her own body. Her expression was completely unchanged: releasing her from whatever place she had disappeared to hadn't brought her attention any closer to the job in hand. She appeared to be able to function physically on automatic pilot while her brain still floated in some vapid limbo.

She dealt with the lettuce without glancing at it, but then I jumped as she suddenly sat up straight – or as straight as the strictures of her trapped figure allowed – and, unnervingly, what I can only describe as interest flickered across her face. Not, unsurprisingly, directed at me, but at someone or something behind me.

I turned to see a young man of thirty or so, with extremely neat, short black hair, striding towards our till. The hair was, indeed, so short, particularly about the ears, as to make his head look too small for his rather gangly body, and the ears themselves curled outwards towards their reddened tips, gnome-like. These, together with his Adam's apple, were his most outstanding features, in the literal sense of the word. As he approached I could read on the badge pinned to his navy double-breasted jacket that, on this occasion, it was 'Warren Chipstead' offering his assistance to all within reach.

He made a sort of smooth, confident swirl of the hips as he manoeuvred himself round the end of the checkout and came to rest beside me in one swooping movement. 'Yesssss, Stacey,' he said with his lower lip pulled away from his teeth, followed by a sort of clicking of the tongue against the roof of the mouth, effectively conveying in the brief words just what a busy man he was. It certainly seemed to impress Stacey, who was looking at the young man now with far more than simply interest. She was gazing at him with something approaching animated approval – even her voice seemed to have acquired a new vivacity as she addressed him.

'Oh, Mr Chipstead. Sorry to bother you: no code.'

'Another one, eh, Stacey? Rightio, let's take a look. Yessss, chicken fillets . . .' A little more clicking, then a swift scoop of the packet out of Stacey's hand and a further smooth swivel out of the checkout area. 'Won't keep you a moment, sir,' he threw back over his shoulder as he went, then, louder in the other direction: 'Denisha! Find me a six-pack chick. fill. and take it to checkout three please.'

A man with a surname on his badge was clearly one to be reckoned with, and an aura of self-imposed superiority wafted after him as he moved briskly away from the till. Poor Stacey. The light faded from those pretty eyes as quickly as Chipstead's back shimmied its way over towards the frozen peas. At least I could see now that life as we know it did exist somewhere in the depths of the girl's vast frame, even if it took the presence of Warren Chipstead to allow one a glimpse of it. I wondered if I could use this insight to achieve a little communication.

'Seems a nice sort of chap,' I tried. 'Efficient, I expect.'

'S'all right.'

'Have you been here long?'

'Eleven.'

'What? Eleven years do you mean?'

It didn't seem possible: I couldn't believe even SavaMart, while allowing for its clearly demonstrated profits-before-quality ethos, could find the benefits of employing child labour worth the risks of prosecution.

'I begun at eleven, didn't I? My shift. Eleven till seven.'

'Oh, I see. No, I meant, have you worked here for long? In this shop?'

'Yeah.'

I could see I wasn't going to get much further, and I was quite relieved when a pretty Asian girl appeared with a pack of chicken fillets and handed them to Stacey.

'Y'are.'

Stacey took them without a word, and I had to stop myself telling her to say thank you, as if I were talking to one of the children. I could understand Judy's objections to her manner, which seemed purposefully designed to be as unfriendly as possible. Denisha — as I assumed it was — didn't seem to notice though, and had already disappeared by the time Stacey had successfully scanned the pack and dropped it into my open carrier bag.

'Thanks,' I said. 'All successfully stock-coded, then?'

'Eighteen pounds forty.'

'Right.'

Was there a thin girl inside this one, trying to get out? It was hard to equate a word as active as 'trying' with this passive creature. And was it possible that, linked to the thin inner girl, there was a happy, positive personality also just biding its time until the opportunity came along to burst out in a surge of joie de vivre? I put a twenty-pound note into her hand and watched her as she listlessly punched in '20', opened her till and looked up at the '1.60' displayed in green on the tiny electronic screen. Even the small mental effort of calculating the change was denied her; everything that surrounded her conspired to deprive her body and soul of exercise and stimulation.

I felt quite frustrated to be leaving the store with my crusade to evoke a response in my fat checkout girl no further advanced than when I had gone in, and was, again, almost reluctant to go. I pictured myself grabbing her by those huge, rounded shoulders in a desperate attempt to get through, to make her look me straight in the eye, as I shouted: 'Is there anyone in there?' or some such. What was she feeling, this apparently indifferent human being with whom I had briefly shared the same small place on the planet? Perhaps she, too, was shy: perhaps the total lack of interest in her surroundings was merely a cover. I had, after all, seen it crack a little at the approach of the manager.

I would describe all this to Judy when I got home, perhaps make her laugh at my description of the girl's words and expressions, and of her semi-awakening in the presence of Warren thingy.

Warren. Yes, now there was a challenge. Surely, he couldn't be the only person capable of provoking a reaction. I felt – not jealousy, surely? – more a small challenge to my male pride. No, I thought, it can't be just you, young man, who can make that tiny light come on in her eyes.

I smiled to myself as I fantasised briefly about how one might go about searching for the switch.

Stacey

My dad always said it was my fault. My size, I mean. But he didn't understand – you only got to look at my mum to know I can't help it. She's big too – not as big as what I am, but she's big. No one understands what it's like: even my mum tells me not to moan about it. But it's the aching – I ache so much all the time. That's the worst bit – the aching. It's the weight on my joints, the doctor says. They just ain't meant to carry that much around. He says I've got arthritis now, too. Well, thanks, great. That's all I need. And the last time I saw him he said I was lucky not to have diabetes. Lucky? What does he know? I asked him about them new patches I've read about that you stick on your arm and sniff and then you don't wanna eat. He just had this kind of smirk on his face and said I'm being stupid again. No – not stupid. What was it he said? Gullible. He said I was being gullible again. And he says the arthritis won't go unless I lose some weight – and there's only one way to do that, he says, and just hands me out another diet sheet.

I've been overweight my entire life. There ain't never been a time when I wasn't fat. I can prove that, too. My mum says I'm remembering it wrong, but if I show her the pictures she can see I'm right. She doesn't like to know that, see, because I think she overfed me, because it made her feel good when I ate so much. But when I show her the pictures now I can see in her eyes they shock her. There ain't that many of course. Dad never bothered much with pictures. But that one of us on the beach at Bognor: I'm next to my mum and we've both got swimsuits on and you can just see how fat I am. I look more like her sister than a daughter. I'm as big as she is but half her height. It's horrible. Why am I so fat? I don't know.

I don't behave like other fat people, I know that. I watch them and I see the way they move and the way they look. I'm not like that. It's different for me. I think it's an illness I have – I know I shouldn't eat as much as I do, but it's not just that. I'm trying some herbal supplement that I read about in the paper, and it said that some people react different to food than normal people; we don't burn it off and our metabolisms don't work right. These herbal things are going to regulate it. They cost a bit but I put in overtime last month at work and I got a bit saved so it's OK. I didn't tell the doctor because he'd just say I was being stupid again.

It may be genetics. That's the other thing. They're finding all these genes now, and my friend says they've found the fat gene and if they can take it out you won't get fat any more, she read it in the paper. But I asked the doctor and he just laughed. He said I need to exercise more, but how can I exercise when it aches so much? Fucking useless he is.

Mum says I was a normal baby but then what does she mean by normal? I know I wasn't normal when I was going to school, because I can remember going to buy school clothes. I must've been about seven or so and we had to get the clothes that was meant for twelve-year-olds. Mum didn't know how much I minded the way the assistant looked at me. It's only a tiny memory but I know how ashamed I felt.

And another memory is splitting my jeans. I was playing with my friends in the playground by the church and I was always ever so careful not to move about too quickly because I didn't want to fall and rip my trousers. We was playing 'it' and I tried to touch one of the boys and I fell and, sure enough, I heard that horrible noise of the fabric ripping. Just giving up under the strain. I went home and found another pair but when I went to put them on they didn't fit so I squeezed myself into them as best I could but my thighs was so large the crotch only came about halfway past my knees.

That old guy came to my checkout again today. That's the fifth or sixth time running in about a week. Tried to chat to me – I knew he was but I pretended not to notice. I hope he ain't one of those weird ones.

'Hello, Stacey,' he says, 'how's it going?'

'S'all right,' I says, trying not to look him in the eye. I didn't want to encourage him, see, and also I could see Mr Chipstead hovering round Sheila's till and I wanted to keep an eye on them. I just hoped the old bloke wasn't going to bring up the bogof thing again. That's four times he's done it now. If I let on I know exactly what he's talking about it'll only encourage him, but if I go on pretending I don't know what he means then he's gonna go on saying it every time. Can't win. Stupid, that's what he must think I am.

'S'cuse me,' I says, before he could say no more, 'Mr Chipstead!'

The old guy smiled a bit and turned round to look the way I was shouting. God, Mr C looked gorgeous: his arse looks so good in them navy trousers he wears for work, and you don't often see it because it's hidden under that long jacket of his, but he was leaning over Sheila's till and you could see it under the suiting, all round and lovely. Two apples. Braeburns? No — more Pink Lady, although that don't sound quite right for Mr C. Not that I can see the colour, of course, although, God knows, I imagine it often enough, but Pink Lady's much too poofy for Mr C. All man, he is. Gala, maybe — that sounds good. A Gala arse, that's what he's got. I'll write Crystal that in my next letter: she'll enjoy that — she's always on about great arses. Muscly, she likes them — what does she call it? Sinewy or something. I like them a bit rounder, myself

Anyway, he come over at last and the old guy was just stood looking at him.

'Yes, Stacey?' He's got a gorgeous voice, too.

'Can I go for lunch now, Mr Chipstead? Only I'm doing late shift and —'

'Stacey, you don't have to call me over for that, you know you don't. Check it with Mrs Peters.'

'Yes, but I never had my lunch break Tuesday and Mrs Peters said I should ask you about taking extra time today to make up.'

'All right, Stacey. If Mrs Peters said so then that's fine – go for lunch when you've finished this customer and I'll send Janet over. Now get on with your work, this gentleman's having to wait. You've got to get your speeds up, Stacey – I've told you this before.'

It's funny but I don't mind when he tells me off. I just mind when he don't talk to me. Or when he talks to Sheila. I can't stand that.

'So, Stacey,' the old guy says to me, 'you've got your lunch break then. That's good. Your manager – Mr Chipstead, isn't it? – seems like a nice sort of chap.'

'You said that last week.'

'Did I?'

He looked pleased when he said that. I wondered for a moment if he was gay, but I don't reckon he's the type. Just happy that someone's remembered something he's said, if you ask me.

'He's all right.'

There was a bit of a pause while I checked the vegetable on the belt. Funny-looking thing it was, and I couldn't find it in the idents for a bit. While I was looking he was watching me again, but I never let on I knew.

'Is there anything I can do?' he said.

'Well, you can tell me what it is.'

'No, I didn't mean that. I meant – well, is there anything I can do for you – sort of – generally. You just looked a bit upset. When Mr Chipstead was here.'

'Sweet potato,' I said. 'Found it.'

What a weird guy. One of those that fancies big women, as they call it. Really creepy. I wondered if I could call Mr

C back to get rid of him, but there wasn't really nothing I could put in words, just a feeling that he wasn't coming to my till every time by chance. I was coming to dread it, really, when I saw him approaching with his little basket with four or five things in it. Why don't he do a big weekly shop in a trolley? It wasn't like he was short of the cash or nothing, you could tell that just by looking at him.

'No, I meant – is there anything I can do to help, Stacey? I mean, if Mr Chipstead is worrying you about your speed. Perhaps I've been a bit slow in unpacking my basket or something. I always find you very efficient – would you like me to put in a word?'

I felt like telling him to mind his own fucking business, but I knew he was just the sort to complain about things and get me into trouble so I kept quiet. I finished off his basket and waited for him to pay.

'Here you are, Stacey,' he said. 'Sorry to interfere – I was only trying to help, you know.'

I took a quick look up at him as he give me the money and I have to say I felt a bit mean then for not answering and all that. He was watching me with ever such a worried expression, and it didn't seem so creepy after all – more like my mum looks when she knows I'm hurting and stuff. Maybe he really was just a friendly old guy who was a bit lonely.

'S'all right,' I said, and I smiled at him. Not so's I was encouraging him or nothing – I wasn't gonna thank him 'cos I never asked for his help, did I? – but the least he deserved was to be let off the hook. In any case, I thought I'd better keep on the right side of him – I didn't want him going home and plotting something nasty. You never know with customers – they can be a dodgy lot if you ain't careful.

Ben

Sometimes I can see life in the simplest possible terms, and I feel as if I've discovered the answer to everything, and then at other times I'm completely at sea and out of control. It's scary, and I'm not sure which is true. It started with all the stuff we had at school about the uncertainty principle — at first I didn't bother to take it in much, just wrote it all down so I could learn it for the exams, but when I really started thinking about it I could see that it made life impossible. If nothing really exists — or at least not in a decided form, kind of thing — until you observe it, then surely nothing exists at all? Or at least it's as good as if it didn't. And if things change just through you looking at them, then nothing I see, hear or feel has any reality, because it's reacting to me observing it. So what I see is unreal, and what I don't see doesn't exist. It makes me feel quite frightened at times, and it's not easy for me to talk to anyone about it, because when I'm in the really bad moods then I have to be by myself so that I don't change anything by communicating with it.

Even on a mundane level it affects the way I look at things. It's like Mum and Dad getting so brittle with each other: I'm never sure how much of that is due to my watching them. Were they easier with each other when Sally and I were little, or was it just that I wasn't consciously judging them then? A while ago I'd have talked to Mum about feeling so strange, but she always seems so busy with her work now, and when she isn't she's either lying down in her bedroom or rushing about the house being tense. Or she gets into those weird moods when she's really hyper. Does things like hovering about downstairs for the post in the mornings as if she's waiting for something. She always says it's just a magazine or a catalogue she's expecting, but she goes all girly and happy for a bit and buys us things and gives us treats. Sally and I used to wonder if she was having an affair, but it doesn't seem like that, somehow. Anyway, I can't see it.

Trouble is, thinking about what objectively exists makes me want to stop working, because in a way everything I'm doing is a waste of time. When I'm sitting there at school it all feels really pointless because I'm observing it and changing it. And all the books and theories and mathematical formulae and religions and portents are worthless. I'm not sure if it makes me want to commit suicide or live for ever. Who was it said there was only one real philosophical question – whether to kill yourself or not?

It's not that I'm always gloomy – more confused. Sometimes it's like I've discovered the key to everything and it feels really good, because if nothing has any true reality then nothing matters, so there's no need to get upset about anything or to hurt about the way things are. But I still don't know what I'm going to do about these thoughts. I feel rather like I've been given a very important message to deliver but they've forgotten to address the envelope.

I started to talk to Holly about it today in the dining hall, but I didn't get very far. I thought it might help if I could explain it to someone else and get it out of my head for a bit, but I could see she didn't understand how important all this was. She was looking really cute, with her hair up in one of those grippy things – and she kept smiling back at me as I tried to explain.

'When you measure something,' I said, having decided I should start from basics – Holly's doing languages for her

A-levels, and science has never been one of her strong points — 'you're never sure if your answer is right. Never. That's why it's called the uncertainty principle.'

'Well, obviously you can never predict things,' she said, dipping her head to look down at her hot chocolate. She tipped a sachet of sugar into the plastic cup and stirred it. 'It doesn't take a scientist to tell me that.'

'No, it's not exactly that,' I went on. 'It's more that — oh, Holly, for God's sake, that stuff's already sweetened: it'll be disgusting — no, it's not so much that we don't know how atoms and particles and things are going to behave when we look at them, it's more that we don't even know the rules. I mean, even if we could measure things without affecting them, we're probably judging them by all the wrong rules. Common sense doesn't really work any more, at least not once you try to look at both quantum and macroscopic physics at once. They just don't gel, you see. And it makes my life — all of our lives — pointless.'

She had that sweet, patient smile on her face again, and the weird thing was that it made her look as if she understood far more about all this stuff than I did, while at the same time I knew perfectly well that she hadn't got a clue what I was on about. Holly always does that to me — whatever I'm trying to tell her she always seems to be one jump ahead, even though she doesn't really know a thing about quantum mechanics.

She put one elbow on the table and rested her chin on her hand. 'I don't see that at all,' she said, still smiling and pretending to be interested. 'Of course your life isn't pointless, Ben. Try and explain.'

'I'm trying to tell you something really important here, and you've got that "let's humour Ben" look on your face. Forget it, Hol.'

'No, go on. Don't be so touchy. I will try to understand, I promise.'

'It's really simple – but it frightens me. I just feel sometimes that everything round me is unreal because I can't look at it without changing it. I suppose that's what I'm trying to say.'

'How's your dad, by the way?'

'My dad?'

'Yes. You haven't talked about him much, lately. You used to all the time. I just wondered if he was OK?'

It really made me think, when she said that. It was true – I did used to tell her about Dad's cases and things. They were always pretty interesting when he was dealing with divorces and stuff: he was cool about telling me some of the really strange things people get up to and how he had to question them about all the intimate bedroom things that went on. But he hadn't been telling me much recently, and I hadn't realised until Holly asked.

'I think he's OK,' I said, 'but he is a bit quiet, now you mention it. Just working hard, I suppose.'

Judy

Charlie's been a bit strange lately. All this volunteering to do the shopping is most out of character: I know he says he's interested in the fat checkout girl and seeing if he can cheer her up, but I find it very hard to believe that's really what he's up to. It must be six or seven times he's gone back there now, over the last couple of weeks. Maybe he feels guilty about me: I know I've been working too hard and it worries him. Rather sweet really, the way he's trying to take the pressure off me. But I do wish he'd go back to

Sainsbury's or Waitrose, even if it would spoil his experiment with the girl. I think we're all getting rather tired of the small selection he finds at SavaMart. I'll have to put my foot down and insist I do the shopping again for a while.

Meanwhile, I think it's time I did something about the way I look: I caught sight of myself in a mirror on the wall of the gym at the school I'm inspecting and I was quite shocked. I thought I knew exactly how I looked – after all, I stare into that mirror in the bathroom every morning and evening. But there was something about the way I was standing or – I don't know; I looked more like sixty than forty-eight. And yet, when I'm at the school, I feel far more in tune with the children than I do with the staff, almost as if I'm pretending to be grown-up when I'm discussing things with the head. She's probably feeling exactly the same. I know when I was teaching I felt utterly different from the way I used to think teachers felt when I was a girl; they looked so secure and smug and certain about everything they said or did. How I longed to be like them. They didn't look as if they could ever feel frightened of going to the dentist, or being late with giving work in or wearing the wrong thing. All the things I was so scared of. I could see it would all be fine once I was past the age of twenty or so.

Now I know you feel exactly the same, of course, but you pretend that you don't. So why should I go round looking like a mature woman of sixty-something when I feel the same as I did at fourteen? There has to be a happy compromise, surely. I know I can't go round in a short, tight skirt and strappy top like Sally does, for heaven's sake, but there has to be something in between that and these sensible suits I seem to have crept into wearing. And there must be a way of doing my hair and make-up that's a bit more –

well, a bit prettier. My figure's not too bad, and although my hair's thinner than it was, it's still —

Oh, for God's sake — listen to me! I sound like something off the pages of a women's magazine. Is this it? Am I going through a mid-life crisis, just when I thought I was skimming over the surface of the menopause so successfully? A confident, modern, professional woman, that's what I am — how bizarre to find myself worrying about all this stuff, like a teenager. I haven't got time for all this.

I wish I hadn't gone off sex. Not just for all the obvious reasons — that I enjoyed it and it kept Charlie and me close and made me feel wanted and all that — but also because it spoils so many other things. I was Christmas shopping today, for example, in Oxford Street, and it struck me how many aspects of life are geared to the business of physical attraction. When I buy clothes and the odd bit of make-up now it's just like stocking up on anything else, and I know it's since sex has gone out of it that it's stopped being fun. Well, it was — terrific fun, to sit in front of the mirror and dress and paint my body to make it attractive. Now I dress simply to look neat and tidy for its own sake, not to be actively attractive to the opposite sex. Clothes, make-up, shoes, hair and all the other nonsense become far less interesting when they don't give you that little frisson of feeling potentially desirable — it may be unfashionable to admit to thinking that, but I do.

Charlie has never minded that I'm less proactive in our love-making — it's not as if I can't get any pleasure out of it. I can — it's just that if I were honest I'd probably rather be reading a good book. I miss so much that wonderfully desperate need that I had in my youth: it was so energising and animal to be dominated by my physical urges. Probably the only time in my life I've really enjoyed being out of control.

I remember how Charlie used to stay at my parents' house when we were going out together. We lived in one of those tall Victorian houses in Highgate, and he'd just got himself attached to chambers as a junior of some sort. He had rooms, of course, but half the time he'd come and live with us. For my mother's food, he used to say, and she'd beam with pride and my father would shake his head in mock despair and mutter about being eaten out of house and home. They loved it really, not having had a boy of their own, and it suited Charlie and me very well to have him treated as a surrogate son. Made him my surrogate brother, I suppose, but – my God, he certainly didn't treat me as any self-respecting brother would. It wasn't the food he was hungry for in those days – and he wasn't the only one who was starving either.

We had a very simple system. His bedroom was on the top floor, in what would have been the servants' rooms when the house was first built, I suppose, and my room was on the floor below, just above where my parents slept. There was no bathroom at the very top and Charlie used to have to come down to use the one next to my bedroom. It would have been far too risky to creep into my room, so he used to leave a little note or drawing in the bathroom when he felt like a bit of hanky-panky, as my father would have put it. The notes were never rude, naturally: in fact they were devised to be as innocuous as possible and if discovered would simply have looked like scraps of paper dropped accidentally and inscribed with odd jottings about law books or train times. But when I went to brush my teeth the sight of one of those bits of paper would set me on fire and I'd be up those stairs in a flash – or, at least, in as near to a flash as I could manage while avoiding the creakier stair treads. It wasn't only one way, either – there were many times I'd make sure I got to the bathroom first, and left notes of my own, signalling my impending visits.

The habit continued as a silly part of our foreplay for several years after we got married. A note inscribed with something like 'Gaston's Matrimonial Property Law Book IV' or '6.40 Waterloo to Haslemere' left on my pillow would send me into smug swoons of delight and straight into his arms. What fun I had choosing nighties or underwear that I knew he would enjoy, dressing myself up like a present for him to unwrap slowly in the soft light of our bedroom. How I miss it.

Ben shut himself in his room after school today, and when I knocked he said not to come in because he was working. That's not like him — I hope he's OK. I always used to think he was the tough one when they were little, but — it's funny — he's grown up to be the one I worry about the most. I just wish he didn't have to pretend to be all right, all the time — I'm sure it's the mixture of trying to look cool and in charge with being so unsure underneath that's getting to him. I've never felt that with Sally. Maybe Holly can talk to him about it — perhaps I'll ask her.

I hate it though. Having to give my little boy over to the care of another woman when it really counts. It's not the empty-nest syndrome they should warn us all about — it's the empty heart. Sounds ridiculously soppy but it's true: it's so hard to have Ben still here in his physical presence, but gone from me in so many other ways. I felt like screaming outside his door today: 'Don't you realise I wiped your bottom and fed you at the breast and washed your snot and vomit and tears off the shoulders of all my clothes for years? I was the centre of your universe, the most perfect, necessary being; now I'm an embarrassment.' But of course

I just said, 'Oh, OK, darling' or something feeble like that and went back downstairs.

Crystal

Dear Stacey,

Hiya! Guess what!!! I finally gotta date!! So I'll be going on to the other side soon after you read this – or maybe I'm even there already. I guess your British post takes forever, huh?

Anyway, pray for me, Stacey. I know you will, and I know the Lord is gonna take good care of me and I've got the cute little teddy you sent and he's gonna go in there right alongside me and I've got my angels praying for me too, so it's like – hey! – it's all gonna be just cool. No – I am NOT gonna send you a picture – you'll just have to wait until after, when I'm thin and gorgeous (and pigs will fly, huh?)

You remember I'd seen my PCP beginning September? Ooops, sorry, I forget you don't call them that over there – you'd say your general doctor, I think. Is that right?? Anyway – you know what I mean. And – whaddaya know?? – I got a referral. So I saw the WLS guy early October – hey, maybe I told you all this, but I'm just so excited!! – look, here's one of my real smiley faces to show you how happy I am – cute, or what, huh???? Anyways, I had real high BP so I had to have medication for that and then a pap smear and all kinds of stuff, and he told me to come back in a month, so I did and he was real pleased with me and said my BP was down and now I'VE GOT A DATE FOR THE OTHER SIDE!

I got my approval from the insurance real easy, too. Some people have all kinds of trouble, but when they heard my weight and my history and I told them who my surgeon was they were real sweet and I got approval right there and then over the phone. I feel kinda scared, too, but I just know everything's gonna be fine. I was real surprised it was so easy, 'cos I'm not like their usual — well, it's hard to explain, but let's just say I'm a little different. And no — I'm not gonna tell ya 'cos I like my little mysteries!

Pray for me, Stacey, and I'll pray the Lord will find a way to help you over to the other side too, sweetie.

Yours with the peace of the Angels to watch over you

Crystal

Charlie

I can pinpoint almost to the second the moment everything changed. I was feeling so fatherly, caring and — I don't know — sort of smug about my relationship with the checkout girl until then. I'd been back many times to SavaMart, making sure I chose Stacey's till of course, and getting her to open up to me that little bit more each visit. I'd get home and describe progress to Judy, enjoying the fact that I now knew more than she did about the whereabouts of various goods in the store. I knew it was irritating her that I insisted on doing the shopping at SavaMart rather than Waitrose or Sainsbury's, which, admittedly, do have a far better class of produce, not to mention service and choice. But Jude can be very understanding when she wants to be, and when I explained that this wretched checkout girl had become a bit of a project, if not challenge, she put up with the unexciting selection of goods I invariably returned with, and relaxed into the unusual luxury of not having to shop.

Meanwhile, I determined to help Stacey — as to why, I find that very hard to answer. Looking back on it, it's difficult to rid myself of the way I now inevitably see things, and to try to remember what originally prompted my innocent and uncomplicated interest in the girl is almost impossible. I know I had become fond of her: making genuine contact with her had become a bit of an obsession, I can see that – it was certainly more than an amusing challenge, which was how I presented it to Judy and Ben. I keep coming back to the word fatherly. Yes – paternal, quite definitely. I think, in spite of the gross physical differences between the two of them, Stacey somehow reminded me of Sally, or, at least, of Sally when she was still at an age to need her dad in a real, physical way. Stacey's disguised but – to me – quite apparent vulnerability stemmed from her size and Sally's was simply because of her youth and inexperience, but the protective response they both produced in me was the same.

So, a middle-aged attempt to replace a beloved daughter? No, not replace: Sally, however changed and grown-up, will always keep that particular place in my heart that a first child has. But my feelings – and I use the word lightly in the context of those early days – for Stacey rekindled the caring, nurturing part of my character, if you will, that had previously been reserved for my offspring. One reads so much about the unhappiness of today's youth – and, indeed, I come across its manifestations only too often in court – but it's rare for me to come slap bang up against it in real life, so to speak, and I was determined to do my little bit to change the fortunes of at least this one unfortunate creature. I was also aware that since I had begun to take an interest in her, the bouts of depression, or boredom, that I had been experiencing increasingly often over the last few years had entirely ceased. Something about the girl fascinated me, and took me out of myself so much that I noticed I was worrying about her rather than about my own problems.

Each time I saw her I wondered whether her size bothered

her in any way — she seemed so bored by everthing around her, apart from the brief flicker of life I'd seen in her eyes at the appearance of the store manager, the smooth Warren thingummy, that I really wasn't quite sure if there could be any sensitivity to her own condition buried deep within the parcel of flesh. But, having seen Judy and, more markedly, Sally worry obsessively about their figures over the years, I knew that Stacey's apparent indifference was almost certainly hiding a miserable awareness of her own unattractiveness. I thought a compliment couldn't go amiss, and might just chip away at the defensiveness she wore around her like an impenetrable shawl.

'What a pretty ring!' I said to her on about my tenth visit to the store. On the middle finger of her right hand she wore a small gold ring, sporting a swirling design of filigree work and tiny blue stones. Inevitably it was partly submerged in the fleshy roundness of what still tended to remind me of a sausage, but it was true that the little points of blue against the gold, nestling into the cushions of pale, smooth skin, as in folds of cream satin in a jewellery box, made a sweet and surprisingly touching sight. I wondered briefly if the adored Warren had perhaps had a moment of madness and presented it to her as a birthday gift, or, more likely perhaps, if it came from a doting mother or father.

'QVC,' said Stacey, mysteriously.

It never ceased to surprise me just how often this girl came out with words or phrases that made no sense to me whatever. My brain, in a desperate attempt to cobble some sort of meaning out of the apparently random and disconnected three letters, struggled for a moment with the mad idea that the girl had said 'QED'. Could Latin have acquired street cred without my being aware of it? It hardly seemed likely; close proximity to Ben and Sally kept me reasonably up to date with modern parlance, and, in any case, it would have made no sort of sense as a reply to my compliment. I hesitated, loth to admit I had no idea what she was talking about. I felt like one of the mothballed judges I sometimes encounter in court ('Tell me, learned counsel, just what is this *BOGOF?*').

'Sorry?'

'I bought it on QVC.'

'Ah!' I was none the wiser, of course, but nodded briefly as if in approval. Clearly, to buy a ring 'on QVC' was something positive – nothing to be ashamed of, at the least – so that an acknowledgement of her wisdom could do no harm. I assumed that it was some sort of hire-purchase agreement. It was clear, however, I didn't fool the girl for a second with my pretence at understanding.

'Shopping channel,' she said flatly, looking up at me with a mixture of boredom and sympathy in her expression.

It all suddenly fell into place. 'Of course!' I laughed. 'QVC shopping channel. Yes, yes, indeed, my wife and daughter have shown me that on Sky. Fascinating. Strangely addictive, my wife tells me. Do you know, Stacey, I thought you meant you'd bought it on some sort of hire pur- chase: I mean that QVC was a type of credit loan or something.'

Did I see a hint of a smile? Yes, I did – I was sure of it. The dimpled folds either side of her mouth deepened a fraction, and the toffee-coloured eyes, as she looked back up at me, definitely twinkled.

'So did you buy it for yourself? Or was it a birthday present or something?'

'I bought it myself. Off QVC.'

'Yes, I see. So tell me,' I went on, as I packed a net of sprouts into the plastic carrier, 'how does it work? Do you

66

phone them up or what? I mean, how do you order what you want?'

'Yeah, you just phone them up with the credit card.'

'Amazing.'

'No – s'easy.'

And then she smiled. Genuinely, wholeheartedly smiled. And all the clichés in the book couldn't describe the change that smile made to the girl's face: yes, the clouds parted; the sun came out – it all happened, and more. It made her look quite extraordinarily pretty – the softness of her round, plump face was, in an instant, made charming rather than podgy, and the eyes, brightened with the touch of warmth, were more startlingly golden than ever.

I was desperate to capitalise on this moment of break-through, and, on impulse, leant over the checkout belt and picked up her soft, warm hand to take a closer look at the ring. She didn't appear to mind; she looked down at her own hand in a detached, vaguely interested way and then back up at me, still smiling.

'Nice, innit? You just phone, you see. Even you could do it.'

I laughed out loud. 'Yes, I deserved that, Stacey. I didn't mean to be patronising, I assure you. It really is a bit of a mystery to me, all this TV ordering and stuff. Buying over the internet and so on. My wife does it frequently, but I'm afraid I'm a bit out of date when it comes to all that.'

This was real progress. I even got a grudging 'Bye' out of her as she handed me my receipt, and I carried my shopping home, if not with a song in my heart, at least with a few random crotchets.

Over supper later I told Ben and Jude of the breakthrough of the day and made them laugh at my pathetic attempts at communicating with the poor girl.

'But don't you see?' I said, made enthusiastic by the wine. 'I got a smile! That's the first one. You have no idea just what a triumph that is – until now only Warren the smooth has elicited any response at all – let alone a smile.'

'Oh, come on, Dad – that's not true. She's been speaking to you loads – you never stop telling us.'

'Well, yes, Ben. She has been speaking to me. I can't deny it. But if you knew this girl – Judy, back me up on this, she really is the most unfortunate creature, isn't she? – if you knew her, Ben, if you actually had to go and do the shopping as I do –'

'Charlie, you don't have to do it,' Judy interrupted. 'You know perfectly well you don't. That just isn't fair: it's been you and this bizarre project of yours that's led to this current shopping craze. I've never known you do so much. It's quite marvellous, in fact.'

'That may well be right, my dear,' I went on, aware that Ben was looking at me with that slightly jaded expression he wears when I'm a little drunk. 'That may well be true. But that is entirely beside the point. The crux of the case, I submit, is that I was challenged to make contact with this fantastically large and non-communicative person, and I have succeeded beyond all my wildest dreams.'

'Who challenged you?' Judy asked with a smile, helping herself to another glass of the Burgundy.

This stumped me for a moment, but I rallied quickly. 'I did. I did' – and I jabbed a finger in her direction – 'and I may tell you, my dear wife, that to be challenged by yourself is perhaps the toughest assignment of all.'

There was a short silence, and then Judy suddenly snorted into her wine and giggled. 'What are you talking about, Charlie?'

'I really don't know,' I said, starting to laugh myself. My

mind flashed back over the conversation and it seemed terribly funny all of a sudden. 'I guess I'm just thrilled that I made fatty smile.'

This made Judy giggle even more, and Ben joined in too.

'You're really weird, Dad,' he said, grinning at me across the table. 'It's like some *Pygmalion* trip or something. What the hell are you hoping to get out of it?'

'I am aiming to communicate with someone less privileged than your good self, my dear son. My challenge,' I went on, as we all laughed louder than ever, 'is to create a little happiness within that – how shall I put it? – extraordinarily overadequate physical specimen.'

When I think how I used to speak about her it makes me shiver. May God – and she – forgive me.

Sally

I always thought I'd leave home as soon as I finished school, but somehow I seem still to be here. It's partly for economic reasons, of course, and although I've taken enough part-time jobs over the past three or four months to pay for clothes and going out, it would be quite different if I had to find the rent and food and all that. But it really is time I started planning what I'm going to do with the rest of the year before I go up to Leeds. I know I want to travel, but I don't want to stop my music, and lugging a cello round Europe would be a nightmare. It'll work out.

Funnily enough, I think I'd miss Ben quite a bit as well if I was to move out. Although we used to row like hell when we were little, we get on OK now, and he's actually quite a cool guy. He's always been off his head, though, and lately he's been even more strange than usual – shutting himself in his room instead of watching TV with the rest of us after supper for instance, and not really laughing when I do the silly jokes that used to make him giggle. I worry about him a bit.

As for Mum and Dad – it's getting quite heavy the way they constantly needle each other. They've never been the sort to have arguments, and they still don't, but Mum's sarcasm and Dad's annoying way of talking as if he's in court all the time are getting on my nerves, and I can just see how they irritate each other. I used to envy my friends at school when they told me how their parents yelled and shouted and even threw things – it sounded so dramatic and kind of Italian, when my home was so quiet and boring. Sometimes I'd make things up about Mum and Dad fighting just to make them sound more interesting – I really wanted them to be divorced so's I could be sent from one to another like Annabel. She used to get amazing presents from her father.

But now that it's not quite so sunny at home I feel differently. I wish it could be just the way it used to be.

Charlie

It was to be another couple of weeks before it happened – before it all changed, I mean.

I was in court – a long and rather dull case that had been dragging on for days. I was examining my own client: a woman who, if I am honest with myself, I knew quite clearly deserved never to see her children again. I was attempting to secure her some sort of limited access.

I was trying to convince the judge that the woman's

prolonged absences abroad away from her children had been justified by the demands of her work or some such, and, as I questioned her, I had been watching her elegant, manicured hand playing with her expensively streaked hair, forcing her to tilt her head as she peered at me resignedly from behind the shining blonde curtain.

I was far from confident that my client, vague and uninterested as she had appeared to be in our briefings, would remember our policy of explaining by her work schedule the weeks and months at a time that she had spent away from her family over the course of the previous years, and I had been irritated by her lack of cooperation in a process that I myself was not at all sure was valid. As I waited for her to answer, her head still now, her hand fiddling with a string of pearls round her neck, I found myself watching the way the ring she was wearing glittered as it caught the light. It reminded me of something, and gave me an uneasy feeling I couldn't fathom. As she began to speak – detailing some justification that we had conjured up between us for her extensive holidays – she thrust her hand back into the blonde tresses, arranging and rearranging the fall of hair, clearly a nervous habit that was helping her to cope with the stress of her court appearance. The ring moved in and out, twinkling sporadically and mesmerically. What memory, lurking at the back of my mind, was being triggered by the sight of this gold and sapphire piece of jewellery?

It was, of course, Stacey's ring. Remarkable how the mind can make connections without letting you know, how it can carry on a private conversation between memory and the subconscious until the nagging irritation of the discussion can no longer be ignored. That I should be surreptitiously reminded of a shop girl's cheap bit of vulgar jewellery by the obviously expensive sapphire ring of the woman I was examining in court was strange enough; what was inexplicable was that the connection should be so disturbing. What should have merely caused me to smile in recognition made me frown in dread.

I pictured Stacey's hand, and the ring half buried in the flesh. And it was then – I'm sure of it – exactly then, as I recalled the soft, white skin and the twinkling of those cheap little blue stones against the ludicrous rococo swirls of gold, that I knew everything had changed. Gone in one microsecond of terrible knowledge was all vestige of the so-called fatherly feelings that I'd professed for the girl. Gone, to be replaced in the same instant by a searing stab of desire so intense that I had to dip my head in sudden dizziness for fear of fainting. The shock was total. How could I possibly trust the bizarre message that every nerve in my brain and body was screaming at me: that a girl whom I had met – no, not even met, encountered at most – a mere dozen or so times, and with whom I had had the briefest of conversations, was affecting my emotions so suddenly and drastically? It was a moment that needs poetry or music to attempt a description – no mere words can convey that kind of emotional attack. Not because of its beauty – far from it: the realisation was closer to horror than to delight – but because the force of such a moment, that takes one's heart in its grip and squeezes it until life itself is threatened, is beyond account.

Stacey

'What are you doing later, then?' I asked Sheila.
Sheila's always doing something, and sometimes she'll let

me go too. Denisha says it's to make her feel smug, 'cos she knows I never go nowhere otherwise, and it makes her feel like she's doing something good, like for charity, you know. But it ain't that – I know that. She likes me going with her sometimes 'cos it makes her look better than she really is next to me. She dresses like she's really something, does Sheila, but I know she knows she ain't really. If she goes out with Janet you can see the difference. It's all make-up and tarty clothes with Sheila – if you see her without all that you can see how horrible she is. No wonder she never keeps none of the boys more than once or twice of going out. Once she sleeps with them that's it. I know she tries to keep her make-up on 'cos I've seen her in the morning when she's come back from a night with one of her fellas and her eye make-up's all smudgy. You can tell she's tried to wipe it off from under her eyes when she's woken up. But it don't fool them none – they know what she really looks like. If you ask me they know that anyway, but they think she's worth a quick fuck or two. But they ain't never gonna give her their babies, I can tell you that.

So, anyway, I fancied a drink or two so I asked her what she was doing. I'm always hoping a bleeding miracle'll happen and I'll get myself laid, too, if I'm honest. I've had guys come on to me, mind, but it's always in a freaky kind of way – they're turned on 'cos I'm fat. I can always tell, even when that guy at the club that night I went with Sheila come out with all that about me being pretty.

Denisha always says they don't mean nothing of what they say when their cocks are stiff and they'll do anything just to get you to let them do it, or to get you to suck them off and that, and I knew what she meant when that little runt was telling me all that shit about being gorgeous or whatever he said. I could see he was just dying for it and he was all sweaty and disgusting and I knew he wanted to rub himself. I nearly let him do it to me, too, just 'cos it was so good to hear him say all that shit about my eyes being so pretty and that. And I wanted to do it once, in fact, 'cos I ain't never done it proper. Not really proper fucking like in the films – there's been a couple of times when I was smaller in the old days that boys got their thing half in but each time they both came so quick I never felt much. Anyway, what with this creep telling me my eyes was pretty I nearly let him just so's I could say I done it but then he said about my mouth being – what was it? – not lovely – luscious! That's it – luscious! That put me right off 'cos it was so stupid.

I told Denisha that one after and she laughed like anything. She's right, of course: my lips ain't nothing like luscious. You'd think with all that fat all over me and under my chin and hanging on the sides of my cheeks that at least I'd have good, fat lips and big boobs. But I don't – I've got this little tiny mouth that's half buried in blubbery stuff and my boobs ain't really big neither. It's just all that fat hanging about all over my chest that makes them look as if they must be from the outside. I'd like to have some of that stuff injected into my lips – what d'ya call it? – collagen or something, but Sheila says she read in *Heat* magazine that the woman off *EastEnders* had it done and her face all swelled up and went purple and now she can't eat nothing except soup. Mind you, if that's true then that might be a good thing in my case. Big lips and only soup and I'd be looking good in no time.

I'd got right depressed after that letter from Crystal. I love

Crystal and I want her to be happy; I really do. It's just that it makes me feel more alone when one of them over there gets on the other side. It ain't never going to happen to me, that's for sure.

'Might go up the high street later. Wanna come?' Sheila said.

'Yeah, OK. Are you with anyone?'

'Nah. Might meet Vinny later, but nothing's fixed.'

'Oh, shit, not Vinny, Sheila. He's a right drag – you know that.'

'No, he ain't. He's a good laugh. It ain't that though anyway, is it, Stacey?'

'How d'ya mean?'

We was sitting at one of the tables in the staff canteen. It's not bad there, as it happens. Quite bright and cheerful, as my mum would say. They done it all out fresh the other day, and the walls are a sort of bright yellow orange. Dead cheerful. And we get to buy all kinds of packets of stuff real cheap that get damaged in the store, so there's always a bargain or two. Don't help my diet none, of course, but it don't come down to little things like that, you see. It's the metabolism that's to blame.

'How d'ya mean?' I said again. She can be right irritating, can Sheila, when she tries. She was just sitting there, giving me one of her clever looks. 'Come on, Sheil,' I said, 'don't fuck about – it's not what about Vinny?'

'It's not 'cos you think he's a drag that you don't like it when he comes out with us.'

'Well, why then?'

'It's 'cos he's dead funny about you, innit? It's 'cos he makes us laugh. You gotta have a sense of humour, Stace. That's your trouble – I know you don't like us

75

sending you up but Vinny's right funny about everyone, you know that.'

'It's all right for you, Sheil. You don't know what it's like.'

'Oh, come on, he's the same about all of us, is Vinny. He should be on telly, my mum says. He's got a right sharp tongue on him.'

I was eating a fish supper. I'd finished at six o'clock and I always have my dinner about six thirty in the canteen when I'm on this shift to save my mum having to cook. She ain't a born cook, my ma, so it ain't like I'm missing much when I eat at work. Fish is good for you and not so many calories as some of the pies they do in the canteen, so I have the fish when it's on. With chips and salad. Salad's good for you too.

'Your boyfriend been in?' Sheila had a mouthful of coleslaw, and there was bits hanging out of her mouth but I could still hear what she said. She likes asking me about the old guy. I know she gets a thrill from talking to me about most anything really: it makes her feel so much cleverer and better when she talks to me. It's funny really – I know her brain's not a patch on mine but she thinks she's the clever one. I can see through all that stuff though, but all she understands is just the outside of everything. She don't see the inner life, that's her problem. Not that my inner life is much cop, but it would be if I didn't have such a fucking nothing outer life – I've got the wherewithal for it, I've got the equipment. Sheila don't have none of that at all: her inner life's a bleeding airy desert. Tumbleweed time, if you ask me. But as far as she's concerned it's what you see on the outside that matters. My life is just the shop and my mum, apart from her, and she loves to be reminded of it. Makes her feel brilliant it does: a right social whirl, her life is, compared to mine.

I squeezed a bit more ketchup onto the fish. Ketchup's good for you too. It's made of lycene 'cos of the tomatoes, you see. Crystal told me that in one of her letters. Or is it lycepone? Something like that, anyway.

'Course he has.' I smiled back at Sheila. I wasn't gonna give her the satisfaction of looking upset about it. 'He's been in three times this week.'

'Truly weird, that's all I can say. I wouldn't want some old guy getting off on me, I can tell you.'

'No, you just want young ones getting off on you, Sheil.'

She looked right pissed off at that, and I felt quite pleased with myself. Who's she kidding? Her and her tight, low tops. 'Do up your overall please, Sheila,' Warren's always telling her. 'Oh dear, Mr Chipstead – however can that have happened?' she says. 'Must be too tight for me across the top.' Silly tart.

I looked out of the window. I hate December. The nearer it gets to Christmas the more I hate it. They'll be putting up the tree in the shop soon, and all the customers will start buying Christmas cakes and packets of mince pies and stuff. I hate to see the checkout loaded with all that, it makes me feel right depressed, I dunno why.

'No, he's all right, that old bloke. Fuck knows why he comes to my till all the time – he must know I'm twice as slow as you or Janet. I'm slower than any of you. But he don't seem like one of those who has a thing about – you know.'

'What d'you say, Stacey?'

I looked back at her and I could see she wasn't really interested anyway. She was looking at something over my shoulder and I turned round to see what it was. It was hard to turn 'cos the seats in the canteen are fixed to the floor and I can only get on one by sitting sideways on the edge and not getting my legs under the table at all. And I was sitting the wrong way to look round, so I had to try to twist myself about a bit to give my neck room to turn. And twisting's not really my thing, you see. Well, anyway, I managed to see what she was looking at. Mrs Peters was having a coffee with Denisha, and they was chatting to each other like real friends.

'Ooooooh!' I said. 'Now what's all that about?'

'Dunno,' said Sheila, 'but I don't like it. If she's gonna give her my overtime I'll kill the cow. Anyway, what was you saying about your posh old friend, Stacey?'

'He doesn't seem like one of those who's funny about – you know.'

'What?'

I sometimes think I like to make things more difficult for me than what they are already. I mean, I know Sheila likes to get me to talk about my problem – I know that by now. So why do I sit with her? And why do I bring up stuff when I know what she's gonna do? Make me say things. It give her a kick to make me say them. So maybe all along I want to say them. That's Crystal's theory anyway. She says she heard that on the telly or somewhere, that you make yourself talk about the things you don't like or something. Well, if that's right I should be talking about my weight problem all day and all night, that's what I wrote her back. Well, maybe you do, she wrote me then. Maybe if you shut up about it and didn't think about it you wouldn't feel so bad and you'd stop minding. Well, I wrote back, you try not thinking about it when your skin's rubbed raw and your knees ache so much you wanna cry and you can't buy no clothes except them that's like tents and you can't get on a bus so you stand on the step part and everyone has to push past you and you can't fit in a seat at the cinema and nobody wants to go out with you except to have a laugh. That shut her up for a bit.

'You know what I'm saying.'

'No, I don't. What?'

See what I mean? Just had to make me say it, didn't she?

'He don't seem like one of those what likes big women. That's what I meant, and you know it.'

'Oh, right. Well, I don't know about that. He looks like he has a right old wank when he gets home thinking about you, if you ask me.'

'Don't be disgusting, Sheil.'

Old sharp-ears Peters was just passing the table with Denisha and must have heard the 'w' word, 'cos she stopped and looked at us with that daft expression on her face that she thinks makes her look as if she's in charge and knows what she's doing. As if. I could see her thinking about whether to say anything or not, but then she got distracted by my plate. Always a good one for a comment or two from Mrs Peters, is my plate.

'Do you really think you need that, Stacey dear? All that batter is full of fat, you know. Why don't you just have a nice yoghurt and an apple?'

Fuck off, fuck off, fuck off, you interfering cow. 'No, I'm off dairy produce, Mrs Peters. My doctor said I wasn't to eat no dairy produce, you see. But I'm to have plenty of lycene.'

Ha! That got her. I could see she hadn't a flying fuck of a clue what lycene was, but being the stuck-up cow she is she wasn't gonna let on. So she daren't say much else in case she give herself away, you see.

'Oh, well, I'm sure he knows best, dear.'

I didn't say nothing more 'cos I just wanted her to go away really, and I wanted to see if Denisha was going to walk out with her, but she never. Mrs P kind of nodded at us and turned away – I could see she was scared I'd say something more about lycene and she'd have to come clean about not understanding what I was on about – and Denisha sat down next to Sheila.

'What was you sitting with Mrs P for, Denish?' I asked once old nosy was too far away to hear us.

'Oh, never mind, Stacey, nothing for you to worry about. Nothing important,' she said, and then she turned and whispered something in Sheila's ear and Sheila laughed. It's not like I think it was about me or nothing – I know it wasn't 'cos Denish ain't like that – but they never include me in their jokes and stuff unless they want something from me, and it makes me feel ever so lonely sometimes.

'So are we going up the high street, then, Sheila?'

'Yeah, OK, Stacey. But piss off when I give ya the word, will ya? If Vin gets in the mood I don't want you getting in the way, OK?'

'OK,' I said. But you wait, I thought, it'll be me telling you to piss off one day, Sheila. And even you, Denisha. There'll be no more whispering and keeping me out of your jokes then, will there? Once I'm sorted I'll be telling you all to piss off.

Charlie

By the time I got home after my appearance in court and the dramatic revelation that went with it I'd more or less pulled myself together. I managed to spend a fairly normal evening with the family – or at least one of the many different 'normal' types that have evolved over the years. Luckily there isn't one definitive norm – like most families, I suspect, the four of us in concert produce a creature that is more than the sum of our parts. Or sometimes less, depending on the combined moods of the participants. There's the jolly, story-telling, happy-ish kind of animal that appears when all of us have had a good day – that's a fairly rare specimen. Quite often Ben, Judy and I are in reasonably good fettle, but Sally has always enjoyed being confrontational, and when the rest of us are in a good mood that normally sends her in the opposite direction, so the existence of a contented foursome has to come from her lead, so to speak. And she has to be in the sort of good mood that will be exaggerated by surrounding jollity rather than irritated out of it. Which doesn't often happen. Especially as Ben has been very moody himself lately – not at all the chatty chap he used to be.

There's the openly hostile evening, of course, that I assume is not unknown outside our particular family circle. It amazes me that we survive these, in fact. It's quite chilling just how much unspoken (and sometimes spoken) loathing can be exchanged between so-called loved ones who go on to wake up the next morning and talk about cornflakes. But there you are: apparently expressions of disgust and pitying sarcasm are all part of the rich pattern we call family life. I'd love to think it's simply some sort of valve, that we are releasing tensions and having a frank and full discussion of issues, or whatever the politicians call it. It's not, obviously. I'm pretty sure it's just that we basically hate a certain number of things about each other and, at times, that seeps into the open.

Thankfully, more common is the sporadically silent but reasonably positive atmosphere that contains a mix of semi-argument and relayed mundane facts punctuated by the occasional laugh. That's the nearest we get to an average evening, and it was a relief to find that the mood when I got home that night was of this kind. I used the spaces between discussions to calm myself further, and kept up an appearance of mild irritation and boredom that fitted in nicely with my attempt at mimicking normality. I resisted the temptation to go to bed so early as to arouse suspicion, but made an excuse soon after loading the dishwasher and downing a quick cup of coffee and went upstairs. As I got undressed I pushed to the back of my mind the disturbing revelation I'd had in court and tricked myself into ignoring it by taking an inordinate amount of trouble in cleaning my teeth. I'm not usually a floss man, but on this occasion I used it to excess, causing my gums to bleed in the process but succeeding in distracting myself from the thoughts that part of me was dying to explore.

As I turned over and prepared to sleep, the images I had conjured up in court inevitably dominated my thoughts, but they had already acquired a hallucinogenic quality. I felt unsure as to whether I had really had that strange vision of Stacey's hand or whether it was some mad exercise my brain was going through to stop me falling asleep. How did I usually go to sleep anyway? Now I came to think of it I hadn't a clue. Did I drift off in the middle of a thought or empty my head of all reflections before slipping into blankness? It suddenly seemed impossible: a nonsensical idea, in fact, that I could slither into unconsciousness every night with virtually no effort. I listened to my breathing. It sounded ridiculously loud. Loud and rasping. Was that really me?

My brain is merely a processor, I thought. A high-functioning computer that needs to go into sleep mode for a few hours to recharge its batteries and file some of its data without any new input. Right. I can easily switch off my PC and send it into limbo for the night, so I simply have to do the same thing here. I enjoy turning off the PC: I find the descending whine of its innards as it settles down for the night very soothing. All I have to do is find the 'off' switch for my own deeply personal computer, I thought – I am clearly pressing restart instead.

After letting my mind drift aimlessly over the subject of bits and bytes and RAMs and ROMs for several minutes I must have bored myself to sleep. Surprisingly, I don't remember dreaming at all – in any case, not about the emotional upheaval that I had gone through in court – but, equally, by the time I woke the next morning, I didn't feel as if I had spent a particularly peaceful or energising night. I felt vaguely uneasy, as if something untoward had taken place during the hours of darkness in which I was somehow involved but couldn't remember. But it wasn't the thought of yesterday's revelation that disturbed me. Strangely, considering the extraordinary force and clarity with which it had attacked me the previous day, by the time I was wide awake and lowering my feet onto the well-worn patch of carpet, it had acquired the characteristics of an interesting and vaguely amusing dream. I thought with relief of the vision I had undergone as being a mild hallucination of some kind, in all likelihood caused by tiredness or boredom with the case I had been defending.

My relief didn't last long. As my feet touched the floor I instinctively flinched and looked down at them, aware, in an instant, that something was very wrong. I had one sock on. Trying to ignore the irritating phrase 'what's afoot?' that I was muttering to myself, I concentrated on possible explanations. I always always get undressed in the large cupboard next to our bedroom that we euphemistically refer to as my 'dressing room', bundle my socks into a pair — one tucked inside the other — and throw them into the laundry basket in the corner. There was no possibility of my having left one on my foot: even when drunk I had never skipped my tucking and throwing routine; the target might have been missed and pairs of socks scattered well beyond the confines of the basket, but the feet had been disrobed every time, without exception.

Then I saw my shoes. A few inches from the side of the bed, they lay casually abandoned, the right one on its side, a single black sock stuffed into the other. I still refused to believe that the night before, utterly sober, I had abandoned my regular routine of undressing next door, and as I would hardly have been likely to carry the shoes away from their place on the rack and into the bedroom, there could only be one explanation: I had worn them during the night.

Ben was sitting at the kitchen table when I came downstairs. He turned to look at me (unusual in itself for that time of the morning: a grunt from the back of his head is the most in the way of greeting that I can normally expect) with an expression in his eyes that I can only describe as wary. I had just a split second to take it in, before he turned quickly back to his Frosties or Choco Flakes or whatever other sugar-drenched breakfast he was putting away. I moved towards the kettle under the window.

'What?' I said.

'How d'you mean?'

'Were you going to say something? I thought for one rather terrifying moment that you were about to say good morning to me.' I paused to give him a chance to retaliate with something equally sarcastic, but nothing was forthcoming. 'No? Oh, well, why break the habit of a lifetime?' I went on. 'We don't want to start establishing precedents, do we?'

'Dad, do shut up,' Ben muttered wearily into the bowl of soggy nourishment. 'I'm not in the mood. Anyway – you know.'

'Sorry? I mean, sorry. Yes, sorry about the sarky comment, but I also mean – sorry? What do you mean, "you know"?'

'Well,' and he looked suddenly sheepish again as he pushed his bowl away and sat back in his chair. 'You know – last night.'

Now this really chilled me. Nothing that I was aware of had taken place before, during or after dinner the previous evening that could possibly have engendered the morning's odd reaction in my son, and I instinctively and instantaneously linked his reference to 'last night' with the mystery of my shoes and socks.

When I was a child I was a frequent and adventurous sleepwalker, occasionally being woken in mid-journey by an anxious mother to find myself, terrifyingly, in a place some way from the warmth and security of my bedroom. I never had any memory of the walk itself, and later could only recall the shocking moment of coming back to consciousness clad in pyjamas in some unexpected corner of the house. But, once I'd been told, many times, about what I had been doing on my nocturnal adventures, innocent though it invariably was, I became extremely frightened by the whole idea. The fact that my body could act independently of my conscious mind was the ultimate in loss of control. Who was the boy who walked? If his actions had no existence in my memory, then what part of him was me – or what part of me was him? Did we have the same personality, or was this alter ego the Hyde to my

Jekyll and did he perpetrate unknown horrors in the hours of darkness?

I found myself reading about doppelgängers, scratching in morbid fascination at the sore that worried me, rather than ignoring it and letting it heal. I became scared to go to sleep, like the wretched children in those horror films whose only way of keeping out of the clutches of the abuser is to stay awake. My tormentor was myself, and I hated to let him loose by drifting out of consciousness. But I went on walking, not often but fairly regularly, and I went on worrying every night as I lay down to sleep.

They told me of one night when my great uncle was staying with us and had been given my bedroom to sleep in. I visited him unannounced in the early hours, to find him sitting on the edge of the bed unstrapping his wooden leg. It didn't appear to worry me in the least, or so they told me in the morning, and I chatted quite happily to the old man about the stump and why it looked the way it did. Now wouldn't you think you'd remember something like that?

I know my parents considered not telling me when I'd been on my outings, but I begged them so relentlessly every morning to let me know, and put up such a good appearance of not minding, that they were persuaded to be truthful. I think my father, a stickler for honesty, could also see that if they kept the walks a secret there just might be some I remembered and their lie would be exposed and I would never be able to trust them again.

And now it all came flooding back in an instant. I was suddenly sure that I had visited Ben last night. The relatively calm mood in which I had descended the stairs abandoned me and I felt an unpleasant little chill pass across the back of my head. I was reminded horribly of those childhood insecurities: what had Mr Hyde been up to this time? I knew

I had to tread carefully if I was to find out without causing more problems than I could handle.

Ben

'Holly, can you come over? I really need to talk to you. It's important or I wouldn't ask. What? Yes, I know . . . I know, that's why I wouldn't have bothered you unless it mattered. Please, Hol – just for a short time.'

I felt better as soon as I put the phone down, and almost rang her straight back to tell her not to come, but I knew I'd only regret it. This was always a puzzle to me – how the idea of being able to talk to Holly was enough to take all the pain out of me, but that once I was face to face with her I didn't really want to go through with the actual conversation. Rather not, in fact. But if I didn't then the next time she wouldn't come, and that would be fair enough, after all. And also, if I didn't, then I'd know inside that I wasn't really going to tell her my problems after all, so the magic of thinking I was going to wouldn't work any more, would it?

I knew she'd promised herself she'd work all afternoon, so it was even more important this time that I made use of her visit. At least she'd listen without that distracting look of anxiety in her eyes that made it so difficult to unburden myself to Mum. Not that I could in this case, anyway, of course. She was the last person I could discuss it with.

Holly was looking beautiful, I thought. She'd rushed straight over and hadn't bothered to put on her make-up or even to put her lenses in, and with her glasses on and her hair pulled back in a ponytail she looked wonderfully fresh and scrubbed. I knew she hated me seeing her like this, however many times I told her I liked her face looking sort of naked. It reminded me of the few times I'd seen her first thing in the morning, when we'd been backpacking and shared a tent.

She was worried, of course, but in a comradely sort of way: non-judgemental, I suppose you'd call it. Mum had let her in, and I checked quickly to make sure she wasn't hovering outside my bedroom door before I closed it again and sat next to Holly on the bed.

'It's my dad. He's being really strange and I'm frightened. I wouldn't say this to anyone else but I wonder if he's going off his trolley. I couldn't sleep last night just thinking about it.'

'What's he done?'

'It's more what he's said. He's not really done anything, I don't think, although he doesn't seem to be himself at all. He's not been telling us about his work, or complaining about things like he usually does, or telling us terrible jokes he's heard from his colleagues. I thought he must just be having some sort of mid-life crisis or something, but now I wonder if it's more than that. He came into my room last night and said some truly weird stuff.'

'What?'

I was finding this hard. Putting these things into words has the strange effect of making them both more real and, at the same time, much less so. I find myself listening to myself as I speak, as if I'm replaying my words from a distance, or as if I'm acting everything out and judging my performance as I'm giving it. Did my father really say all that stuff to me, or was I making it up? And if he did say it, so what? Perhaps I was making something out of nothing and being melodramatic. Suddenly I felt foolish and childish.

'Hol, I'm really sorry. I think I'm wasting your time.

I don't know what's the matter with me. I expect I'm worrying about nothing. Forget it – get back to your revision or whatever and I'll see you tomorrow.'

'It's OK, Ben. You always do this, you know. You might as well tell me now I'm here. Maybe it's nothing and maybe it isn't, but you'll worry about it in any case. You'll feel better if you talk about it. And don't feel bad about my work: to be honest I was thinking of stopping and going out to do some Christmas shopping. I wasn't getting anywhere.'

'That's not what you said on the phone.'

'No, but that was just to make you feel bad. And to make sure you really did need to talk and you weren't just looking for an excuse to stop working, like I was.'

There was a bit of a silence, so I used it to give her a kiss. It was funny to bump into her glasses and it made us giggle.

'Sorry.'

'Don't be. I love you in your glasses.'

'Oh, you can't! They're awful – really geeky.'

'No, I like them. And your eyes look different without your lenses. Not so fishy.'

'I beg your pardon? Fishy?'

I kissed her again, and moved a hand to slip up inside her T-shirt to have a feel but a noise from the landing outside made me nervous and I pulled back from her.

'So, anyway, go on. What did he say?'

'It was about twelve thirty. I was deep asleep: I'm not always at that time but I was really tired after football practice. I'd been listening to my mini-disc and I think I must have gone to sleep with it still going, or at least with the earphones still in, because I didn't hear him knock, and he always does. Although – I've only just thought of this – perhaps he didn't this time. Like I said, he's been doing really strange stuff lately. Maybe he just walked straight in.

In any case, he was standing next to the bed, just looking at me. There's always enough light from the street for me to see in my bedroom, even if the light's off, and —'

'I know that, dimmo.'

'Yeah, of course you do. So you can picture it — me waking up and him just watching me. But he wasn't looking creepy or anything, like in a film, I don't mean that. I mean, it was just Dad, you know.'

'And?'

'And he said something like, "You are all right now, aren't you?"'

'What did he mean? All right about what, after what?'

'Well, I was half asleep, of course. You know what it's like when you just wake up: there's a bit of you pretends you weren't really asleep at all, and behaves kind of extra awake and sort of knowledgeable and intelligent to cover for the fact that your brain isn't making any sense of the world for a bit. And I wasn't sure if I was in the middle of a conversation with him or where I was or anything, really. But I just said, "Yeah, I'm absolutely fine, Dad. Yes, I'm totally all right now," or something as I sat up and took out the earphones. And he kept looking at me and said, "No, but you'll manage from now on, won't you?" And by that time I was more awake and realised that I didn't understand what the hell he was on about or why the fuck he was in my room. So I told him. I asked him why he'd woken me up and what did he mean, and then he sat on the bed and gave a great big sigh and shook his head. This was all really odd, I can tell you. I wondered if someone had died. My gran or someone.

'"Sorry, Ben," he said, and that made things even odder, because he never uses my name unless he's calling for me up the stairs or telling me off. "I'm so sorry." "What for?" I said.

"Is someone ill, Dad, or what is it? What's the matter? Why did you wake me up? Is Mum OK?" Then he looked down into his lap and said "Mum" several times, as if he couldn't work out what it meant. And he sort of shook his head next and turned back towards me. He smiled at me, and looked a bit more normal then. "Sorry, old chap," he said, "didn't mean to frighten you. Everything's fine. Go back to sleep." And he took the mini-disc off the bed and put it over on my desk, winding the earphones neatly round it. And then he went out again.'

'I shouldn't worry – it doesn't sound all that strange to me. Maybe they'd had a row or something. Your mum and dad, I mean. Mine do all the time and they're not even in the same house. I can tell straight away when they've been arguing on the phone because afterwards my mother looks at me in that sort of pitying way as if I'm a poor semi-orphaned child who's never going to feel the love of her father and all that stuff. I keep telling her, it doesn't worry me one fart if they're together or not. I see more of him now than when they were, anyway. It's not really me she's worried about, of course. She just enjoys the martyrdom of it all.'

'No, I don't think it was anything like that, Hol. I know them when they're rowing and it was different. And it wasn't like when he's worried about work – I'm used to that, when he goes all moody and difficult. This was – well, he was like someone else, that's the only way I can put it – and after the way he's been so different lately it really got me. There's something going on.'

Sally

God, I'm really putting on weight, I've got to watch it. I tried on a pair of trousers in a size 12 today and they were so tight I could hardly get the zip done up. It's my thighs that are the problem: I'm getting that horrible pear shape that just wrecks the outline unless I wear something that covers my hips.

I hadn't meant to start trying on clothes: I'd really gone to do some Christmas shopping and I was finding it so difficult that I took a break and thought about what I might ask Mum to get me as a present instead. It's funny – I usually find it so easy to buy things for them but because everyone's been so moody lately it's quite put me off. Since Mum's been spending so much time upstairs with headaches she seems to have lost interest in clothes and things – I keep asking her to go and see the doctor but she insists she's OK. So when I looked at some of the scarves and belts I might usually have chosen for her I got quite depressed and couldn't imagine her being pleased with them at all. Or any of the lipsticks or perfumes either: they just seem totally irrelevant somehow. And it's a bit the same with Dad – I usually get him a silly, funny kind of present: a singing dog turd sort of thing or beer glass that burps when you pick it up – but his sense of humour is completely unpredictable at the moment and there's not much less funny than opening a singing dog turd on Christmas morning if you're not in the mood.

I caught him looking at Mum today with an expression that quite gave me the creeps. I guess I've always taken for granted that they love each other in that unembarrassing, friendly kind of way that you hope your parents do – the last thing I'd want is for them to start being openly romantic or anything — God forbid! But recently I've begun to wonder: they almost seem as if they don't like each other any more.

Crystal

Whoa, Stacey!!!

How're ya doin??? I'm writing this one week post-op and I'm feeling great! I thank God so much for blessing me in finding such a loving and kind-hearted friend as yourself. I have been blessed to meet many of my angels in person, but you're my kinda favorite even tho' we're only pen buddies.

You have been a very big part of my life over the past year as I began this journey and this quest to be a better, more healthy human being. And I just want to say thank you for being there!!! I'm praying for you, honey, that you may reach your destination in WLS as I have and live a whole and complete life as God intended for us all to have. May the love of God keep you, the peace of God surround you, and the grace of God be ever present in your life. There are some things in our lives we can't change — and I sure as hell should be the one to know that if anyone does — but with the Lord's help I am changing my body shape and finding the person I was always meant to be.

It all went great last week and thanks to Jesus and my family I am on the mend now. Already as I type this message, I swear my arms are closer to my body and I can actually see the keyboard on my lap without straining. The swelling has gone down around my ankles too. I have gone from asking if I needed to have my brain examined to knowing this is the most important thing I have done for my health.

Get over here, Stacey! Get onto the Other Side — you won't regret it.

Love and kisses

Crystal

Stacey

When I read the letter from Crystal it really made me think. I was sitting at the kitchen table with my ma, and I was finishing a virtually fat-free organic yoghurt. Well, in fact I was finishing my third one – they just don't seem to fill me up somehow and I read that you can eat as much of the fat-free ones as you like and they don't give you much calories. My mum said she couldn't get the totally fat-free in the flavour I like and in the organic so she got the virtually fat-free instead. I like the organic because they don't use the chemicals and that in them and you never know what's gonna make allergies. Allergies can cause weight gain 'cos they upset your metabolism and that. So I always get the organics when I can. Don't s'pose the virtually makes much difference. Each 125g carton is pure and natural and contains 0.1g of fat and 97 calories, so that's OK. And they contain as much calcium as a full-fat one so that's got to be good for my joints.

So I was finishing the yoghurt when I read Crystal's letter. The post comes after I leave for work if I'm on an early shift so, if I get any letters, I read them later when I get in and have my tea. The girls at work had been talking about going on an outing all together to see a movie so I was in a bad mood anyway: not that they didn't ask me, but they know I can't fit on them seats at the UGC one where they're going. Last time the manager found me a space at the back where he could pull up the arm and give me a double seat, but I'm not doing that again. Not unless I'm on my own at any rate. God bless videos, that's what I say. Whoever thought of videos gets my vote, that's for sure.

They know, of course, about the seats. The girls. They pretend they want me to come, but they just want to see what I'll say. Or they want me to come with them and then they'll act all surprised when I've got a problem. 'Oh, sorry, Stacey – we didn't think.' Oh yeah – pull the other one. Mrs Peters has enough trouble squeezing in herself; it's only beside me she looks normal – she's quite a fat old bag herself in fact.

So Crystal's letter was a real eye-opener as they say. I looked down at the yoghurt pot and the way I'd scraped it clean. Well, licked it clean, if truth be told, as my mum says. Looked like it'd been washed. Not a speck of pink on it; not a hint of rhubarb virtually thingy anywhere in sight. It made me fucking depressed. This ain't gonna work, Stacey, I said to myself. This just ain't gonna work. I suddenly saw it so clear. It was like one of them revelations people get when they find God, like Lorraine did when she got born again. Mind you, I'm not so sure our Lorraine did see things clearly once she'd found Jesus – not like you're s'posed to anyway. I always thought she went a bit daft. She walked round at work with this shining look in her eyes all the time and nothing I could do would annoy her. That was weird for a start, 'cos before I used to be able to get her going with no sweat and it always give me a kick 'cos she got so worked up. 'Oh, sorry, Lor, was you waiting for me to take over?' I'd say, all innocent, when it was my shift. Just two minutes late and she'd be in a right state, slamming her cash drawer in and flipping the carriers about as she closed up. Perfectionist, is Lorraine. Changeover at four means exactly four with her, and she likes to get her till all sorted and prepared, so if she has to do another customer once she's ready for the changeover it gets her right thrown. But once she'd found God she'd just look at me all dreamy and not say a word. I got later and later just to see if I could get her to blow, but she never. Till Mrs P pulled me up with one of her sarky comments and I had to be on time again.

And that's another thing: the swearing. Lorraine used to eff and blind with the best of us but it seems Jesus don't like her swearing so that all stopped once she went to the classes. And she'd turn that stupid dreamy look onto me when I said fuck or something and shake her head just that tiny little bit the way she does that makes you want to press your mouth right up against her ear and say every bleeding word you can think of. Just to get rid of that understanding fucking smile and those shining fucking eyes. She's still like that now, although the shine's worn off a bit over the last year. I guess it's tricky to keep up all that peace and understanding stuff when the highlight of your life is listening to some old bird complaining about mould on her Jersey royals. Must begin to wonder when God's plan for you is gonna reveal itself.

Crystal's a bit heavy on the Jesus stuff, too, but I don't mind with her somehow. Anything that gets you through the night when you're a big girl like Crystal and me, you see. I can't wait now to see that picture she promised me – I want a before and after, I told her, like in the magazines, so I can see how quick she's changing. It's funny the way she's never let me see one before – mostly I've found with all the girls I write to they're dead keen to send pictures. That's half the point really, of writing to others who're obese – you don't never have to feel shy about it 'cos we're all the same. It gets almost like a competition to see who's the biggest even.

I envy Crystal the way she feels so looked after by Jesus and her angels and all that. Double angels, in fact, 'cos she's got the ones like me who's ordinary friends and then she thinks she's got real ones as well. The ones with wings up in the sky flying about and blessing her and stuff – keeping an eye. Must make her feel she's worth something, mustn't it? Self-esteem, that's what they're always banging on about in my diet magazine. How can you esteem someone you can't stand? They don't explain that one. If I catch sight of myself in a mirror it makes me feel physically sick; no way can I esteem that. When they try and get psychological they talk a lot of shit in them magazines if you ask me: feel good about yourself, they say. And try to find your inner child. Crystal started some of that too in one of her letters and I says no way — if there's an inner child in there it's gonna take so long for me to find it I'll die in the attempt. She got quite upset when I wrote that — I sometimes think Americans don't have no sense of humour.

I hadn't never really taken the surgery stuff seriously before. I'd thought I had, and thought it was only 'cos I knew I'd never be able to get it done that I didn't find out more about it, but reading her letter I suddenly saw the light. All the diets and gadgets and supplements in the world wasn't gonna help me — I was too far gone. Crystal had done it and already she felt the change — I knew just what she meant about her arms, too, and I looked down at mine on the table. Once I looked at them I could feel them, and I knew the insides was sore and red where they rubbed against the sides of my chest. I wanted a space between, like Crystal's getting. I wanted it so much it made me get a bit tearful. Thousands of people get the weight-loss surgery in America, Crystal says. We get all the good things they have over there in the end, whether it's McDonald's or Nike trainers, so we're bound to start doing the WLS soon, I thought.

'Ma,' I said.

'Yes, love,' my mum said. She was sitting in her chair by the fire reading *Hello!* She loves that chair — it's sort of moulded to her bum after all these years and she don't like to leave it much really. She's not as big as me, anyway. Not near as big, in fact, but I wouldn't say so to her. That last time I went to the doctor's and he said all that about losing weight I told him I was just big like my mum. (I didn't go to be told to lose weight – I don't need a doctor to tell me that, do I? I just gone to get something for my joints, you see, 'cos the aching was so bad.) Anyway, that's when he said I was much bigger than my mum and if I didn't lose weight I'd be dead within a year. I was about 19 stone then and what he said scared me so much I hardly ate for a week. Didn't last long, though, and I haven't dared go back since 'cos I know I'm much heavier than that now.

'Mum – what do you know about weight-loss surgery?'

'You mean that liposuction – you want to be careful about that, Stacey. My friend Terri's daughter had that done on her thighs and they're like two bags of laundry now: all ruckles and dips and folds. Revolting. You wanna be careful, Stace.'

'No, I don't mean liposuction, Mum, I mean stapling. My friend Crystal – you know, the one I write to – she's had this stapling thing on her tummy and she's told me stories of all these friends of hers who've had it and they lose all this weight ever so easily.'

She's not really one for new ideas, my mum, so I knew this wasn't gonna go down too well, but I just wanted to say it out in the open. It's much easier to take things seriously if you've heard yourself say them out loud, and I've had this surgery thing in my head for so long I wanted to get it out and share it. It didn't seem so crazy once I said it.

'You don't wanna touch anything like that, Stacey. Terri read about this woman who had her jaws wired together and she went mad.'

'What are you talking about, Mum?'

'She did, Stacey. Terri says this woman went mad and attacked her dog with a spoon 'cos she was jealous of the dog eating dog biscuits, when she could only eat mush through a straw. You ask at the doctor's, they'll tell you about wires and staples and that. It's diet and exercise that'll do it. That's the only safe way.'

I didn't say nothing more but she hadn't put me off. My mum comes up with all kinds of scare stories when you ask her things. Seems like if it ain't the papers it's one of her friends what's heard something terrible that can happen, even if you're just thinking of changing your toothpaste. But to me it all seemed possible, suddenly. I was going like Crystal: I was going on to the other side.

Charlie

I never did discover exactly what passed between Ben and myself the other night, but I'm absolutely certain that I must have walked into his room and spoken to him. I managed to put it to the back of my mind and set off for work feeling far more cheery than I had when first getting out of bed. Indeed, the memory of that odd experience of waking to find myself unilaterally clad, sock-wise, soon faded into insignificance and became a dream-like part of all the experiences of the previous twenty-four hours. Rather amusing, in fact, and most probably simply a manifestation of the tension I had been putting myself through over my current case.

Much as I dedicate myself utterly to the client I am representing at any one time, it is naturally something of a strain to fight on behalf of someone when one's sympathies tend to the other side. I'd never admit it to anyone, but even if I don't positively favour the opposition, I more and more often find myself seeing all angles of a case, and feeling uncomfortable in maintaining the one-sided approach necessary to conduct a successful defence. The awareness of there being two sides to every story has always been at the back of my mind, of course — as it would be in any reasonably intelligent person's — but I seem to be consistently more conscious of it these days, so that even as I ask a question of my own witness I am horribly aware of the opposite point of view. This makes it very difficult to summon up the dogmatism to make a really good case, and the strain of pretending to feel something I don't is bound to tell.

By the time a couple of days had passed, I'd pretty much concluded that the Stacey ring 'vision' and the sleepwalking were easily explained in terms of overwork. I decided to set myself a little test: I'd promised Judy that I'd pick up some Paracetamol at some point during the day (she was in bed with a headache that morning), so I thought I might as well get it at SavaMart. I could easily pass by on my way to Lincoln's Inn, say a cheery hello to my fat friend and bring a little light into her life before closeting myself in the dimness of court no. 4 in the family division.

Could it ever have been that simple? Perhaps, if I'd left it alone and gone straight to work, I need never have faced the truth; I could have continued to believe that my revelation had been an illusion, and that the feelings it had conjured up had been transitory. My relationship with Stacey could have remained as insignificant as it then seemed to be — a passing aberration that meant nothing and would quickly fade. Or was it only because I knew I was bound to see her again that I felt so deceptively peaceful and unconcerned?

The sun was shining as I turned into Victoria Street, catching the tinsel decorations strung across the road as sharply as spotlights, making them flash and sparkle. I glanced up at them when I reached the supermarket, and remembered with a jolt of guilt that I hadn't yet ordered the new set of tableware that I was planning to give Judy for Christmas. I was left with dancing after-images in my eyes as I entered the store and at first found it hard to see clearly in the comparative gloom of the interior. Having picked up a basket and headed towards the chemist supplies via the bread aisle, I glanced back at the checkouts and it took me a moment or two to take in what I saw. Amazing, really, that the absence of something so enormous should take so long to register. She wasn't there.

Two of the tills were unattended, and at the other four were girls of average, if uninspiring size. Where was Stacey? She was usually on this shift – I'd seen her many times as I'd popped in on my way to work and bought a newspaper. Extraordinarily, and totally unexpectedly, I was almost knocked over by a wave of panic, and had to hold on to a shelf to steady my balance. I dipped my head and took a couple of deep breaths in an attempt to pull myself together, then, bracing my shoulders and assuming what I hoped looked like a normal expression, I continued down the aisle, putting a couple of packets of scones unthinkingly into my basket as I went. It was all I could do to stop myself rushing to the checkouts, grabbing one of the bored-looking girls by the shoulders and demanding that she tell me where Stacey was. I managed to stall myself for a few more minutes, but after a half-hearted examination of a plastic-wrapped German rye and pumpernickel loaf, I could bear it no longer and walked back, as nonchalantly as I could, towards the tills.

I wasn't sure whether to be disappointed or relieved to find that they were all empty of customers. I could have done with a few more minutes to collect myself before having to face anyone, but equally I was desperate to find out whether Stacey was lurking somewhere on the store premises and might be appearing any moment for her shift. I picked the till with the least unfriendly-looking girl ensconced next to it, and unpacked the contents of my basket onto the belt as I cleared my throat. The girl and I both listlessly watched the two packets of fruit scones gliding slowly towards her, and it struck me that they would in all probability never be eaten. Judy makes extremely good scones and would never dream of buying them ready-made, and there was no way I could explain my sudden decision to do so. Unless I could eat eight scones myself before returning home at the end of the day I was going to have to throw them away, and as I couldn't imagine being able to eat anything ever again I was sure they were doomed. Even as I opened my mouth to inquire casually about Stacey's whereabouts I considered grabbing the packets just before they reached the girl's outstretched hand and changing them for something more useful – fascinating that I should find myself worrying about eight wasted fruit scones when my life was in chaos. All this was going through my head as I struggled to maintain an appearance of normality.

I cleared my throat again. 'Morning,' I volunteered, nodding casually at the girl.

'Hi.'

'No Stacey then, this morning, I see,' I went on, feeling sure I was bright red and grinning like an ape.

'No, not s'morning.'

Oh, Christ – the scones were scanned and the till was

showing my total. I had only a few more seconds while I paid and took my change before I would run out of excuses to talk to the girl.

'On holiday, is she?'

She looked up at me and I swear she was smirking. In spite of my studiedly casual tone I could tell she sensed the urgency behind it, and it made me feel a fool. It suddenly seemed obvious that my constant visits to the supermarket and my use of one particular till had not gone unnoticed by the rest of the staff. It might have been only recently that I had become aware of my addiction to Stacey, but I now felt certain that to everyone else it had been crystal clear for some time. My body prickled with the humiliation of it and with the feeling of being watched: apart from the other checkout girls eyeing me right now, I could just imagine the dreadful Chipstead having a laugh about it with them all in the staff room, or whatever they call it in supermarkets.

'Nah. She's off sick. One seventy-two.'

'Oh, dear. Poor thing,' I managed to mutter, as light-heartedly as I could, as I pulled a couple of pound coins out of my pocket. 'Expecting her back soon, are you?'

'Dunno.'

I quickly shoved the scones into a carrier, picked up my change and made my way out into Victoria Street. I felt almost unbearably sad: I knew that my life really had irrevocably turned some sort of corner, and even though I couldn't yet begin to see what might lie ahead on my new and unexpected path, it was clear that it was not going to be an easy one. I looked for something to ease the distracting ache inside, and found myself gazing into the window of a greetings card shop. A get well card – that was something. An excuse to think about Stacey while I picked out a pretty, extravagant card to lift her spirits.

I chose something very pink and flowery. It reminded me of her — the roses and sweet peas pictured had a fleshy, blushing, luscious look to them that made me think longingly of her cheeks and of the hints of enormous bosom that always peeped out of the top of her overall. Roses in her cheeks, I thought to myself as I gazed at it soppily, but the phrase conjured up the delicate blush on the pale skin of a Victorian heroine. No — my girl's cheeks had room for a whole vase of the things. Plus a few giant chrysanths. My love is like a red, red sofa, I mused. And yes, of course — newly sprung. How very suitable. I laughed to myself as I paid for the card and watched the young man slip it, together with a fuchsia-coloured envelope, into a paper bag. She's going to love it, I thought happily. How many cards is that poor gigantic creature going to get when she's ill, apart from this one from a demented guy who's going through some sort of mid-life crisis? It didn't occur to me at that stage to wonder how on earth I was going to get it to her. I think I was just delighted to have found a small way of distracting myself from the deep sadness that was still threatening to well up inside.

I stopped outside the store, put my briefcase and SavaMart carrier down on the pavement beside me and pulled the card out of the paper bag — it made me smile again, just to look at it. What kind of madness was this? I shook my head and took my fountain pen from my upper breast pocket, then, before I could think too carefully and end up abandoning the whole idea, wrote 'just hoping you get better soon' at the bottom of the inside page. I hesitated as I wondered how to sign it: 'Your checkout friend'? 'Mr Baguette'? but, utterly unable to make a decision, left it blank, hoping I'd be able to hand it to her personally in any case. I slipped it back into the paper bag, then paused as I saw the bright-pink envelope.

I pulled it out and stared at it. Another nightmare. How would I address it without knowing her surname? 'Stacey' seemed intrusively intimate, but 'Miss – or Ms – Stacey' sounded patronising and hierarchical. I stood dithering for a moment or two, then popped it into the carrier bag and went on my way to work.

Stacey

'I don't feel too good, Ma,' I said. It was true; I'd felt right rough since I woke up. It wasn't like me not to go into work, neither. I had this pain on my left side and every time I tried to get up out of the chair it fucking killed me.

'You sit there, Stace,' said my ma. 'I'll get you a cup of tea and a slice.' She's good to me like that. We may have our problems, her and me, since my dad left, but we don't do too bad. At least I don't have to worry about what she's thinking when I'm sitting having a relax. Not like at work, when I'm always wondering about the others. They think I don't see them looking at my legs and bum and all that when I come in the canteen. Mind you, I'm careful about when I go there: if Mr Chipstead's already in there I'll wait. I don't like him to see me moving around more than I can help. It's better when he finds me already in my sideways position, then I can tuck as much of myself behind the table as possible. I kind of twist round and drape my arms on top of the table and try to hide the other bits and let him concentrate on my boobs. I've seen him looking at them and I can tell he's interested. And I never get up from my till when he's looking, neither – not unless I can help it.

I was watching *Jerry Springer* to take my mind off the pain. It always cheers me up that programme, in any case, seeing all them other big people. I'd like to live in Florida, really. I'd be more like all the rest there: Crystal told me my kind of size is quite common out there, and there are stores and places just meant for big girls. When I read her letters I get to feel as if I'm not that bad, really – but then I see myself in the mirror and I know I've got beyond the kind of thing that could ever look normal. And, anyway, Crystal's gone over the other side now, so she's not like me any more. Or she won't be soon. That's really hard to think about: she's been my friend for so long and now she's going to be just like all the others. I won't be able to tell her stuff like I used to.

'Come on, Stace!' said my mum as she put my mug and plate down next to my chair. 'You're all right, love, you know you are. You'll be right as rain by tomorrow, sweetheart. You've had these kind of pains before, haven't you, love?'

Now I ain't usually much of an emotional type. Denisha says I'm as cold as a block of ice, but then she never did have much in the way of a brain, if you ask me. But when I watch Jerry and all them screaming women on his show it's true I feel right embarrassed: I mean, I like watching them 'cos it's so weird, but I can't imagine letting go like that, let alone slugging some bloke in front of twelve million people. But maybe I was feeling sorry for myself or something, having just thought about Crystal and how she wasn't gonna understand me no more. And then with my mum's being so sweet like she always is – well, I dunno, but it all just got to me somehow. And I suddenly burst into tears and howled.

My poor mum. She didn't know where to put herself, I could tell. I couldn't stop crying, but all the while I was thinking: I've gotta stop this, 'cos my mum just don't know where to put herself. She's ever so clingy to me, is my mum, and I've never minded 'cos she's not a bad old thing and she had me ever so young so in some ways we're more like sisters, I sometimes think.

'You gotta get yourself back down the doctor's, Stace, love,' she said. She tried to get herself down next to me on the floor so she could put her arms round me. That made me feel like crying even more, 'cos the thought of her poor old knees trying to manage on the floor was awful: her arthritis is even worse than what mine is, you see. The doctor says they might have to give her new knees one day, but my mum says she ain't never gonna let them do that to her. She managed it, anyway, even while I was trying to raise myself up a bit out of the chair so she wouldn't have to go down so far, but I was still sobbing so hard it was making me shake and I couldn't get the energy to give myself the heave it takes to get me up. A right old pair, we are, when we're waddling around together, I always say. She reached her little arms out and got them round me a bit and it felt really good as she gave me a hard squeeze.

Dunno what I'd do without my mum, I really don't. I slag her off a lot to the girls 'cos that's what they all do about their mums, but I don't mean it. She's the only one that loves me. That's the problem. They always say you just need love and it's true. If my mum wasn't here there'd be not one person that loves me. Except maybe my dad. I think he loves me, wherever he is, but when you ain't seen someone for twelve years and you don't really know what they look like except by the old photos and you was just a kid anyway then you can't really tell, can you? I mean, he may have loved that kid, but who's to say whether he'd love the grown-up Stacey? Especially since she's grown up so big.

I don't like to think of that, though. That he might hate the sight of me if he saw me. I like to pretend that he knows

I'm still big but he loves me anyway. And it ain't so stupid to think that, because my mum was big when he loved her – he liked a good handful according to my mum.

'Did he go because he didn't like you being fat?' I used to ask her.

'No, Stacey – if I've told you once I've told you a thousand times, it wasn't to do with that. He liked a good handful, did your dad.'

That's how she always said it, and it made me feel right cheerful. I could picture him from the old photos, and in my mind I'd put him on the beach with my mum and he'd be grabbing a big handful of her backside, and smiling like anything, and she'd be looking all pretend cross and loving every minute. That's what I want. A man who'll love me just the way I am.

'You gotta get yourself down the doctor's, love,' she said again, and I stopped crying then and tore a piece off the loo roll that was with all my other things on the table next to my chair and I blew my nose. It was really loud and that made us laugh – I blow my nose like a navvy, my mum says – whatever that is.

She's right. It's about time I went to the surgery again. My joints are hurting like buggery, and, in any case, I want to ask him something.

Ben

I had this really strange dream last night. I was a computer protocol. Don't ask me how the fuck I could *be* a protocol because you wouldn't think you'd know you were one, really, as it's impossible to begin to imagine what one would feel like. If they could feel, that is – which they patently can't. No, I can't explain how I knew, but not only was it definite that I was one – and it wasn't at all unexpected or surprising, just the way those truly odd things never are in dreams – but I was a particular type. I was a TCP/IP protocol: the thing that connects up to the internet or whatever. And my friend – it could have been Holly or Maxim or anyone I know, really: it didn't seem to have anything as identifiable as a sex or name – was an IPX/SPX protocol. So to make any sort of contact with my friend, this other protocol, I had to work out how the TCP/IP protocol communicates with the IPX/SPX networking one. And I just couldn't begin to work it out or remember how to set up a way of them understanding each other.

It must be from listening to Hol going over the stuff she's been doing on JavaScript. She's been constructing a website for her dad's golf club and taking courses on loads of computer stuff. She's way beyond anything I can understand, but what she was saying must have reminded me of the time I was studying networking and all that in the IT class at school, and although I didn't think of it when I was with Holly, all the protocol business must have been dredged up while she was talking. Emerging from the depths of my memory and getting ready to invade my head in the night.

This guy at school says it's all about trying to communicate with my family. He would. It's only because I was telling him about my dad the other night and how strange he was. I don't think dreams are so obviously symbolic, myself.

There are times when I think we must be one of the most dysfunctional families around, but then I listen to my friends and we seem pretty average. From the outside I suppose we look relentlessly middle class, boring and normal: barrister father, ex-teacher and Ofsted inspector mother and two children both privately educated. But the way we can sit round the table and talk about nothing when half the world is starving and the other half is wrecking the planet with its greed really gets to me sometimes. I'm going to volunteer in Africa for my gap year. And I may stay out there and not bother with uni at all. But I haven't told anyone except Hol yet – and she just says I'll never go unless she goes with me. I have to say women do have an inflated idea of their importance.

Mum had one of her migraines this morning. She was still in bed when Dad left for work – really unusual that, as she's normally the first down. Mind you, Dad was up and dressed very early, and he looked a lot more positive this morning. He was humming to himself as he made his toast, and, after he'd taken Mum up a cup of tea, he bounced off to work looking really quite jolly.

It was when he came back that things went a bit pear-shaped again. I was doing some homework at the kitchen table – I normally do it in my room on the computer, but I was starving and while Mum made me a sandwich I thought I'd make a start – and he came in looking a bit depressed. He kissed Mum in that absent-minded way he does without saying anything and then plonked his things on the table and walked over to put the kettle on. I could see his manner had irritated her – she clanked the knife into the butter dish and then threw it down onto the worktop as she moved over to the table.

'Yes, thanks, Charlie – I am feeling a bit better. Thank you for asking,' she said as she picked up a plastic supermarket bag he'd brought in and tipped the contents out onto the table. 'I don't see any Paracetamol,' she went on. 'Is it here or –'

'Oh, bugger!' said Dad, and he turned quickly round

looking quite shocked. He rushed to the table and reached out almost as if he was going to snatch the bag out of her hand. 'Oh bugger, Judy! It's not in there — I didn't —'

'No, I can see that,' said Mum. 'You forgot it, I'm sure, didn't you? And why on earth have you bought all these scones?'

'I went in there to get the Paracetamol, darling — what an idiot I am — I just saw those scones and —'

But Mum suddenly smiled and picked up a flowery card that was under the packets of scones. How easy it is to make a woman happy — they're right in the mags when they tell you to buy something for them every now and then. I've seen Holly when I get her some tiny present — it's ridiculous how much it seems to mean to her. I felt quite embarrassed for Mum when I saw how she changed when she picked up the card. Dad had completely forgotten to get the one thing she really wanted, after all — and now she'd gone all forgiving just because he'd bought her a pathetic card.

'Oh, Charlie — thank you, darling. What a wonderfully ghastly card — I love it!'

She opened it and read out loud, the way she always does when she gets cards. Most people just skim through the verse or don't even look at it at all, but my family likes to read the verses out and have a laugh. It's pretty patronising really. I'm sure some people take them seriously.

This one finished with something like, 'And days of health restored for ever'.

'Wonderful poetry!' she said, laughing up at us, then she looked down at the card again. 'Just hoping you get better soon,' she continued. 'Very formal, darling! Glad to see you're not letting your emotions run away with you. No — only joking,' she added, as she saw Dad's expression. 'Thank you darling, it's really sweet. I almost forgive you for not getting the Paracetamol. Luckily for you I've got a couple left, or I'd send you straight out again right now.'

Dad was being weird again. He wasn't laughing, or even smiling, really. He was just looking at her. 'I said I'm sorry,' he said. 'I'll go out and get you some now.'

'No, darling, I said — it's OK, I've got enough to manage. I've taken plenty of the migraine stuff and I only wanted the other as a back-up in case it went on. But it's much better and I probably won't need anything more tonight.'

'Sorry about the scones.'

'What on earth made you get them? You know I hate the shop-bought ones — if you wanted me to make some you only had to —'

'You don't like the card, then?'

'What?'

'You said it's — what did you say? — that it's wonderfully ghastly, was that it?'

'For God's sake, Charlie — are you serious? You're not really offended about that, are you? I love it, I said so. I only meant —'

'I know exactly what you meant. It's obviously not the right card for you, is it?'

Mum glanced over at me, but I looked away quickly. No way was I going to get involved in this. I knew I ought to defend her really — he was being fucking stupid about the whole thing and he knew exactly what she'd meant about the card, but I couldn't bear to join in. It always annoys me the way my family sends everything up and I'd hated the way she read that poem out — it's like she's back to being a teacher when she does that sort of thing. I wasn't going to help her by taking her side. She could get out of this one on her own. Fuck knows why he was taking it so seriously, though. I even wondered for a moment if he was joking and was pretending to take offence to give us all yet another family laugh, but it was going on too long for that.

'Charlie, don't be ridiculous. Are you annoyed because I took it out of the bag before I was meant to see it? Look – here's the envelope: it's a gorgeous subtle pink that goes beautifully with this wonderfully tasteful card. Now, for God's sake, put it in the envelope, stick it up and give it to me later or whatever you were going to do. Let's start again. I won't interfere and I won't criticise your choice, OK?'

Dad shut his eyes for a second and swayed a bit – I almost thought he was going to fall over. But he opened them again, sighed and rubbed his face with his hand. 'It's not your fault,' he said. 'I'm just a bit tired, that's all. It's nothing to do with you, and I apologise.'

Judy

And then Charlie walked out of the kitchen and shut himself in the little box room we call his study. He really is behaving most oddly – I wonder if he's going through some sort of male menopause, or whatever they call it. I took the get well card up to the bedroom, because I was embarrassed to let Ben see that I was about to cry, and put it on my dressing table.

Once it was there, standing open on the glass surface, it suddenly looked unbearably pretty and touching. I sat on the stool and gazed at it. It wasn't odd of Charlie at all to behave the way he did, I thought – why had I been so dismissive and cynical about such a thoughtful gesture? Sometimes I feel sick of myself, I really do. It's all very well putting on my smart little business suits and collecting my papers together and going round all these schools with my teams and so on, but I'm never sure what gives me the right to judge anyone, let alone write reports on them. It's all an act, the way I look as if I know what I'm doing. I'm sure that's partly the cause of my – what shall I call it? – my headaches. Why not? I've called it that for so long now I'm almost beginning to believe it.

I remember my mother saying something many years ago about never feeling grown-up. It shocked me deeply and left me feeling very insecure. 'You think I know what I'm doing,' she said, after I'd been particularly cheeky to her and she was letting me out of my room after half an hour's banishment. 'I don't, you see, Judy. I feel exactly the same as I did when I was your age – it's just that I've learnt to pretend I have a kind of authority. If you push me too far you'll find there's really nothing there for you to lean on, and you won't like that, will you?' I couldn't understand it at the time: she'd always been my rock, and, together with my father, had surrounded me with a cushion of certainty about the world. I definitely didn't like the idea that my cushion might just collapse if I put too much pressure on it. Very unnerving, and really quite hard to take in.

Now I know exactly what she was trying to say. If I look into myself too deeply I find a frightened little girl, and it's only by keeping firmly on the surface and relying on the practicalities of life to float me along, so to speak, that I can appear to all around me to bear any real responsibility. Sometimes I think Sally can see this perfectly well: she is a very canny child – always has been – and, whereas Ben has always been my baby, Sally often seems more like an equal.

At that moment, though, as I looked at the pink roses on the card, I felt about six. He's such a dear, my Charlie, I thought. Just a little boy himself, really, for all his high-powered job and greying hair. I must take more care of him. It's all very well looking after all the practical things – and thank God I do, at least as far as finances go, because otherwise he'd – but I shook my head hard and managed to snap my mind away from *that* – quite enough on my plate without delving into all that just now, I thought – but I must be more careful with the other side: emotions and all that. I know how bossy I get some of the time, and how briskly sharp. I've got to stop it.

I looked into the dressing-table mirror and reached for a stick of blusher and a lipstick. I laughed to myself as I realised I was doing exactly what I tend to sneer at nowadays: prettying myself up to keep my man happy. Never mind, I thought, it's not just that, is it? It's more about your own self-esteem and confidence, isn't it? Well – sort of, anyway. With a bit of the other as well. 'You've come a long way, baby,' I whispered to my reflection as I leant forward and inspected the lip colour, 'but not quite far enough to give up worrying about looking reasonable for your husband. Well – too bad.' I felt almost skittish as I turned my head this way and that and practised a couple of smiles. I reached for one of the perfume bottles and sprayed a bit under my chin and onto my wrists – I hadn't bothered to wear it for a while and it smelt surprisingly strong, so I tried to wipe some of it off with a tissue, then stood up and took a quick look at myself in the full-length mirror on the door of the wardrobe. Boring, I thought. The brown skirt and sensible blouse and jumper were extremely dull. Right.

I was quite enjoying this. Maybe the card fiasco had been a good thing: a little jolt at the way I took my family life for granted. I opened the wardrobe door and quickly shunted the hangers to and fro in search of inspiration. The navy skirt – that was more like it. A better fit and slightly shorter. Plus my white polo neck, if it was clean. I looked at my watch and thought about putting the baked potatoes in – plenty of time to change first.

I felt really quite pretty by the time I came downstairs. Ben was still sitting at the kitchen table, and the crumbed plate next to his books reminded me that I never did finish the sandwich I was making him. He glanced up as I came in. 'Hi, Mum,' he said, 'you look nice.'

'Thanks, darling,' I said, 'just thought I'd freshen up a bit. Sorry about the card stuff before, I –'

'It wasn't your fault, Mum. Forget it. Dad's out, by the way.'

'Out? Where?'

'Dunno. He didn't say. He came out of his study and went straight out, soon after you went upstairs.'

I tried not to show that this had, quite unexpectedly, taken me aback. I suppose I'd imagined a loving reconciliation after the little tiff over the card, with Charlie teasing me about my change of outfit and giving me one of his dry kisses. I felt suddenly rather foolish in my smart clothes and lipsticked face. The perfume, too, still smelt far too strong, and I was aware that Ben must be smelling it too.

'Oh, right. He didn't say when he'd be back, then? I mean, I assume he's in for supper?'

Ben didn't answer, and I stood there not quite sure what to do. I knew I ought to put the potatoes in and then go and work on my reports, but I just hadn't got the heart. I was worried about Charlie and wanted to know where he was.

'Ben, I'm just popping out for a few secs, won't be long.'

'OK, Ma.'

He didn't look up, bless him, or comment on the fact that I never normally 'popped out' for no good reason in the late afternoon. I gave him a little squeeze on the shoulder, collected my coat from the hall and left.

I didn't have a clue what I was doing or where I was going to go: I just knew that I couldn't stay in the house for the next hour or so. Ridiculous — I was behaving like a teenager let down by a boyfriend. I had that panicky ache in the pit of the stomach that propels you to chase after someone who'd probably far rather be left alone.

I turned into Victoria Street and the wind hit me in the face. It had a deep chill to it and I shivered and tilted my head up to check for any sign of rain. It was dry, but the sky was already dark and my breath was steaming. Might even be a white Christmas, I thought. Only three weeks to go. I really must finish off my shopping.

It was then I saw him. Standing still just a few yards along the street from me, his hands in his pockets and his coat collar turned up, looking into a shop window and frowning slightly, apparently deep in thought. So — you were almost home again anyway, I thought. Good. I'm obviously overreacting to our little row and you came out to stretch your legs and now you're on your way back. I decided not to say anything, but to go home and wait for him, with luck not having to let on how childish I'd been. I watched him fondly — it's not often you get the chance to really look at your own husband without his knowing, except when he's asleep, of course, and that doesn't count. I've never thought he looks like himself when he's asleep, anyway — far from the peacefully angelic faces of the children when they were young, Charlie, at least once he was over thirty or so, always seemed to me to move out of his face and leave an unfamiliar shell behind once he was snoozing. He sleeps with his mouth and eyes both slightly open and his hair strewn wildly on the pillow, looking like an uninhabited, dilapidated house. His essence doesn't seem to live there any more until he wakes in the morning and, as he stretches and squirms, it seeps back in and his face looks like Charlie again.

But the man I quietly observed in Victoria Street was undoubtedly and completely my husband. I knew he'd be considering his work as he stood there unmoving: when he was halfway through a case, as he was then, he regularly got that look of abstraction in his eyes, and the family knew not to attempt any communication until the moment had passed. Another reason, I realised, for me to have been more patient over his odd reaction to the card – his case was obviously not going too well and he was touchy.

He moved and shrugged his shoulders a little (I'm sure he was giving a sigh, but I couldn't hear above the traffic) and began to turn away, not towards me but in the opposite direction. I forgot my resolution to go back home undiscovered and called his name out loud. He didn't seem to hear and I walked quickly towards him and called again: 'Charlie!' I saw now that he was carrying something, and I felt a slight unease. If he'd just gone out to stroll around a bit and collect his thoughts, why had he brought something with him? And why was he continuing to walk away from home? He must have been gone at least three quarters of an hour, while I was fussing and preening myself in the bedroom, and he couldn't possibly have got only this far in that time. So where had he been before, if he was still walking in the opposite direction to the house?

As I caught up with him I put a hand on his arm and he turned towards me wearing the most extraordinary expression. I can only say it seemed full of – what? – hope, I suppose. But hope in such an exaggerated form that he looked more like a drowning man spotting a life belt than someone being greeted by his wife.

But the look didn't last long, and was quickly replaced by one of resignation, almost anger. 'Judy,' he said, 'what in Christ's name are you doing here?' The tone was so unfamiliar it quite shocked me. He was about to say something else, but obviously changed his mind and looked away from me.

'Charlie, what's the matter? What are you doing?' I asked, feeling anxious again. 'I only came out because I felt miserable after our stupid little row and when Ben said you'd gone out I just wanted to see if I could find you and say sorry. I know it was stupid, and I never really dreamt I had a chance of finding you, but it's not like you to be so huffy about something like a card and it worried me. What were you doing, anyway – and where were you going when I stopped you?'

'I really don't know, Judy. I simply felt like – no, I'll tell you exactly what I was doing. If you must know, I was taking the wretched scones back.'

'What – the scones?' I laughed. 'You're not serious?'

But I could see in a flash that he was. Very serious. He lifted up the plastic bag he was carrying and held it open under my nose. 'See?' he said. 'Scones.'

And there they were, and as I glanced at the shops alongside me I saw that we were standing just a few doors away from SavaMart.

'But how did it take you so long to get here?' I asked. 'You must have been gone nearly an hour and home's only five minutes away.' I glanced quickly down at the carrier bag. 'And why didn't you go in to SavaMart? That was where you got them, wasn't it? And where were you going to just now when I called to you? You were walking away.

What is going on, Charlie? Is the case going really badly? You can tell me, you know. It always helps you when you talk about it, darling. It's just so difficult when you're touchy like this.'

'I am not touchy, Judy,' he said quietly. 'I've told you – I was simply going back to the shop to change the scones. It really isn't worth discussing any further.'

There was something very odd about his tone of voice: it was almost as if it wasn't Charlie speaking at all, but a sinister stranger who had inhabited his body without my noticing. It changed the way I saw everything around me, and at the same time it was as if a tiny shifting movement under my feet made me want to reach out to steady myself. The ground on which I stood, whose support I had always taken for granted, was suddenly made of quicksand.

Crystal

Hiya, Stacey!!!

How're ya doin'? How d'ya like the cute angel picture I've put in this letter? I'm doing just great – it's two weeks after surgery now and I've lost 20 pounds and gone down 2 pant sizes!! Yeah!

Thanks for your last letter – I just loved it. You're so funny, your letters make me laugh out loud, with those British expressions you use and all. Let me know as soon as you've talked to your physician about weight-loss surgery, honey – there's gotta be someone in that crazy island of yours that can do it. Ask your angels for help – and I don't mean the buddies that support you through the surgery, I mean your real angels. They're all around you, Stacey – even tho' I know you don't always believe in them, they're there for you, honey, just watching over you like Jesus is.

There have been many times when I believe that my life

has been touched by angels. One time I was watching TV and a psychic talked about children and the fact that "imaginary friends" were actually angels that only children could see (I had three when I was a child). I had a load of problems when I was a kid and I was very miserable at that time about my weight and all kinds of other stuff, and wishing that I had an angel. Suddenly, while I was watching the show, I felt a warm puff of air on my cheek and neck and a warm, strong hand on my shoulder, and a male voice in my ear telling me: "See, we were here all along, you just forgot about us." I turned around, and there was no one. I know now that they are with me always.

Angels have never experienced physical life. They retain their Divine Memory and work with anyone who opens themselves to that high, pure vibration. My friend says they're made of silk, but I don't agree about that. I think they're made of pure spirit, and that's kinda more see-through than silk, I guess.

Look after yourself, honey, and God bless you
Crystal

Stacey

I went to the doctor's this morning. I waited nearly an hour in that bleeding awful waiting room. I thought if I watched them fish swim about much longer I'd go mental. The girls on reception have that look on them – they peer from the back through that little open frame at me so I know they know I'm there, but they make me stand at the desk until I'm taking root before they can be bothered to move their arses and get out the front. Then they start filling in forms and that before they look up at me. They want me to blow a fuse and start yelling at them like I done that time all those years ago when my mum was sick and they wouldn't pay no attention. Then they'd be able to make a complaint about me and get me out of their faces. But I ain't gonna do that. I ain't gonna give them the satisfaction. So I just stand there, shifting my weight one way and the other to try to stop my knees hurting while they fill in their stupid forms and ignore me. When they finally have to give in and look at me they make like they've only just seen I'm there, like they've only just happened to notice this giant 300 pounds of flesh standing about three centimetres from their noses. Yeah, right.

'Well, you'll have to wait a bit, Stacey,' they say, once I've finally got them to write my name on their stupid lists and stuff. Or 'Is it urgent, Stacey, because there are a few waiting and it may be some time?' or something.

'Yeah, it's urgent,' I feel like saying, 'so isn't it lucky that you asked me that straighta-fucking-way or I'd probably be dead by now.' But I don't, of course. I just look back at them and say, 'Don't worry, I'll wait,' and then go and find a chair that looks as if it might not break when I sit on it.

Now, wouldn't you think they'd have a decent chair at the doctor's that's not gonna collapse when someone of my size sits on it? No, that would be too easy.

Instead them girls watch me − suddenly their forms don't seem to be so urgent, funny that − as I go over to the bleeding fish tank and look at the chairs out of the corner of my eye till I spot the strongest. We all remember the time that I sat on one that began to give way and the girls rushed over as if that chair was the most expensive and precious chair in the universe and said, 'Oh no, dear, you mustn't sit on that one − it's not designed for obese patients.' I'll never forget that. How humiliated I was, I mean. 'Obese patients'. Thanks for nothing. Anyway, now they watch me with their beady little eyes and we all know what they're remembering. I hate going up the surgery. I hate it.

Still, the wait wasn't so long as sometimes. Bet the girls were disappointed — I've had to sit there nearly two hours some visits. This time the doctor seemed to get through his list quite quick and suddenly it was my turn. I really didn't feel like a lecture — I just wanted him to make my side stop hurting and give me my mum's prescription for her pills but he can't ever leave it at that. So I sat through all the stuff again, although he never said about me being dead in a year and that — although he made me go on the scales again and I'm bigger than when he told me that, so I know he's still thinking it. But he had a good go on the dieting and stuff, before I asked him. About the surgery.

He give me one of them sarky smiles then, when I tell him about it. I knew it was doomed as I was telling him — he had that face on him that means he thinks everything I'm saying is rubbish.

'And where did you hear about this, Stacey? The stapling operations have all sorts of unfortunate side effects and I really wouldn't recommend them.'

When I told him it was my pen friend in America his smile got so much bigger and sarkier I thought he might burst out laughing. Cunt.

'Ah, yes — our American friends,' he said. 'No, Stacey, you don't need any of that nonsense. No gadgets or pills or operations. All you need is sensible diet and exercise. Less food, more exercise. Simple!'

It may be simple to you, mate, but it's the most difficult effing thing in the world to me, I thought. D'you think I'd be sitting in front of you here, after waiting outside with that chair heaving and creaking under my weight and your snotty receptionists looking at me like something that's been dredged out of the river, if it was simple? I felt like hitting the stupid shit.

'Do they do it over here?' I asked. I decided to ignore his smile and his obvious bleeding comments and try at least to get some useful information out of him. 'Is there anywhere that does it?'

'I believe there are a couple of hospitals here, Stacey, yes, that do the operation, but, as I say, I really wouldn't advise it. It's still relatively untried here, although you'll find your friend in America will no doubt tell you how wonderful it is and so on. Forget all about it, Stacey, and work a bit harder on your diet. Here — take one of these.'

He pulled a sheet of paper from off a stacking tray thing on his desk. Another of his diet sheets, of course, and I felt like chucking it straight back at him, but I never, 'cos I need him for my pain pills and my mum's blood pills and all that.

'So what about the pain in my side, doctor? Only it's been real bad lately or I wouldn't have bothered you. I had to go off work and I don't never do that except when it's serious. Can you give me something stronger for it?'

Don't know why I bothered to ask, really, 'cos I know it's always gonna be the same old stuff about weight and strain and my frame not being designed to hold all the fat it was supporting and that. At least he didn't get out his pen this time; once he starts drawing them diagrams of joints and stuff I really get pissed off. I'm not stupid, I feel like shouting, I don't enjoy being like this, I just want you to stop the pain. Don't give me the bleeding lecture again — I don't need it.

Anyway, I managed to get myself onto his table with a bit of a struggle and after he'd done his prodding and listening and things he said there was nothing wrong. Apart from the fact my body's about as wrong as it could be in every other way, of course. But I don't need you to tell me that, I thought.

'So you can't give me nothing stronger for the pain, then, doctor?' I said once more.

'Only the same as I always do, Stacey. I really want you to try and get that weight down. I don't want to put you on any stronger anti-inflammatories as I can't see it being a short-term measure unless you make an effort. The pain is telling you something important, Stacey, and I want you to listen to it.'

So I'm like, 'Hello? Do you think I haven't been listening to it for twenty years or more, doc?' But I never said it, 'cos there's no point in getting him all annoyed. I didn't mention the op again neither, for the same reason. But I can't get it out of my mind, somehow. It just sounds so right for me, like it did for all them girls in the States. Stateside, as little Andy at work would call it. He sounds really thick when he calls it that; he thinks it makes him sound cool and like the guys on the TV when he says 'Stateside' but he doesn't realise we're all laughing at him. Poor little sod, he wants so much to be a rock star or a film star or something and he's about as far from that as it's possible to be. Kinda like trying to imagine a clam becoming prime minister: just not an effing hope in the world of that guy doing anything with his life except maybe – just maybe – getting out of the back stores and onto shelf-stacking. Maybe.

I'm different though, you see. That's what really pisses me off: if it wasn't for this body of mine I coulda done something with my life. I just know it. I'm not like the others: I see things they don't see. I coulda been someone.

I just can't get that op out of my mind, like I said. All that stuff Crystal and the others tell me: that could be me. I could get over onto the other side, just the way they done. That other me is just waiting to be let out, I can feel it.

I guess Crystal's right. I need an angel.

Judy

Perhaps if I hadn't been so caught up with my little trouble I'd have noticed sooner that something was very wrong with Charlie. I thought at the time that everything was pottering along pretty normally, but now I look back on it I wasn't seeing things clearly at all. It was a bit like those times I've had flu or a bad period or something and didn't realise until I was better that I hadn't been myself and hadn't been handling things or coping properly at all. I think I'd been in a really bad way all through the beginnings of the crisis and ignored the warning signs that I'd now find obvious. I'd almost got to believe that the headaches were real – well, of course they were, if you call having the pain real. But I know perfectly well now why I had them. Or rather why I brought them about. Because that's what I was doing, I have no doubt about that whatsoever. When I needed a little 'fix' from a quick indulgence in the hobby, I'd have a headache. A genuine, painful, one-sided migraine, complete with the flashing lights and the horrible shadowy aftermath, but one that I concocted all the same. It made it so easy to spend time up in the bedroom without anyone questioning it, you see.

You'd think that my problem and having to get through it might have made me more tolerant when I did begin to notice what was happening to Charlie. It didn't though, not at all. In fact it just made me more angry, because I felt I'd kept mine entirely to myself and hadn't let it interfere with anyone else's life – well, not at that stage, anyhow. And I knew that I would in time get myself out of it and I had never accepted that it should be indulged in the way he appeared to be indulging himself in his weird situation. I felt it was possible to come through these things and it seemed to me that he just wasn't making any real effort. And mine had been going for far longer than his. And did less harm. Apart from financial considerations, it was all between me and the cupboard, so to speak.

In my case – and maybe in Charlie's as well – I'm never sure about all that 'cry for help' theory: why would I have managed to keep it utterly secret for so many years if I'd all the time wanted someone to notice and come to my aid? Because it had been years. From very small beginnings, admittedly, and the growth had been subtle enough for no one to notice and for me to ignore just how much it had taken over, but it had been quite some time. No, I think some of these things are far more complex, and I've never found a satisfactory explanation for mine, that's for sure.

At any rate, whatever the reason, I didn't see what was going on with Charlie until things were pretty advanced. I blamed everything on his work: his strange silences, his moodiness and his obsessive shopping trips. And then, of course, when things got really bad it was inevitable that my own difficulties would be exposed. What a terrible word – it sounds as if I was to be written up in the *News of the World* or somewhere. Not that it doesn't have the perfect ingredients for such treatment.

The evening of the get well card argument was the first time I was consciously aware that something was up. Even when his work was going badly, the old Charlie could always be brought round with a bit of coaxing – certainly by Sally, if not by me – but that night nothing would bring him out of his black mood. I did try. In spite of his strange manner and my own uneasiness, I insisted he came back home with me from the supermarket, complete with wretched scones, which I knew they'd never take back, in any case. I planned to open a bottle of wine and forget the whole silly business.

It was a miserably strained walk back. I tried all manner of jokes and diversions to jolly him out of his silence, but really didn't seem to be getting anywhere. I was telling him about some of the other people I'd been working with on my most recent inspection, and I thought I was being quite funny about them, when, a few steps from the front door, he turned and looked at me.

'Shut up,' he said, quietly, but horribly seriously.

I would never have dreamt that such a mild and commonly used insult could be so utterly shocking. For a moment I didn't know how to react, torn between laughing out loud and hitting him.

'You're joking,' I said at last. 'You've got to be joking. I've put up with your ludicrous, unpleasant huffiness ever since the ridiculous card business at home; I've come out to find you and jollied you along all the way back through one of your tiresome black moods, and now you're telling me to shut up? Why the hell should we have to put up with your bad temper just because some stupid case is not going the way you want it? I don't take it out on you when some crappy headmistress plays up on one of my inspections, do I? You're selfish and —'

'For God's sake, shut up, Judy,' he said again.

This time I felt quite unnerved. He was still looking directly at me, but his eyes seemed strangely unaligned, as if the pupils had got out of synch and were straining away from each other. Funnily enough, something in his expression reminded me of the way I felt when I needed to get to my cupboard. It did shut me up – quite took the wind out of my sails – and I just stood there watching his face and waiting for him to say something.

'It has absolutely nothing to do with my work. I am going through a situation at the moment which is causing me some anxiety' (in times of stress, Charlie invariably reverts to talking like a barrister) 'and I'd be grateful if you'd just leave it alone. It is entirely not your fault, and I'm sorry to be the catalyst for this period of difficulty, but I suggest we carry on as normal – or as near to what we describe as normal – as possible, and I will endeavour to sort myself out.'

I felt quite sorry for him then, although it was a bit like being addressed by an intolerant Martian, in the way he used such odd, formal language without appearing to know what he was saying, but I'd got used to that over the years. I knew it didn't necessarily mean there was no feeling or emotion lurking underneath the rhetoric.

I tucked my hand into his arm and tried to steer him towards the front door, but he pulled against me and backed away a little.

'Sorry, Judy,' he said. 'I can't come in just yet.' He turned and began to walk away, then looked back at me over his shoulder. 'I have to buy another card.'

At that I did laugh. It was surely an understandable reaction – it would have been bizarre in the extreme to take him seriously. I was quite sure it had to be a joke: a way of making me feel all right about my reaction to the infamous get well card. So even when he moved off again towards Victoria Street I simply chuckled to myself and opened my bag to take out my front door keys. I planned to tell the children that all was well and that we were to prepare ourselves for another card and an evening of good old-fashioned family fun.

Charlie

'Hi, please could you give this to Stacey? It's just a get well card. I'd be grateful if you could give it to her as soon as possible. Obviously once she returns to work she'll be better enough to come back so will presumably be over her flu or whatever it is and the card will be redundant, so if you could get someone to take it to her while she's ill I'd be grateful.'

I knew I was overtalking and sounded like an idiot but I didn't care. It was a relief to know I had no choice but to get the card to Stacey: I could see now that it was absolutely the right thing to do, and the risk of Judy and the children finding out was justified by the intensity of my need for Stacey, and the lack of the family's need for me. Judy was perfectly happy in her world of the children and her work and was merely irritated by me most of the time. When she wasn't at work or cooking for the kids she was increasingly often shut in her room with one of her headaches, in any case. If I was to be out of the house more it could only be a good thing for the family. Stacey clearly lacked friends, and I lacked Stacey. So for me to contact her was not only sensible but necessary.

I'd walked all the way to our nearest Hallmark to give myself a better choice of card, and had found a wonderful one – very different from the flowery one Judy had commandeered: this was modern, bright and funny, and I could imagine Stacey laughing over it and her wonderful eyes shining with pleasure. I hadn't hesitated in signing it this time, either, boldly adding under the printed text: Best Wishes for a Speedy Recovery from your Bogof friend – Charles Thornton.

The Chipstead chap – Stacey's hero, I regretfully remembered – was looking at me suspiciously. I put on my best 'respectable barrister' voice and smiled at him. 'Just a card for a valuable member of your staff. Stacey has been very helpful to me on my shopping trips while my wife has been unwell, and I simply wish to send her a little greeting in thanks.'

I could see that the alien concept of Stacey's being actively helpful to a customer had quite thrown his smooth assurance for a moment, but the mention of my sick wife had achieved its purpose of allaying any suspicion of my intentions that he might previously have entertained.

'I'll see that she gets it, sir,' he said. 'I'm sure it's nothing serious and that Miss Salton will be back with us in a day or two. Very kind of you to take the trouble.'

He smiled silkily and took the card from me, spinning on one heel and executing one of his hip-swivelling shimmies as he unfastened the chain that hung across the empty checkout, swung through to the other side and then looped the chain up again behind him. 'Brenda!' he called as he headed for the freezer cabinet. 'Brenda, dear, can you do me a favour on your way home tonight?'

A dim-looking girl with frizzy brown hair and wearing thick leather gloves straightened up from bending over the frozen food. The lenses of her spectacles were misted with condensation and she held a packet of peas in one hand and pushed the glasses up her nose with the other one. So this is Brenda, I thought. Brenda the messenger, who will be taking the card to Miss Stacey Salton. Well now, Brenda, I muttered quietly to myself, I think you and I may be having a little word before too long. I watched as he handed over the card and said something to the girl that I couldn't quite hear, then I looked away as he turned and shimmied back across the store towards the delicatessen counter.

I pottered about the store for a while, smiling benignly at Mr Chipstead whenever I glimpsed him across an aisle, placing an object into my basket regularly enough to make my behaviour appear innocuous. I kept an eye on Brenda: she was still dipping in and out of the freezer cabinet, straightening up the piles of fishfingers and beefburgers and adding extra packets from the large canvas-sided wheeled bin at her side. She had stuffed my card into the pocket of her SavaMart overall, and it irritated me to see the edge of the envelope bending into a crease every time she leant over. I strolled casually over and positioned myself next to her, resting my basket on the edge of the cabinet as I peered down at the misty packets. I bent and picked up a packet of frozen pancakes, then smiled at the girl as I held it towards her. 'Do you have any chicken ones of – oh!' I broke off in apparent surprise. 'I see you have the card that Mr Chipstead was very kindly arranging to have taken to Stacey! I do hope it's not too much of a bother.'

Brenda seemed mystified for a second, then reached into her pocket and grasped the envelope in her thickly gloved hand. I was dismayed to see that, as she looked back at me, a small smile of recognition – no, not smile: more of a smirk – was making the corners of her mouth twitch a little. I had to face the uncomfortable fact that my favouring of Stacey when choosing the checkout on my many recent visits to the store had been noticed even by thick Brenda. 'Oh, yeah,' she said, 'you mean this? A card, is it?' She pulled it out of the pocket and looked at it, then back up at me, her thick lips still contorting in their struggle to contain the giggle evidently bubbling behind them. The envelope was not only creased but now dampened from the wet glove. I could see that the edge of the capital 'S' was smeared and fuzzy under the girl's thumb.

For a moment I considered taking the exchange further, perhaps suggesting that I post the card instead, thereby getting Stacey's address, but I was aware of Mr Chipstead's lithe figure still moving silently around the store, and caution curbed my impatience. It was also clear that this exchange was to be reported to the other girls (and in all probability to Mr C himself) as soon as I left the store, and from the look of interested amusement on this stupid girl's face, I could tell that I was still the subject of their gossip. I would have to work hard to appear squeaky clean and of no possible threat to Stacey, although it was hard to believe that they could imagine anyone wanting to violate the depressed, gargantuan pile of flesh that had become the focus of my obsession.

Maybe I was wrong – maybe hordes of fat-loving perverts queued up to make attempts on her cushioned ramparts, and I was simply yet another weirdo fascinated and challenged by the hugeness of this extraordinary girl. Was that me? Was I succumbing to some primitive fantasy triggered by Judy's busy thinness? No. From the very beginning, from the moment when my awe-inspired examination of Stacey at the checkout had matured into the unexpected and unreasoning desire I now felt for this girl, I knew it was far more than mere physical need that underpinned it. No matter how many others had been in her life, I knew instinctively that I was the only one who had needed her in this way: totally and without criticism. I must tread carefully with this messenger and ignore the impulse to snatch the precious card out of her hand and demand Stacey's address. I would have to wait a little longer before tracking it down.

'It's very kind of you,' I said, then stopped myself moving away as I remembered my original excuse for talking to her. 'Oh – I was going to ask if you had any pancakes with the chicken filling?'

Brenda gazed at me for a few seconds without speaking and I tried to decide whether the smirk that still twisted her mouth was one of wry insight or utter lack of under-standing. She wiped her smeared glasses once again with the back of her sleeve and returned my dimpled envelope to her pocket. I pictured wistfully the state it would be in by the time it reached my adored Stacey.

'Nah,' Brenda at last replied, 'only cheese.'

Stacey

I made myself go back into work this morning, even though I still felt bad. They was picking the employee of the month today, see, and if you don't show up for work you can't be picked. I know I ain't never going to win it – goes without saying – but I can't stand the others to think I'm not there just so's I can use that as an excuse for not being chosen again. Mr Chipstead did tell me once that I had as good a chance as anyone, but I'm not that stupid. They're not going to have a picture of me in *Sava News*, are they? Not even in close-up, not even with all the rolls round my neck cut out. I'd still look like a pig, and that's not going to raise company morale or whatever they call it, is it? Look at our lovely Stacey – this month's pin-up girl. No chance.

It's secret how they do pick them, mind. I used to think it was how much money you'd taken on the till, but then that Jeb boy got it that time, and he'd never been on a till at all. Just shelf-stacking and sorting stuff in the back, like what

Andy does now. Denisha said Mr Chipstead fancied him, but I never believe those things about him. He only likes girls, I'm sure of that. And he says the picking ain't nothing to do with him anyway.

Mr Chipstead was manager of the month once. He looked wicked in *Sava News* – he takes a lovely photo. His hair was a bit too short, mind; he'd cut it specially and I like it when it curls a little over his collar. But he had such a cute smile on him. 'Warren Chipstead runs a lively store in the heart of London's Victoria,' it said. 'Popular with his staff and appreciated by local customers, Warren regularly initiates innovative fundraising schemes and has raised over £525 in the last year for Children in Need.' I cut it out and put it in my knicker drawer. Not so sure about the 'popular' bit though. Although we all fancy the pants off him, some of the girls are right bitchy about him; and he's very sharp when he wants to be. I wish I didn't like him so much really – I wish I liked someone I stood a chance with, someone who'd be kind to me, if you know what I mean, and like me for who I am. In all the mags it says over and over how it's inside that's important and it don't matter what you look like and my mum always says it too and I try ever so hard to believe them but then I see the way Mr C looks at Sheila and I know it ain't true. Not for a fucking minute, it ain't. On one page the mags are telling me how it's my inside what counts and on the page opposite they're telling me how to get a perfect fucking lip line. You don't fool me. I says to me mum, they don't fool me; they think we're stupid 'cos we're ugly, but it don't make us stupid. I got just the same brain behind all this fat, you know – no, a better brain than that Denisha for a start.

I tried to buy myself a new bra after work. I swore I wouldn't let it upset me like it did the last time but it ended up making me cry again. It's just so humiliating the way they treat you. I swear they get a kick out of it: 'Oh, no, I'm afraid that doesn't go up to a 46EE', they shout across to the cubicle. I try to look as if I don't care, but they know I do. At least I managed not to cry until I was out of there. I'll just have to send away again to the OS place, but their stuff's all so dreary. It looks more like medical contraptions than pretty sexy underwear.

It made me so depressed I went straight to the internet café near our store and I typed in 'weight-loss surgery' in the Yahoo thing to see if there's a place that does the weight-loss op over here. Took me hours to find it – I can see why Crystal got hers so easy: if I'd wanted it in America or Australia or Mars or somewhere I'd have been spoilt for choice. There's only one or two here – pathetic, ain't it? We never do catch up with the Americans. One of them's up north, but it's not like that's the end of the world. They give all kinds of info on the site and it's just like Crystal said – they do that Roux-en-Y thing. Staples and Y-shaped intestines and all that sort of weird crap. I've wrote down the number, anyway, so I'm getting nearer. Mind you, I've got about as much chance of the doctor sending me up there as one of Crystal's bleeding angels landing in my cornflakes, but I ain't gonna give up.

I saw that old bloke that fancies me today. He was in the store again and looked ever so nervous as he came through my checkout. Denisha told me the day he came in and gave Brenda that card for me he was stood outside the front of the store looking in for about half an hour. He'd been in earlier as well, she says, and asked where I was. Janet was on the till in the evening and she says he looked a bit peculiar, but then what else is new, I says. I hate it when the girls talk about him, 'cos it's like they're pretending it's a good joke this crappy old gent having the hots for me but I know they think it's 'cos no one normal would wanna know. Well, fuck them, that's what I say. Still, it is a bit creepy. I wish I didn't have to go home on my own every night – supposing he's watching me, like them stalkers?

I don't think he means no harm though. Denisha says I should be careful but I think he looks OK. I feel quite sorry for him, in fact – he can't get up the courage to say anything to me except all the boring stuff about prices and that. I know he's dying to stop and chat; I can see it in his eyes and the way his hand gets all shaky as he puts the stuff on the belt, but he just can't do it. I'd even laugh now if he tried to bring up that bogof stuff he used to, just to make him relax a bit, but he don't do that now.

'Good morning,' he said as he put down his basket. He never looked at me though, he was just looking down at the food. I waited for him to say something more – I was sure he was going to ask me if I'd got the card, but he never. I s'pose I shoulda thanked him for it, but I couldn't quite do that, somehow.

'Oooh, these peas are cold,' he said, or something like that as he took out the frozen stuff. I said 'yeah' or something. I mean what else can you say? Frozen peas ain't gonna be hot, are they? I'm not gonna help him to say whatever it is he wants to say – that's his problem. Specially with Mr C and the girls watching – I'm not letting them think I'm sad enough to let some old weirdo chat me up.

Charlie

I can't stand it any more. When I saw her again today I couldn't even get a smile out of her. I can't stand being here at home and having to make conversation with Judy and the children when all I want to do is to sit and think about *her* and how I can get to see more of her. I couldn't go in to work this morning. I set off but I couldn't face having to read the briefs and put up with David's awful jokes and pretend everything's normal. I phoned in sick again and said I had to take a few days off. I hung about the store a bit, then sat in the park and thought about it all. I know what I have to do now.

I'm only a burden at home, I'm sure of that: they'll all be fine without me — it's better for them. I'll get out of their way.

Next

Sally

The night Dad left was truly terrible. So many of my friends' parents have split that I'd always thought it would be quite easy to accept – and he and Mum had been so strange with each other lately that you'd think I'd have seen it coming.

But I had no idea how bad things were until I took the call from Dad's office that morning. I was lying on the sofa watching *Neighbours* and thinking I ought to start planning the famous trip abroad I keep saying I'm going on, when the phone rang. It was David thingummy – Stevenson – Dad's clerk of chambers or whatever he is. It was so strange to hear him asking where Dad was – it was like a mirror image or something, 'cos usually it's us asking him the same question: he always knows Dad's schedule and is brilliant at organising him.

'How d'you mean?' I said, or something equally dim. 'Isn't he at work?'

'He hasn't been into work regularly for some time, Sally,' he answered, and I felt a tiny little quiver of panic – not just because of what he was saying, but the way he said it was scary, like a headmaster, as if he was going to have to expel me or something. 'He's hardly been here at all, with all the sick leave he's been taking, and the unexplained absences – and today is especially difficult, as we had an important appointment fixed up. Have you any idea where he might be?'

'No – no, I haven't.' I didn't like to let on that I

hadn't even known he'd been ill — what the hell was going on? 'I mean — I hadn't really thought about it, but I suppose I assumed he was with you. I'll — get Mum to ring you, shall I?'

'If you would, please, Sally.'

When I rang Mum on her mobile (Dad always said they were a waste of money so he'd never bothered to get one) I was still in a bit of a panic and I asked if I should start calling round hospitals or ring the police or something. She was just weirdly calm about it and said it didn't surprise her a bit and that I should do nothing and we'd talk about it later. So his going that evening shouldn't have been that unexpected now I look back on it. But it was — both Ben and I were utterly shocked by it. I felt like a little girl again — no, that's not right; I felt horribly adult, but I remembered how it felt to be a little girl, and that's what made it so sad and so frightening. Because Dad had just always been there, and always been so kind and so funny — I wanted to be able to talk to him in the way I did when I was seven or eight, in the way that always made him laugh and pick me up and tease me. He'd get that amazingly proud look on his face when Ben and I did things or said things — just anything, really. I hadn't realised how much that meant — Dad's being so ridiculously proud of anything we did. All the little things like learning to swim, or speaking a couple of crappy lines in the school play or having a smart-arse argument over the kitchen table — he'd get really turned on by it in a way I used to think was pathetic. Mum always loved us, of course — they both did — and it was her we went to when we hurt ourselves or needed help with sorting out arrangements for things, but it was Dad who kept us feeling we were truly special.

It began with yet another row. Ben and I were in the kitchen and I was peeling some potatoes because I wanted to watch something on TV – I can't even remember what it was now – and Mum had been up in her bedroom again and I could see it was going to get late so I thought I'd make a start on the supper. Then suddenly Dad came home and slammed the front door behind him as if he was trying to break it or something. I went out into the hall and I was going to tell him about David ringing because that seemed like a good way of bringing up the fact he'd been missing from work. And I wasn't just being nosy and wanting to let him know that I knew about his being off work – I really thought I might be able to help if he was having a problem. But he just kind of brushed past me.

'Dad?' I shouted up the stairs. 'Are you OK?'

He yelled back something like, 'What does it look like?' and went into the bedroom. He'd come home in bad moods before – specially in the last few weeks – but this was different.

I went back into the kitchen and spoke to Ben, who was sitting at the table with his homework in front of him looking as scared as I felt.

'For Christ's sake, what the hell is going on?' I said. 'We've got to do something, haven't we? Or say something? Did you know he's been taking time off work?'

'What? Dad has?' said Ben, and I felt quite relieved to see I wasn't the only one to be surprised.

'Yeah – I wasn't going to tell you until I'd talked more to Mum about it – or at least told Dad. It seemed a bit disloyal somehow, because I'm not sure he'd want us to know. But if he's just going to push past me and shout at me like that – then, what does he expect? This is like a bad TV soap, all this door-slamming and Mum disappearing into her bedroom for hours. We can't let them go on like this; it feels like this is happening to someone else. Mum and Dad don't do this stuff, do they?'

I knew Ben was trying not to let me see that his eyes were watery. Poor guy – I know how he felt – all this was just so scary. It was like living with aliens or something.

'What can we do, Sal? If you try and say anything, it'll only make them worse, you know that. They prefer it if we pretend it isn't happening. I can't believe he's been off work – that's just amazing. What's he been doing? Did Mum know where he was? When he was off, I mean. Is he having an affair or something, do you think?'

'Christ knows. They said he'd been on sick leave – but I'm sure he hasn't been ill. And I've no idea if Mum knew – she's being almost as weird as he is. But I don't care what they prefer. I'm not letting them carry on like this, for God's sake. It's not fair on us, for one thing. How do they expect us to cope with this hell going on? I'm going up to talk to them.'

I do so so much wish I hadn't done that, now. I always think I'm so clever, that's my trouble. I was so sure I could bring them to their senses, kind of thing, that I never thought twice about going up those stairs and confronting them, but I can see it was really stupid.

As I reached the landing I could hear the shouting going on behind the bedroom door. It had been bad enough when I heard it downstairs, but up here it was terrifying. I wonder if kids whose parents row all the time get used to it, if they don't get frightened any more by the loud voices and the horrible anger in them? Maybe it's easier for them. For Ben and me it was just so different from anything we'd known, and I was very frightened – I don't mind admitting it. I felt like rushing downstairs again and asking Ben if he'd come up with me instead of doing it on my own, but then I remembered his tearful face and thought better of it. I'd always looked after him and I wasn't going to let him down now: big sister would sort things out, like she always did. I walked across to the door and leant my forehead on it for a second or two, with my hand on the doorknob. I could hear the words now.

'I know it's my fault, you stupid woman,' Dad was saying. 'Don't you see I'm not denying that for a second? But it's not going to change – that's what I'm trying to tell you.'

'You can't just expect me to accept this – you can't possibly expect me to carry on as if –'

'I'm not expecting anything. Do listen, damn you! I AM NOT EXPECTING ANYTHING – I'm merely stating the facts, for Christ's sake.'

'Well, don't! Don't just "state the facts".' She was mimicking him now, half crying but still managing to mock him in that unbearably irritating way she had when he started using his barrister voice. I knew this simply meant more trouble.

'SHUT UP, WOMAN! SHUT UP AND LISTEN!' I squatted down outside the door and covered my face with my hands as he went on. 'I thought I could go on living here even though I'm going through this catharsis, but –'

'Ooohh – going through a catharsis, are we? You shit!'

Oh God, this was so awful. I'd never heard Mum talk like this. I just wanted to die. But something gave me the bravery to stand up and turn the familiar flowery china handle and push open the door. As soon as I saw their faces I knew it was hopeless. They had turned at the sound of the door catch, and the anger and hate that I saw on both their faces made me cry out. I can't even remember what I yelled at them – something like, 'Oh, do stop it, both of you' – but it didn't help. Now I think it was probably the worst thing I could have done. If I'd only left them alone to get through it maybe he wouldn't have gone.

But my entry into the bedroom did do something. It changed things in a flash — if not for the better at least for the different, if you see what I mean. The anger sort of crumpled away from their faces and they stared at me in — oh, how shall I describe that look? I can still see it now, and it makes me want to cry all over again. A sad horror — that's the best way of putting it, as if they'd unexpectedly come across an unspeakable accident. A child who'd been run over or something — well, in a way they had, but then that's just me being self-pitying, I suppose.

It certainly stopped them shouting, that's for sure. Dad collapsed in a heap on the bed, holding his head in a way that reminded me of the way I'd sat outside the door a few seconds earlier, and Mum moved towards me with her arms open. Dad was muttering, 'I can't — I can't — I can't', or something, and Mum put her arms on my shoulders and then turned to look back at him. Then she said something that was more unbearable than anything that had happened before (and I know things can't be more or less unbearable: you can either bear them or you can't, as Dad would say in his corrective moods — but they can in my book, as all of this was unbearable to me, but some was worse than the rest). She turned to look at Dad, still holding me by the shoulders so she had to twist her head right round on her neck, and said, 'I love you so very much, you see, Charlie. That's what makes this impossible. I can't live without you.'

I'd never heard anything like that before. Never. Yes, of course they often said they loved each other, but in that casual 'I love you, darling' way that was about as meaningful as saying good morning. Kind of comforting but not ever embarrassing or emotional. Like the way they kissed – very loving and all that, but not (oh Christ, I hate even saying the word in the context of my mum and dad), not sexy. Just quick dry-looking brushes on the cheek, or quick meetings of pursed lips. The way she told him she loved him that horrible evening was like seeing her French-kiss him. It made my insides shrivel up in a spasm. Not because I was embarrassed; things were far past that stage by then, but because it made me so – so stricken. It was utterly wrong that I should be seeing into her heart in this terrible way, and I wanted out. But her hands were gripping my shoulders so tightly I couldn't move, and she was controlling me with her feelings just as much as with her muscles.

Dad didn't look up and I wondered if he'd heard her: she hadn't spoken very loudly and he was still muttering something into his cupped hands. Mum suddenly let go of me and I turned and started to run down the stairs, but halfway down I saw Ben coming out of the kitchen. I knew that seeing me in the state I was in would only scare him even more, so I stopped and went up again, feeling foolish in spite of myself. I was terrified that Mum or Dad would come out of the bedroom and see me creeping back up and imagine I was trying to eavesdrop outside the door. As I reached my room in safety I heard the front door slam and knew Ben must have gone out, no doubt frightened away by the shouting – he never could stand arguments, poor guy. I tried to pull myself together, but I just couldn't stop my stupid heart thumping up into the back of my throat, so I took a few deep breaths and decided to wait a few moments until it slowed down. As I sat on the bed I caught sight of myself in the long mirror on the back of my door. The weird and horrible thing was that I found myself checking out the way I looked – I don't mean to see if I was still too obviously upset to go downstairs, but as if I was appraising myself as the wronged daughter in a drama or something. Without thinking I even pushed the back of my hair into a better shape where it always goes flat against my head. Does that mean I didn't really care about what was going on? Or does it mean I'm especially vain, like Abby says?

All I know is that if I hadn't stopped and sorted out my fucking looks in the mirror maybe I'd have been in time to stop him walking out of the front door.

Charlie

And, suddenly, it was done. The madness that had been dominating my head for all those weeks had exploded out into the open and I found myself walking out of my own home and into the street. Even as I did so I was amazed at the way my legs managed to place themselves cleverly one in front of the other and my large, adult's body balanced on the small area of my right and left foot alternately. How could they function normally while the brain in charge of them writhed in delirious agony and uncertainty? As I made my way along Victoria Street, inconsequential worries about my lack of clothing and shaving things took turns in flashes with yawning chasms of terror at the thought of what I had done. More unnerving than that, though, was the question that forced itself into my head every few seconds like a painfully probing scalpel. *Why? Why have I done this? For what?* As I would answer — *for her, for Stacey, to be with her* — a hot sweat of horror would overwhelm me in sheer disbelief. It just didn't seem possible — or real. I pictured the fat, stupid supermarket girl and marvelled. But I walked on. Some knowledge at a far deeper level than my conscious mind was reassuring me that I was right — that this madness had a point after all.

I didn't need to think where I was going, what I was going to do next or how I was going to live. All those things would work themselves out as long as I kept going and pushed aside the agonising questions that kept attacking me. I managed to walk past the front of SavaMart without so much as glancing in, surprising myself by my self-control, and I hurried along the alleyway that skirted it on the far side and followed it round into the small street that backed onto the store. I'd noticed and mentally logged the staff entrance a few days previously, and now I found an unobtrusive spot in a doorway opposite and tucked myself into its shadow, leaning against one side of the grubby concrete that framed it and fixing my gaze on the double doors in front of me. A part of me still felt as if all of this was unreal — that at any minute I would pull myself together, understand where I was and laughingly return home, anticipating as I went the jokes and good-humoured teasing that would take place when I admitted that the whole charade had been an elaborate hoax.

'What?' I could hear myself saying. 'Run away from home? Me? Like a kid with a spotted hankie tied on a stick? I'm sorry — what did you say? I don't think I quite heard you — leave home because I've become obsessed with a fat girl who works in the supermarket round the corner? Oh yes, that's utterly believable, isn't it? I mean, that just makes perfect sense — that I, a respectable barrister, should walk out on my own family — quite apart from the comfort of the house I've spent much of my working life striving to pay for — and follow some daft girl I've hardly spoken to.' They'd all be laughing now, of course, amused by my irony, the ludicrousness of my story and the witty way I was expressing it.

I looked down at my feet. They weren't budging, of course. Much as I knew my behaviour and motivation to be incredible in any sane world, in the one I now inhabited it was only too real.

My heart was beating uncomfortably hard, pulsing up into my ears every second or so, and I was aware of the sweat — cold now in the chilly wind that crept into the doorway — on my forehead and upper lip. I wiped it away with my forearm, the material of my jacket feeling rough against my skin, and glanced down at the sheen it left on the black sleeve.

'God — I didn't even pick up a coat!' I muttered, and laughed at the streak of practicality that insisted on poking itself into my crazy world from time to time. I looked across at the double doors and then down at my watch. Five forty: from my regular stakeouts of the store over the last few weeks I'd worked out a rough schedule of the way the girls worked their shifts, but which one she was on today I had, of course, no idea, not having planned in advance — or indeed planned in any way at all — this sudden mad dash into the unknown from the safety of my predictably shaped life. No matter: I would wait until I got some sort of clue. No one would find me here — and no one, apart from Judy and the kids, would even be trying. I would ring the office in the morning and leave another vague message about ill health with the girl on the switchboard to keep them happy for a day or two at least, but for now in all likelihood I would be left alone to enjoy my stakeout in peace.

Although I was cold it didn't bother me; the weather was part of the old external world that had very little to do with me or my present situation. I was able to insulate myself effectively from all stimuli except the all-important information being absorbed and relayed to me by my eyes, which were trained exclusively on the doors opposite. A couple of staff members came and went, and I shrank back into the doorway as they did, frightened that one of them might recognise me and pass on to Stacey or Mr C that the old guy was waiting for her outside. A stalker – I supposed that was what I was.

Then the worst happened: the next person to leave the store was young smoothie himself. As he pushed open the double doors, I noticed that Chipstead's lithe, swooping swagger was far less pronounced once out of the surroundings of his little kingdom. He looked smaller, too, in his fuzzy grey overcoat, and less sure of himself. He paused on the step, looked about him, pulled a pair of woolly gloves out of a pocket and put them on carefully, checking the fit of the fingers one by one and pulling the cuffs of the coat carefully back over the wrists. I moved even further into the shadow and watched him step down from the kerb and cut diagonally across the road, thankfully not looking my way as he scanned for traffic in both directions. He walked out of my line of vision, but I could hear his footsteps receding down my side of the street. I relaxed a little and leant forward to peer out of the doorway to see where he was headed: with Chipstead safely out of the way I would feel easier about waiting for Stacey.

As my head emerged from the safe frame of my grubby hiding place he turned and looked straight at me. Whether I'd made some slight noise as I moved or whether he'd sensed my eyes seeking out the back of his neck I shall never know, but the reaction was instant and unexpected: a broad smile stretched out his mouth and he spun round on the spot – in a flash reacquiring the suppleness of his managerial persona. He made a move towards me that was at once graceful and idiotic – a parody of a mime artist gliding on seemingly motionless feet along the pavement between us. He reached me, still grinning, and stuck out a gloved hand.

'Ah! Waiting for Stacey, sir?'

I felt like hitting him, but was held back by common sense and an instinctive need to keep open all possible channels to Stacey, and I smiled weakly back instead. I hesitated for a moment before replying, but reasoned that, having gone this far in my extraordinary journey, nothing would be gained by fabricating some alternative reason for my presence. Indeed, my chances of progress might well be improved by admitting the truth.

'Yep – that's right.' I beamed, taking hold of his hand and shaking it firmly. Even through the woolly glove I could sense the weakness of Chipstead's reciprocation and was silently thankful for the layer of knitting that separated my flesh from what I felt sure was the clammily cold limpness of his. 'Out soon, is she?'

There was no doubt I had chosen the right tack. In spite of Mr C's rigidly maintained smile I sensed that my jovial lack of embarrassment at being caught staking out the staff entrance of his store had caught him off guard. I wondered how he would have reacted had I shown fear and guilt at his approach: called the police? No, that would have been a move too precipitous no matter what he suspected, nothing in my behaviour having come anywhere close to being criminal. From what I had so far seen of this officious little man he would be well up on his rules and regulations. (I made a quick mental note to refresh my memory on the recent anti-stalking laws.)

'Brenda passed on your card. Very thoughtful of you, Mr . . . ?'

Now here's a thing, I thought. Why is my immediate instinct to hide my identity and assume an alias? I made a speedy assessment of the pros and cons and found myself unable to find any possible advantage in using a false name.

'Thornton. Charles Thornton. And you are?' I said — as if I didn't know.

How quickly we learn to deceive when it matters to us. I've always liked to think of myself as a reasonably straightforward man, and had assumed that my honesty was born out of an innate sense of morality and 'rightness', not that it existed merely because its strength in withstanding a selfish need pulling in the other direction had never been tested. From the very first sign of its being needed to further my progress in seeking the love of Stacey, I was able to undertake this kind of mild deception without any qualms.

'Warren Chipstead. I'm the store manager.'

'Yes, I assumed you were, Warren. And I'm a barrister: family law.'

'Oh, really? Yes, that's very interesting.'

I could sense reluctant admiration fighting with disdain as he nodded briefly and I almost pitied the man. A deeply ingrained side of his character, influenced no doubt by an upbringing surrounded by old-fashioned ideas of respect for authority, for power and for the medical and legal professions, was telling him that the man before him was in some way respectable and safe.

'Stacey better, is she?' I returned, calmer now that the initial confrontation had passed off so successfully.

'Yes, she seems pretty good now, sir. Much better. Or at least' — and he paused for a split second to punctuate his sentence with a smirk — 'as better as she'll ever be.'

A spasm of terror clenched my balls, and I fought to keep the fear from moving up into my face.

'How do you mean? Does she have something serious? Something –'

'Oh, dear me, no, Mr Thornton.' (Was it part of SavaMart's policy that store managers, like Americans or good maître d's, should be required to absorb names and faces on one hearing? Or had he, too, known my name all along, as I had his? I, once again, imagined their discussing me over tea in the staff canteen, laughing at my obvious attempts to chat up Stacey.) 'I merely meant' – and his expression became even more knowing as he leant slightly towards me and spoke man to man – 'that Stacey's body isn't exactly built for health. I don't see her on the jogging machines, do you, sir?'

I was shocked by the violence of the instinctive reaction that fought to overcome my natural physical cowardice and I had to close my eyes and shut out the wretched man's face for a second to prevent myself smashing my fist into it. I controlled myself by thinking of the terrible consequences of letting go, and by the time I looked back at him I even managed to produce a small smile of apparent complicity. I saw a way forward.

'Poor creature,' I said, still smiling and shaking my head slightly. 'I feel rather sorry for her. Dreadful to let yourself go like that. I assume you keep yourself pretty fit, Warren?'

Chipstead's little body went into display mode: he pulled his shoulders back and at the same time stretched out his neck and jutted his chin as if preparing for a fight, making him look like a bird wearing a collar two sizes too small. 'I like to think so, sir: physical fitness is indeed a bit of a hobbyhorse of mine. I've been encouraging my area manager to think of installing a small fitness centre on the premises for the staff, in fact. But space is at a premium in central London stores, as you can imagine. I've considered commandeering part of my back depot but I just can't think where I'd put my bulk dry goods.'

We pondered this interesting question together in silence for a moment. I restrained myself from making a suggestion as to what he could do with his back depot and merely nodded wisely in sympathy. I felt strangely relaxed in his company now, almost fatherly towards him.

Not for long. A spasm of toe-curling delight suddenly zipped through me as I saw Stacey emerging from the entrance opposite. What the hell was it about this enormous child that so gripped my heart? I was reassured to find nothing but love engulfing me as I watched her struggling to get through the space that would have fitted two normally proportioned people with ease. I felt no hint of regret or even mild anxiety at the sight of the girl for whom I was risking everything.

'There she is, sir,' said Chipstead redundantly.

'Ah, yes, so she is.' I smiled back at him. 'I shall go and pay my respects.' Why I was talking like Mr Darcy on a bad day I have no idea; I'm sure I would have tipped my hat, had I been wearing one. 'Please excuse me, Warren, I shall catch up with you later.'

As I crossed the street, Stacey noticed me and stopped her manoeuvring for a second. Her body was positioned sideways-on in her attempt to get through the doorway, but her lovely face was turned directly towards me. She looked startled, and I smiled gently and reassuringly at her as I came nearer. I saw her eyes flick across to take in Chipstead, and I called back a quick 'Good night, Warren,' to him over my shoulder, hoping not only to allay Stacey's doubts by linking myself with a figure of safe familiarity, but also to encourage him to go home.

Surprisingly, and in spite of Chipstead's obvious curiosity, it worked on both counts. He began to move off down the street, usefully returning my farewell with a 'Good night, Mr Thornton' as he did so. I saw Stacey's expression relax a little, causing me a small pang of jealousy as it shifted briefly through obvious regret at his departure on its way to interest in what I was going to do next.

She still hadn't moved and I was able to take a better look at her as I approached. She wore a girly pink-striped dress and over it a black coat made of cheap, shiny leather. The coat was unbuttoned, and one side of it was caught against the hinge of the door where her bulk pushed against it. I held my hand out to her and smiled again.

'Stacey,' I said gently. 'You must let me help you.'

Ben

'Ben, you absolutely mustn't blame yourself. That's just too corny. It's only because your parents have been so stupidly close all your life that you're taking this in such a heavy way. Most of us just view this kind of thing as normal, you see. You wait — he'll come back. Then you'll wish he hadn't, 'cos the rows'll start again and that's much worse than him going off, isn't it?'

Holly looked so pretty I wanted to kiss her but it didn't seem right in the middle of what we were talking about — I was worried she'd think I was only pretending to be upset and I wasn't: I was feeling terrible and I couldn't find anyone to believe me about it being my fault. I don't know what I was hoping for anyway — supposing she had said, 'Yes, it's all your fault and you've broken up your parents' marriage and you may never see your dad again'? Then what? I can't see that making me feel any better. No, I guess deep down I was hoping she'd really manage to convince me that I couldn't have done anything to stop it, but I can't see that that was possible. Or maybe I wanted her to agree that it had been my fault and be really sympathetic and sorry for me and put her arms round me and all that stuff. Anyway, there wasn't any point in going on about it all – I knew she'd never understand – but I couldn't just break off in the middle and start grabbing her tits and all the things I wanted to do. But if I went on moaning about it being my fault Dad had gone off then she'd just keep comparing it to her parents and it wouldn't get us anywhere. They're completely different from our family. I'm always surprised by how little they can say to each other; Mum, Dad, Sal and I have always been able to talk about anything.

At least we used to be able to, but now I think about it we've none of us been the same for quite a while now. I didn't realise until this terrible stuff happened, but it's made me think about everything and I can see we've all changed over the past year or so. Sally seems like the only one of us who's not really much different. Maybe because she's out of the house a lot more than Mum, Dad and me, she manages to chat about college and her friends and everything in the same way she always did. I know I've found it harder lately to talk to the family about what I'm feeling – especially since I've been having all these thoughts about life and what it means and the implications of the quantum physics and so on. And already I can't remember what it was like before Dad started going weird – I just don't know anything, and Ma's been so different since she started her headaches that I guess I'm imagining how good it was. Maybe they've been hiding really bad secrets for years and we never knew.

Maybe they hate each other and they've been keeping up this amazing act.

'I s'pose that, if my other parallel universes stuff is right, then there's a world existing right now where none of this has happened. There's a universe immediately next to us where Dad hasn't gone and Mum's cooking supper and not up in her room all the time and Dad's opening a bottle of wine and I'm panicking about homework and not about my parents splitting. Anything that can happen, does happen. Somewhere.'

'Yeah, right. So that means there's also another universe right next to us where your mum and dad are getting divorced and I got run over crossing the road this morning.'

'Thanks a lot, Hol. That really helps.'

'It's just I can't stand it when you go off into your strange metaphysical things. You've got to learn to live in reality, Ben – and I know that'll start you off again about what do I mean by reality and all that, but you know perfectly well what I mean. I don't care how many universes you're occupying, I'm staying in this one, and it may be shitty and parents may yell at each other and storm off but it's all we've got. Isn't it?'

'I guess so.'

She gave one of her giggles and grabbed my chin with her hand and pinched it.

'Oh, baby, don't look so pissed off,' she said, smiling at me. 'It's OK. You wait and see – it's not as bad as you think. Do you want to know what I think reality is?'

I sighed a bit and reached across the bed for her hand and held it tightly. 'All right, Hol, yes. Tell me. What is reality?'

'This,' she said, and she leant forward, pushed her lips onto mine and stuck her tongue into my mouth.

'Can't argue with that,' I said, once she'd let me go.

Judy

I feel as if I forced him to go. It's outrageous that I should: there's no question that I'm the wronged party in all this (oh, Christ – I'm even talking like him now) but in a funny kind of way I know I am to blame. I don't believe for one minute this bizarre nonsense about him having fallen for the fat girl at the supermarket checkout – that's just too fantastic to entertain seriously, even of a man who's patently into some kind of middle-aged crisis or male menopause or whatever you call it – but I do believe that he craves sex, and I feel so bloody stupid for not having realised just how much. And if the mounds of flesh surrounding that wretched girl have brought him to some sort of vortex of physical desire then I should have seen it coming, if you'll pardon the unfortunate wording.

Oh, God – d'you suppose he has? Made love to her? I can't picture it – if I try to I can only see him suffocating, immersed in her voluminous dollops of flesh. Ugh! It's disgusting – even the thought of it. I can hear the doorbell, see the policeman on my doorstep: 'Mrs Thornton, I'm so sorry to have to inform you that your husband has been found dead, buried alive in a supermarket checkout girl.' God damn her.

After he left I opened the drawer of course and went through eighteen of them in one go. Didn't help much, but it gave me something to do while I calmed down before facing Sally. When I eventually went downstairs and found her in the kitchen I didn't know what to say to her. She looked up at me and it was like looking at myself: her expression reminded me of the one I've seen so often lately in my dressing-table mirror.

'Are you OK, Mum?' she said. 'Is Dad coming back?'

'I don't know, darling,' I said rather feebly. How does one behave in situations like this? Sally's never been a child to accept comforting lies easily: she's always been far too sharp for me to be able to fool her with the usual reassuring clichés. She would soon have seen through anything I could invent to make things look better than they were, and as the truth was equally unbelievable I stayed silent for a moment or two.

'Where's Ben?' I said at last, praying that at least one of my beloved offspring had been spared my humiliation and the sight of his father flying the nest.

'He's at Holly's. But he knows.'

'What do you mean?'

'I told him. I rang and told him.'

I was suddenly enraged. I can see now of course that it was the horror of the situation and my own misery that exploded out of me in the way it did, but at the time I felt nothing but outrage and fury at the girl in front of me.

'I do think a wife and mother should be allowed to tell her own son when his father has left her!' I shouted. 'I don't see why you felt you had the right to take it upon yourself to tell Ben of my humiliation and degradation without consulting me. The least I can ask is that you show some respect for my – for my –' and I went no further but at that point broke down into hopeless sobs.

'It's not just you he's walked out on, Mum, if you want to get selfish about this. He does have a couple of children, you may remember, and, although you may understand what this is all about, believe me his son and daughter don't.'

I was still crying and the more I tried to stop the worse

it was. I could sense Sally's anger: I must have looked like a self-pitying idiot. I couldn't be the comforting, understanding mother I knew I should be in the situation and that just made me feel even more sorry for myself than I already was. Here was a moment when this sometimes difficult and independent daughter of mine really needed me and I was letting her down. God knows, it wasn't her fault that Charlie was going through this breakdown or whatever it was.

'Mum – please stop crying. We need to talk about this. Dad isn't going to do anything stupid, is he? I mean – is he going through some sort of – you know, I mean is he OK?'

'I don't know, Sally. I don't know what he's going through. I'm the last person he'd tell in any case.' I was gulping back the sobs now, desperately attempting to pull myself together and not succeeding. There was an accusative tinge to my voice and I knew it wouldn't help: before I stopped teaching I used to see, over and over again, the damage caused by squabbling parents using their children as sounding boards for their own anger, and here I was doing it myself.

I glanced up at her and saw her face tighten in disapproval. 'Well, I can't say I'm surprised to hear that, Mum,' she said.

'What do you mean?'

'The amount of time you spend on your work or up in your room I'm amazed you know any of us exist, let alone are aware of what we may be going through, as you put it.'

'How dare you speak to me like that, Sally? What could you possibly know of my work or of my problems and what I've had to cope with? How can you pronounce on my relationship with your father when you know absolutely nothing about it — of what I've had to put up with over the years' (oh, God, there I went again) 'or of what we've done for the two of you.' (Oh, no, surely I wasn't pulling that tired old cliché on my own daughter — I'd be starting the next sentence with 'when I was your age' if I wasn't careful.) She'd frightened me, that's why I'd lashed out at her — I hadn't appreciated how obvious my excursions to the bedroom had become. I would have to be more careful. I could see every word of this conversation being relayed within minutes not only to Ben but to her coterie of close friends as well — mobiles and e-mail have a lot to answer for.

'Sally — I'm sorry. You'll have to take anything I say at the moment on a sort of temporary basis: I'm more shocked than I'm letting on, I think. Yes, of course your father and I have had our difficulties: marriage isn't the simple business it appears to be, you know —'

'Oh, Mum, come on, I'm not stupid. I'm only too well aware of how things are. That's why I'm never going to get married — I've told you that loads of times. It's just not natural to expect two people to hang around for zillions of years together. But if you are together you might as well be happy, don't you think? I mean you and Dad always used to get on so well and be good friends and all that crap and then suddenly you both seemed to get irritable with each other and be tired all the time. It just seems such a waste, that's all I'm saying. He's a good bloke, Mum, and you're throwing him away.'

Out of the mouths, etc. I resisted the urge to yell back at her: it seemed hardly fair to accuse me of being the one to throw away the husband who had recently walked out on me, but there was something in what she was saying that penetrated my outraged shell and hit me somewhere very vulnerable and, as I had innocently thought, hidden.

'Was I tired, Sally? And irritable? I was looking after you all just the way I always did, wasn't I? What have I done wrong? Why do you think he – oh no, I can't do this to you, darling. I'm sorry – this isn't fair: you've had your father walk out of your life – even though I'm sure it's only for a little while, darling – and I'm trying to talk to you as if you should be helping me, instead of the other way round. I'm sorry, that's so selfish of me. Forgive me, sweetheart.'

I sat down at the kitchen table opposite her and put my head in my hands. I didn't have the energy to pretend a stoicism I didn't feel, and I sighed deeply. I felt a light touch on my hair and I raised my head to see Sally smiling softly at me, leaning forward across the table with her arm still reaching out to stroke me gently and comfortingly.

'It's OK, Mum. Wait and see – it'll be OK. Just talk to me more, to me and Ben.'

'But I'm always talking to you – and especially to Ben. Have you any idea how much help I give him with his homework? And how else do you think this house functions except by me looking after all the finances and running everything and getting everyone organised and –'

'Yes, of course we know all that. I'm not talking about all the stuff you do to look after us, that's not what I mean at all. It's just that – well, the more you seem to be so capable and able to handle everything and sort everyone out, the less we seem to really know you. It's not enough just to be our mum any more, you see. Everything you did was perfect and wonderful when we were little – and that Dad did as well, in his own way – but now we're adults we need to know you as a person if we're all going to get on and make things work. I've got to know that I like you as a woman, as well as love you as my mother – and that's quite a different thing, isn't it? It frightens me sometimes when I think that maybe we wouldn't get on at all as friends if it wasn't that I happened to be your daughter, because then how can we possibly go on living so closely with each other? Even if I'm off at uni or whatever, we've still got to try and function as a family.'

'This is so unlike you, Sally – in another mood I'd find it pretty sickening, I have to say. All this about getting to know each other – for heaven's sake, child, can't we just get on with things? We've always laughed at all that embarrassing stuff about women being their daughters' best friends instead of just being good mums. Don't you remember telling me about that ghastly mother of one of your friends who insisted on dressing the same way as her daughter and joining in their boy talk? And dancing about and telling risqué jokes and smoking pot with them when they just wanted her to go away or tell them off or something more normal and mum-like? You don't want me to go all trendy like that, do you, Sal? Surely not?'

'No, Mum, I don't. That's not what I mean, either. Not that you need to worry,' she laughed. 'You've got a long way to go before you're in any danger of being "trendy" as you put it. Even the words you use to try and describe it automatically put you out of the picture as far as that's concerned.'

I was amazed to find myself laughing as well as I grabbed the hand that was still stroking my head and gave it a little slap. 'Don't be so cheeky!' I said, and kissed the smooth white back of it. The skin was almost as soft as when she was a baby, and I laid my cheek on it for a second. 'Oh, Sal – I don't know. I really don't. Everything's gone haywire and

I just don't know what to do next, or how to behave. Will you help me?'

As she looked at me across the table I felt more like her child than her parent. We were still smiling at each other and I knew we were closer at this moment than we'd ever been before. I understood what she meant about having to get to know each other as adults – I'd relied for far too long on the natural adoration that had been mine since her and Ben's births; now I had to earn it all over again.

'Yes, Mum. I will. If you really want me to – then I will.'

Stacey

I felt ever so good when I saw the two of them when I come off my shift. For a second it was like they was waiting for me – like when Janet or Sheila come out and there's Gary and Nick and all them others hanging about outside. I pretend they're waiting for me as well as Sheila sometimes – 'cos she likes to come out arm in arm with me in any case, so it don't look as if she's hoping to see the boys. She always looks surprised to see them and it makes me laugh 'cos she's only spent an hour and a half in the loo making up her face, ain't she? And she's not doing that to go down the Chinese with me, I can tell you that for nothing.

So it was fucking great coming out and seeing lovely Warren with the old guy, and the two of them looking at me when I come out. I got stuck again like I always do, and I couldn't hide behind Denisha or Sheila or any of the others 'cos I'd come out on my own as Mrs Peters had let me go early as it wasn't long since I'd been off sick.

'I feel poorly, Mrs P,' I said when I'd got her over to my

bell. 'I'm going all swimmy with the bleeper and I'm starting to make mistakes. Mr Chipstead said I was to take it easy since I've been off sick, so can I go now?'

It always gets her, that. Once Sheila had a fainting fit and when they checked her till receipts she'd sold all this wine and stuff for about two pounds instead of more like fifty. She'd turned off her bleeper and entered all the prices in by hand, you see, and Sheila never was one for knowing about prices. I can't do my adding and stuff but I do know about prices: Mrs Peters says she can ask me for a price on something and I'm quicker than her handheld. I always wish she'd say that in front of Warren, but she never. I've tried to get her to say it but if I ever speak to her when he's around then she just says, 'Get on with your work, dear', or something else fucking patronising.

So, anyway – if we ever want some time off we've only got to say we're having trouble with our bleepers and can we turn them off and they look right shit scared. Denisha said we should get onto that Claims Direct and sue SavaMart for the bleepers making us feel bad but Mrs Peters heard about it and said it wouldn't work 'cos they change us around to different jobs enough for them to be covered or something. And she says Claims Direct has gone bust in any case, but I think that's rubbish 'cos they was always advertising on TV so they must have loads of money. Anyway, that decided me 'cos I don't want to be took off the till more than I am now: it's a right nightmare if I'm put into the back depot to stock-take or something. I can't get between the stacks any more and if they see I could be out of a job – and Denisha says I couldn't claim for unfair dismissal or for them being 'fattist' as Crystal calls it 'cos if I can't do my job then it's not their fault. And they don't like to put me on shelf-filling, I know, 'cos I put the customers off their food and that ain't exactly what you want when you're in the grocery business, is it? They never say that, of course, but I'm not stupid: I know if some cunt's in here looking to buy a dessert for her tea and she sees me standing by the frozen steam puddings it's gonna make her think, ain't it? So I just shut up about that, but if I can get off a bit early sometimes then I do.

My coat was caught on the door again, and Warren was watching so I was trying to make it look as if it was the coat button that was caught like it could happen to anyone and not my tummy that was stuck. It looked like he'd been talking to the old bloke, and when they saw me they said something to each other that I couldn't hear. Then the old guy started to cross the road towards me and I felt right scared for a second 'cos I was stuck and Warren was walking away down the street. I felt like calling out to him, but I knew I was being stupid, and then the guy shouted out good night to him – he even called him by his name so maybe they knew each other or something – and then Warren said good night back to him and I felt a bit better.

The old guy said, 'Let me help you', or something and he took my hand and he sort of half pushed open the other door and held it while I got through. I must tell Denisha this tomorrow, I thought. I feel like a right princess in a story or something, with this guy taking my hand and helping me. He was ever so gentle and he looked at me ever so kindly, as if he really cared about me being OK.

'Thanks,' I said. And I didn't feel a bit scared now, fuck knows why. There was just something in the way he looked at me that made me feel safe and he'd pulled back a bit and was watching me like – oh, I dunno, it's hard to say, but as if – well, as if he was proud of me, that's the nearest I can say. Like when I got my NVCQ and my mum opened the envelope with the certificate and then took that picture of me holding it. She looked just full of love, really, and ever so proud. That's a bit how the guy looked. Not creepy and with those horrible glazed kind of eyes that the freaks get when they look at me, like they want to lick me or something.

'Shall I see you home, Stacey?'

That made me wobble a bit, though. We had such strict instructions about 'not fraternising with customers' or however Mrs P put it, and we'd heard so many scare stories that I couldn't help wondering what he wanted. I had a lovely quick daydream about him trying to rape me and Warren breaking down the door just in time and coming to save me, but then he spoke again.

'We can walk – it's not far, is it? – or I've got my car parked round the corner if you'd prefer. Warren – Mr Chipstead, I mean – said you'd be coming out about now so I brought the car near as it's such horrible weather. Warren and I are old friends, you see, and I knew you'd been ill – oh, did you get my card, by the way? – and I just thought it would be a nice surprise for you if I gave you a lift home.'

He was gabbling a bit now – talking too fast for my liking, and I knew he was feeling kind of panicky. But it was bleeding cold and even though I tried to wrap my coat round me it just wouldn't meet in the middle and keep the freezing wind out. It was spitting a bit too, and I knew it would be just my fucking luck for it to start raining any minute. By the time I came out of the tube the other end it would be pouring, and the thought of the journey was right depressing in any case. Even once I'm down into the tube it's horrible: I always have to wait while they undo the barrier next to the places you're supposed to go through. I have to stand there while all the normal people slot their tickets in and them gates open and shut and I get quite dizzy watching them in their little routines:

ticket-in/flip/pass/flip/ticket-out. The huge sea of people waiting in the rush hour goes through them like when I went on the Thames barrier trip at school and all them little gates let the water through ever so slowly and once it was out and through the other side it rushed like fuck. All them people are just the same: they all have to move forward ever so slowly on one side and then once they're through they're down them escalators like a dose of salts, as my mum would say. But I'm always stood there like a right idiot until they can be arsed to open up the side gate and let me through. And then they give me that look that means 'are you sure you'll be able to get on the train at that size?' and I go through ever so fast before they can stop me. 'Cos it won't be long, I know that. It won't be long before I can't fit into the train any more, let alone into a seat – I've given that up long ago.

So while something in me was screaming not to be stupid and remember all them murders and stuff you read in the papers and they have on *Trisha*, there was another bit of me saying, 'Go on, girl – you go for it. Have a warm comfortable ride in his car, and if he rapes you and cuts you up into little pieces and boils them for supper then that's just something you'll have to cope with at the time.' It made me giggle a bit, thinking that, as it sounded funny and he smiled at me. He looked all kind again, and suddenly I decided to do it.

'Yeah, OK,' I said. 'Thanks. Let's go in your car.'

Charlie

I'd thought to push the passenger seat as far back as it would go before I'd left the car, so I was able to open the door for Stacey and gently help her in without too much embarrassment. I offered to help do up her seat belt, and to my surprise she accepted immediately and simply sat back like a child while I reached over her and clipped it in. It was the first time I had touched her anywhere except on her hand, and even through the layers of fabric of her coat and the striped dress it was a delight to me to feel her softness under my arm. It was all I could do to prevent myself giving her a quick kiss as I pulled back out of the car, but I was just rational enough, in spite of the joy leaping about inside me like a frisky lamb, to keep my hopes set firmly on the future and to avoid doing anything that could jeopardise it.

'Now, Stacey,' I said, in what I hoped was a suitably calm and reassuring voice, 'I know Warren said you lived some-where in Balham, but you'll have to tell me exactly where. Or would you rather I dropped you at the underground?' I added, praying that she'd refuse and that it would simply make her even more convinced of my good intentions.

I slipped into my seat, did up my seat belt and switched on the radio as I held my breath while waiting for her reply. My finger hovered over the pre-set buttons for a second or two in an agony of indecision: should I put on my usual Radio 3 or 4 in an attempt to impress her with a glimpse of the culture I could bring into her life, or Sally and Ben's Capital, Heart or Kiss to show I was — literally — on her wavelength? I opted for a kind of honesty and chose Radio 3. Just as Mahler's Fourth erupted, gloriously, into the small space of the car, Stacey turned towards me and lifted her eyebrows slightly.

'Forty-three Towerbury Street, just off the High Road,' she said quietly, and her voice seemed to blend with that of the soprano singing of heaven. What an extraordinary child this was! Not for a second did she seem to have questioned why this virtual stranger had appeared out of nowhere to whisk her home in his car, or why, indeed, he had sent her a card or presented himself so frequently at her till. And the slight change of expression – which up to now had been either nervous or bland – to one of wry complicity gave me a glimpse of an altogether cannier creature than the one I had hitherto thought I'd known. I started the engine and then looked back at her. She was still watching me, her plump cheeks and the end of her nose red from the cold and her eyes bright behind the glasses. To my astonishment, she suddenly smiled a little and the tops of her cheeks rose up to be twin hills over which her eyes were rising suns. I felt a stab of intense happiness that made me laugh out loud.

'What?' she said. 'What are you laughing at, then?'

'Nothing, Stacey. Nothing at all – everything's fine. Before we set off, though – can I just say one thing?'

'Oh yeah – now what? Now it's coming out, is it – whatever it is you want?'

'Stacey – please, don't look so suspicious. I've been coming to your till for weeks now and if I'd wanted to do anything to hurt you or take advantage of you or whatever, I'd have surely tried it before now, wouldn't I? No, I just wanted to say that I will never ever do anything that you don't like or that makes you unhappy or embarrassed or sad or – this is a very strange situation and you'll have to forgive me if I sound a bit peculiar but I'm staggering about in the dark here.' I took a quick look at her still-wary face and knew I must keep talking if I was to save myself. I hadn't meant to say anything at all other than pleasantries on the way to her house. What on earth had started me on this semi-confession I had no idea, but now I was halfway in I had no choice but to try and dig myself out again. 'I'm just very fond of you, you see, and – oh dear – that sounds bad, too, doesn't it? I really am a perfectly ordinary, respectable, rather boring person, Stacey, and I've never done anything like this ever before.'

'They all say that.'

'What do you mean? Who do?' I was panic-stricken in an instant: who were these 'they'? How many men did my girl have trailing after her besides me?

'The creeps. The weirdos. The ones what say dirty stuff in the street and that.'

'Do they? Who do? What kind of creeps?'

'You know. The men that try to touch you or say stuff. Like the guys that go after Andy. They all say that too. "I've never done anything like this before. This is the first time I've ever felt like this – I'm a happily married man," and all that crap. They're on the common every fucking night, Andy says, with their briefcases and their business suits trying to meet young boys to have a quickie with before they go home to their families.'

'But do you have lots of them after you, Stacey? Do men try to touch you and – say things and so on?'

The noise of the still-running engine, mixed with the strains of the symphony, filled the moments before she spoke. She was looking down into her lap, fiddling with one of the large, shiny buttons of her coat. 'Nah – not really,' she said at last. 'Only sometimes. And it's all right – I know you're not like that, really. Go on.'

She raised her head again and I felt such relief that I almost hugged her. Without any possible justification this girl trusted me. I could see that now.

'I want you to be happy, you see,' I went on, feeling safer and calmer every second. 'I want to – forgive me for this, Stacey, as you'll very probably say it's the last thing you want or need, but – I want to look after you. That's all.'

'Oh, no, it ain't,' she said. 'Who do you think you're

kidding? That's not all you want, is it? I may not be as smart as you, but I'm not stupid, you know. But don't panic,' she went on, as she sensed my dismay, 'I'm not saying you don't want to look after me and all that as well. It's just — let's not kid ourselves — you fancy me, don't ya?'

I couldn't help it — I laughed again. The way I had been pussyfooting around with her; my prissy middle-class angst muddled with my lust and guilt and terror sending me into whirlpools of anxiety in my attempts to try and convey to the girl my desperate, pathetic love suddenly seemed foolish and unnecessary. Yes — I bloody well did fancy her, and if she could accept that then who knows what unexpected joys lay ahead?

'Yes, I do.'

'Well, that's good, you see. Not many people really fancy me, you see, me being a big girl and all that. I don't have a boyfriend, if that's what you want to know.'

'I think you're lovely, Stacey — really. Shall I take you home?'

'Yeah — OK.'

Crystal

Hiiiya, Stacey!!!!!

How're ya doin', gal? I'm real happy 'cos the weight's goin' down again now after my plateau. Have ya heard about the plateau? You always get one sooner or later once you're on the other side and you gotta be ready for it or it can bring you right down. Bring your spirits right down, I mean, not the pounds, ha ha. You just get kinda stuck and the pounds just won't get goin' again. My friend Bobbi got stuck on her plateau real soon after her op, too, and she got so depressed I thought she might do something terrible but the doc put her on some pills and she went to a counselor (councilor??? Sorry, Stace, you know what my spelling's like) and she got over it but it was edgy for a while. I prayed real hard for her for sure and the Lord got her through.

Yea! Stacey, I got myself some new lingerie today – matching panties and camisole. It's made of red lace and Josh says it's kinda sexy and that makes me feel sooooooooooo good. The panties are still tight so I gotta keep on going with the weight loss but I can just get them on and they're THREE SIZES smaller than the ones I bought before I came over, so isn't that cool??? Mind you, I can't wear them very often because – well, that's for me to know and you to wonder . . . I'll tell ya when I see ya.

Now I just gotta get the OK from the insurance for my tummy op. My doc says once I've lost enough they can take away the apron that's hanging down and tighten up the folds under my arms and I can't wait 'cos I still don't feel right without long sleeves and something hanging down over my waist. But I don't have to tell you, gal, do I???

Have you got yourself an angel, Stacey? I mean one of the human ones this time, the ones in heaven are there for you whether you know it or not so you can't get rid of those even if you wanted to unless you do something real bad and then God turns his face from you and Jesus cries and you may find yourself with LUCIFER LOOKING AFTER YOU!!!! And we don't want that for you, Stacey. Even tho' I know sometimes you don't believe what I tell you about the power of the Lord and prayer I shall never give up on you and I pray every day that you may find the help you need.

It's so cool you found that place in Britain that does the RNY. Have you gotten to see them yet? You have some great doctors over there even tho' you're so small. I read about how you invented penicillin and stuff over there so they have to be good at getting you over, huh? Did you like the stickers I put on the envelope? Don't throw them in the trash 'cos they're lucky and the pink one with the glitter on it is to bring you luck in getting over. Cut it out and keep it in your purse – a friend of mine did that with the same sticker and she had her op in two months and her uncle won the lottery (he only had four numbers but he won two hundred dollars!!!!)

Do you see *Sex in the City*? It's soooooooooooooo cool and I get the hots for all the guys. Josh says I'm a sex maniac!!

Write back and may Jesus hold you in his arms.

Lots and lots and lots of hugs and kisses

Crystal

xxxxxxxxxxxxxxxxxx

Ben

Christmas was bloody awful, but then it's never been a favourite time of mine – or at least not since the dim, distant days of stockings at the end of the bed and whispered secrets and all that kind of thing. Before the devastating day when Sally told me that Father Christmas was not real I used to get so overexcited on Christmas Eve that Mum would have to put me in a cool bath to try and calm me down. I'm not sure, in terms of peaks of exquisite pleasure, that anything has quite come up to it since – even sex. The feeling of stretching my toes out to the end of the bed in the early morning and finding the rustling, unfamiliar weight left there mysteriously in the night was so fantastic that I used to lie there moving it around with my feet and picturing it for ages before I raised my head to look at it. And then the brilliant time of slowly opening each wrapped little parcel inside the huge stocking that Mum had made specially. She'd based it on a knitting pattern for a sock and had meant to make it three times the size but because she tripled the measurements it came out nine times instead.

She never was that good at maths. So it had to have some really big stuff inside to fill it up – I always thought they'd be the really good things but they usually turned out to be clothes of some sort: a big bulky jumper or a new dressing gown or something. And what I was looking for were cars or Ninja Turtles.

It lost its thrill once I knew it was Mum doing it. She and Dad used to keep up the pretence, and Sally and I had to take all the stuff into their bedroom and show it to them and they'd pretend to be surprised and I'd feel really embarrassed. I suppose I should have come out with it – told them straight out that I didn't believe in him any more, I mean – because, although they knew perfectly well that Sally had told me (in fact, Sal said there was a huge row about it) we'd never openly acknowledged it. But it's not that easy for a seven- or eight-year-old or whatever I was to tell his parents that they can stop lying now because he's perfectly well aware that this old guy who's supposedly invading his bedroom once a year is invented.

Even though it wasn't quite as exciting, it kept on being fun for a few years of course; it's hard to remember now when it all became a bit of a chore. Probably about the time that I realised I'd rather be out with my friends than doing things with my parents. But this year takes the prize – if I thought I'd been pretending to have a good time before now, then this Christmas I get the Oscar. And Sal, too. I hadn't realised just how much the whole occasion had become an established routine, and when one of the key players is missing it's really hard to pretend it's anywhere near normal any more – let alone enjoyable. Both Sal and I longed to tell Mum just to drop the whole idea for once – to have no presents or Christmas lunch and all that but just a quiet time on our own watching a few films on TV and having some ready meals or takeaways to save her cooking, but of course we knew we couldn't do that. It would have hurt her far more to abandon the celebrations than to stagger on with them as if nothing had changed.

Every other moment there seemed to be reminders that Dad wasn't there: like the terrible puns and corny jokes that were missing as we opened our presents round the tree. Christmas Day was the only time he ever drank in the morning, and he'd sit there with a glass of sherry, eating chocolates and making comments as each parcel was opened — and they really made us laugh. This year when Sally opened the one from Aunt Cherry and it was the same old tin of biscuits that she always sent there was an awful silence and you could tell we were all trying to think of the kind of joke Dad would have come up with. And the carving of the turkey: it was so cringe-making when Mum said, 'You be the man of the house, darling', but I had to give it a go. I could see Sally was trying not to giggle, because I was cutting it into strange square chunks instead of slices, and I couldn't look at her or I knew I'd go too. And it was really sad how Mum was making such an effort to be smiley and all that — I'm not sure I wouldn't have cried instead of laughed if I'd once let go.

Anyway, we got through it, and Dad phoned about four o'clock and we had a strange, awkward conversation without really talking about anything. Mum had answered it, and I thought it must be a distant cousin or something, because her voice sounded so normal but kind of detached, and then she passed it to Sally and Mum had a desperate look in her eye and I just knew she needed us not to make trouble. So we both spoke to him as if nothing had happened and as if we were always separated on Christmas Day and just kind of clocked in with each other and checked on each other's health and so on. It reminded me a bit in a funny way of the years of pretending about Father Christmas, because I found myself telling him what we'd been doing as if he didn't know perfectly well exactly what we always do on Christmas Day. And, in both cases, I never dared say the really big thing – that I didn't believe in him any more.

I was longing to go round to Hol's, which I'd done the year before at about six o'clock. I can remember leaving Mum and Dad sitting in their armchairs in front of the TV; they were still wearing the paper hats from the crackers and they'd drunk a lot of wine. You could see they'd be asleep long before they got to the twist at the end of *Fight Club* so I knew in the morning they'd dismiss it as just another violent film without knowing what the fuck they were talking about. I felt quite irritable about it, because they were already muttering about modern films being all the same and stuff, and I didn't really thank them for the day or anything. I know they didn't expect it, but Mum worked really hard at all that food and wrapping and things, and I wish I had. Because that was probably the last good Christmas I'll get. I can't imagine it ever being like that with my kids, partly because I'm probably not going to have any and partly because, even if I did, I'm not going to lie to them about things – ever. Even about Father Christmas. And I'll let them do just what they want at times like Christmas and birthdays and all that.

On Boxing Day Mum started to talk about him a bit. She really hadn't said anything since the day he left. Sally said she'd talked quite a bit on that day itself, and she thought they might get somewhere, but then after that Mum just clammed up, and Sal and I found it easier to keep right off the subject. It wasn't as if life seemed all that different really – Dad had been so quiet and distant for the weeks before it happened and I was usually working in my room or out with my friends so the house didn't seem particularly empty or anything. But all three of us knew there had to come a time when we discussed it: Sal and I hadn't got a clue whether things were permanent, like in terms of a divorce and stuff, or whether this was just some extended row that would blow over. Sal said she thought there was another woman involved, but I didn't believe that. That's one thing Dad just wouldn't do – he's not the type.

Anyway, on Boxing Day Mum started to talk. She said that she thought Dad was having a mid-life crisis or something (I didn't like to point out that as Dad was forty-eight he might be considered a bit past mid-way) and that if we just sat tight and kept calm everything would sort itself out. Since he left, Sally's said so much to me about how women shouldn't rely on men and how Mum was making a big mistake in not just getting on with her life without Dad and not letting him come back in any case, that I was sure she was going to say something, but she didn't. We both just listened to Mum and kind of nodded and muttered a bit and tried to show some support. But it's all pretty fucking awful really: I've never seen her like this and she looks so sad all the time – I wish I could help her, but I can see it's not Sal and me she needs right now. I never realised before how much she really loved Dad. It's quite shocking.

Stacey

Who'd have thought it? The way Charlie's fitted into my life like he's done. It's hard to believe it's all happened in a few weeks; my mum and I are always saying it's like he's been around for ever, really. I laugh now when I look back to that first day when he drove me home from work: he seemed so – I dunno – kinda quiet and a bit dim. Now he's the liveliest of the three of us. My mum says if it wasn't that he fancied me she'd have a go herself. Gotta watch that, I have, 'cos you can't trust my mum further than you can throw her – and that's not very far neither.

He come in that first time and he took his hat off – he was wearing that boring black thing that makes him look like a doctor – and I could see right away that Mum was dead impressed. He did a kinda little dip with his head as he took it off and she went all simpery and cute.

'Who's your friend, Stace?' she said.

'This is Mr Thornton, Ma. He comes in Sava-Fart for his shopping and we got chatting. Didn't we, Mr Thornton? About bogofs?'

'Stacey – don't be so cheeky – what will your friend think of us?'

'How d'ya mean?' I asked, all innocent. It's good fun getting Ma going, even though she knows I love her really.

'Well, you know,' she said, 'you shouldn't call it – you know . . .'

'What – Sava-Fart, d'you mean? Why not? It's what we call it, ain't it, Ma?'

Charlie was smiling at all this – he hadn't never had a chance to say hello or nothing, and already he was seeing the other side of the Salton household. Dunno why I was feeling so perky, but he'd got me all high on the drive home like I was pissed or downed a tab or something. Fuck knows why – it was something to do with the way he'd been looking at me, and that. It's hard to say how I felt exactly, but I guess it was how Sheila feels when she knows she looks good and the guys are eyeing her and getting excited.

'It isn't the best supermarket in the world, is it?' Charlie said, trying to save Ma from feeling embarrassed. He's nice like that – I know that, now. He don't never like to see people unhappy or uneasy and things, although I don't know how that fits with him having done a runner on his wife and kids. But I don't like to think about them.

'I think your name for it is rather apt,' he went on. (Ooooh – that didn't half sound poncey, but I held my tongue 'cos he might not have understood if I sent him up like I would have if I'd been with the girls. I'd do it now, of course – I send him up rotten the way he talks, but things was different for them first few days before I knew how hung up he was on me.) 'I always have felt that Stacey is too good for it, Mrs – sorry, forgive me, but you are Stacey's mother, aren't you?'

Course he knew straight up that she was, but he was just trying to get me to say it so's he didn't have to leave and he could start chatting and that. But I never – I just looked at him and then at my mum.

'Yes, that's right,' she said. 'I'm Stacey's mum, Lena. I've always said that about Stace and that place, Mr Thornton, it's funny you should say it – I've always said our Stacey should find something better. She's a very clever girl, you know, and she's wasted in that place.'

Yeah – right, like I should be modelling for the magazines or something. Who the fuck does my mum think I am – Posh Spice? I'm lucky to have got the supermarket job and all – I know that. If I was the size I am now when I'd gone for it they'd never have let me in, that's for sure. Even then they took a good, careful look at me, and Warren was none too certain, I could see. But they ain't queuing up to work in Sava-Fart, you see, so I knew I was in with a chance, and I didn't look too bad in them days and it was winter so I was wearing my thick fuzzy coat. I ain't stupid, you know. You can't tell what's fuzz and what's me in that coat, so long as I keep it buttoned right up and tuck my legs under. It was fucking hot in the office, I remember that – and they kept saying wouldn't I like to take off my coat and I kept saying no, it's OK, I feel the cold really badly so I'm fine, thanks, and I was sweating like a pig and I was sure they could see that. But I kept my head tucked right into the collar so them rolls of fat that I can't stand was hidden and I looked up at them under my lashes and it was OK. I wasn't half the size what I am now. I'd seen that film with Eddie Murphy – *The Nutty Professor* – and he wears this fat suit in it and he looks just like he's really big, so I thought if I wear the coat like it's a fat suit then who's to know where the coat stops and the real me starts? If Eddie Murphy can look big, then I can look small, or that's the way I was thinking in any case.

So I got the job and my mum was so thrilled and excited that I got caught up in all that too and felt like I'd won the lottery or something. She had Auntie Ede round and everything – bought some beers and we all had a celebration. So I had to laugh when she said that to Charlie about it not being good enough. I remembered the way we'd all drank our beers and cheered and laughed and that; she was dead thrilled then. And when she come in the shop and seen me in my uniform for the first time sitting at the till I thought she'd start crying or something. I was right embarrassed 'cos they still had a senior standing next to me watching everything I did and it made me so nervous I was punching all the wrong buttons and missing the scanner and fuck knows what else. You kinda lose your mind when you're being watched like that: I was checking on the daftest things when I was still under a senior. Customers was bringing these fruits and stuff in their plastic bags out of their trolleys and sticking them on the belt and looking all impatient and

I'm fucked if I could remember what half of them was. ''Scuse me, Mrs Peters, what's this curved yellow fruit that comes in a bunch called?' Nah, I'm joking there, but you get the picture. So anyway, when my mum was there looking at me all soppy and proud it was right embarrassing. I was trying to pretend I didn't know her and she was just another customer, but I could tell Mrs P was onto her. Ma kept whispering the names of stuff when she took it out of her trolley once she saw I was in a panic. Everything – even all them with bar codes on, so I was trying to tell her to shut up 'cos I only had to scan them, but she didn't get it and kept on whispering '*fishfingers, Stacey*' or '*white sliced, love*' like I'm an idiot. God knows how I kept that job, but then when I see as they have such trouble getting any new staff I guess it ain't surprising. I know how they need me now, see. If Mrs Peters looked at me today like she done then she'd be in big trouble. Stupid cow.

Charlie stayed and had coffee with us that first evening. Mum gave him her sweet, milky coffee and he said it was just how he liked it. We laughed about that after, me and Charlie, 'cos he likes it black with no sugar and he never dared say. He went on drinking Ma's coffee for days before he dared tell me. I knew right off something special was happening, though, 'cos I was listening to him talking to Ma and telling her about his job and that and I realised I'd been sitting there without trying to cover myself up like I usually done. I was enjoying myself, and that don't never usually happen when there's other people in the flat 'cos I'm always wondering what they're thinking and trying to sit in a way that don't look too disgusting.

It was just like when the girl finds her soul mate in the books Ma reads from the library. She reads a lot, you see, and I always know when the girl's getting the right guy 'cos

Ma goes all dreamy-looking and smiley and she don't even want to watch the TV unless it's *EastEnders*. She's right soppy, my mum. I wondered if that was why she was so happy and smiley that first evening with Charlie – was it just like in the books, that she knew straight off that he was crazy about me? (Crazy's the word, if you ask me, as I'm always telling him – crazy to fancy a lump of fat like me. But there's no accounting for tastes, as Sheila says. Course she says it when some guy don't want to get in her pants soon as he sees her. Other way round with me.)

So did Ma know Charlie was Mr Right as she puts it? Or was it just she smelt money? She ain't greedy, my ma, but she been on benefits for so long she gets all excited when she sees someone what's earning. Especially someone like Charlie – however much it pisses me off, she still talks about him some of the time as if he was better than us. I think she saw him right away as the one to drag her fat daughter into the good life.

Well, Ma – you might not be so wrong at that, as it happens. What's it you always say? 'Stranger things have happened.'

Charlie

I know I was walking about looking like a madman. The minute it was done I couldn't stop smiling. I was aware of people glancing at me as I passed them in the street, not liking to look at me too directly or for too long – for fear of my engaging them in some crazy conversation, perhaps. My transformation from having been in a state of persistent longing into one of joyful calm was instant and totally unpredictable – for those first few weeks I felt as if I would never need anything more in my life than the regular visits to Stacey and the evenings of disgusting coffee and unimaginable bliss.

It was all astonishingly easy: Lena accepted me without question, and, even on that very first visit, the atmosphere was so relaxed and uncritical that her invitation to me to call in again the following day seemed the most natural thing in the world.

Stacey on her home ground turned out to be even more adorable than I could have imagined: funny, bright and completely, captivatingly charming. Yes — there is lust, I cannot deny that, even to myself, but there's more, too. I love her. I truly love her, and, for the first time in my life, I understand what that means.

During those early, delirious days I couldn't think about the future: nothing existed but the present. I stayed in a dreadful little hotel in Pimlico, calling in to see her each evening after work. I knew it couldn't last, of course, not in that form, but my happiness was such that it left no room for logical thought of any kind. I was content (content? How can such a mild word begin to describe the bliss of my new existence?) just to get through the days and live for the evenings spent in her company.

It wasn't easy to keep up appearances at work. The sheer heaven of seeing Stacey made everything bearable, of course, but the logistics were never simple. For the first few weeks, when I was staying in that depressing hotel, I did at least have somewhere reasonable to wash and shave and hang up my clothes, but it was still a miracle that I got to chambers or to court most days on time and looking fairly presentable. My room in the hotel was my launch pad, which, together with the occasional takeaway, packet of crisps or chocolate bar, afforded me every physical necessity and enabled me to project myself into an appearance of normal living each day while my mind existed solely for her.

I would wake in the morning to my telephone ringing its pre-programmed alarm call – in my half-asleep state I never did learn not to say 'hello?' every time into the robotic silence – and smile to myself to think that I would see her within twelve hours of that very moment. My breakfast was a quick cup of tea, assembled, rather than brewed, from little packets and cartons on the tray by the wardrobe, possibly accompanied, if I was feeling particularly indulgent, by a tiny, dry, film-wrapped biscuit. My grooming routine consisted of a shower – newly opening each time a sliver of paper-wrapped soap and unscrewing a tiny virgin bottle of shampoo – and a quick shave. Dressing was functional but efficient: I not only made use of the hotel laundry but also, for the first time in my life, discovered the remarkable effectiveness of the Corby trouser press in the corner (how many times had Judy and I laughed at such things as being useful only for salesmen and illicit lovers). At work, although I was aware that my attention was now never fully devoted to my clients and that little things were beginning to slip, I was happy and positive, simply filling in time until I would make my way to Balham and to joy.

I worked more consistently than I had over the previous few weeks, in fact, because it had been made quite clear to me that my clerk wouldn't be suggesting me for any more cases unless I pulled my socks up. For the short time between walking out of the house and the start of the Christmas break, I was committed to appear in various pretty straightforward divorce proceedings. I bought a couple of shirts and some underwear from Marks & Spencer, and, by hanging my suit in the steamed-up bathroom each evening, I could walk into work looking reasonably spruce, without having to face the problem of collecting my things from home. Once in court, with a supreme effort I kept superficially calm. If I'd betrayed even a fraction of the tumultuous feelings that were heaving around inside me during that period I wouldn't have lasted a moment – thank God for the artifice that's always been an important part of the way I present a case. I needed all the skill I could muster during that unreal time just to stop myself screaming out loud – mostly for joy, in those early stages, but, even then, sometimes in terror.

I knew home and Judy would have to be faced before too long. Although I had been surprised by how easily I was surviving with the bare minimum of personal effects (so ironic that most of my time during the day was being spent in argument over the division of the most trivial of goods), I knew soon I would need to expand my wardrobe, and, apart from my clothes, there were books and papers that I needed.

It was easier than I had foreseen. Apart from a dreadfully stiff phone call on Christmas Day I hadn't made contact with Judy and the kids at all for a couple of weeks, and I kept putting off getting in touch for fear of upsetting the rickety little boat of happiness I'd somehow managed to keep afloat since leaving. Bloody selfish, of course, but then I swear I honestly felt that they were better off without me and that Judy and I had never really been a proper couple at all. The intense – no, even that doesn't begin to describe it – the ravaging, all-consuming feelings that I was experiencing for Stacey rendered everything and anything else so irrelevant that I can't see it now as being selfish in any normal sense of the word.

I rang the bell rather than used my key, which I still had with me, sensing some unwritten law of propriety that suggests a certain politesse in warning the abandoned spouse of one's arrival in the family home. Judy answered the door and looked quite startled, poor love. I'd left a message on the machine telling her I was planning to come round and collect some of my things, but she'd been late back and hadn't had time to check it, she said. I'm not sure that was true, in fact – I'm more inclined to think she'd been home for some time, because she had some marks on the side of her face that suggested it had been pressed onto a cushion or pillow or something. My guess is she'd been up in the bedroom with one of her migraines but didn't like to say so in case I thought she was playing for sympathy. Little did she know she could have told me she'd just been diagnosed with stomach cancer and I'd have brushed it off: nothing and nobody other than Stacey could reach me.

Ringing the bell of your own front door and being let in like a visitor by someone you've lived with for over twenty years is a disorientating but not entirely unpleasant experience. As I was already floating in a no-man's land of emotional upheaval of stupendous proportions, to find myself standing like the Frog Footman in front of my own house, on the wrong side of the door, seemed oddly amusing rather than depressing. In more normal circumstances I've no doubt Judy and I would have laughed about it, but at that moment, not surprisingly, she didn't look as if she found it very funny.

'Hi,' I think I said, rather inadequately. 'How are you doing?'

The startled look disappeared in a millisecond and she replaced it with her Ofsted expression, as I call it: one of inspection looking for the worst and expecting to find it.

'How do you think?'

I resisted the temptation to inform her that, given the

huge scope for sarcasm, recrimination and noble suffering that my behaviour had afforded her, this wasn't the most inventive of replies, and merely lowered my head a little in an attempt to defuse the situation.

'You'd better come in,' she went on, and stepped back from the doorway to let me pass.

'Thanks.' I pushed past her into the hall, turning sideways with my back towards her to avoid the potential embarrassment of brushing her breasts as I passed.

'I just wanted to collect a few things, is that OK?'

'I can't stop you, can I?'

As I walked through the hall and into the living room my mind was whirling in a panicky assessment of what I might need in the next few weeks and what could be left to a future, more organised division of our property. I began to appreciate for the first time the problems encountered by my clients: the innumerable piles of objects that belonged to me assailed me on every side, so to speak, and I couldn't think how to begin to choose which to pack up and take away. Judy was trailing after me as if she expected me to make a run for it with something of hers, and I found myself leaving the living room and climbing the stairs to the bedroom without having made a single decision. I had foolishly not thought to bring a case or trunk with me, so I was aware that, even should I be able to make a few rational decisions about what to take, I would have to run the gauntlet of trying to pick a suitcase that might fairly be considered mine. As most of my work was based in London, I rarely travelled alone – Judy was the one who occasionally had to move around the country on inspections or for meetings – and, as I pictured the pieces of luggage stored in the attic, I realised that in all probability they had all been bought by her, even if we had jointly used them on family holidays. I certainly didn't fancy risking a row over something so inessential – I'd rather save it for the time I felt sure would have to come when argument would be inescapable.

'Can I borrow a bin liner or something, do you think? I mean, I didn't bring a case or anything, so I'll need something to take my stuff away in.'

'How much are you planning to take, then?'

'Oh, nothing much,' I said casually, scratching the side of my chin to ease a nonexistent itch. 'Just a few essentials, that's all.'

'Why, are you planning to come back, then? Why not take the lot?'

'That's hardly practical, Jude, at this stage, is it? I'd have thought that was fairly obvious.'

'Oh, I see, it's just the practicality of it. Do forgive me – you see, it may be obvious to you, but we're a bit in the dark here. We rather thought you lived here – that you were a husband and father, in fact, but – as I say, you'll have to bear with me as I've obviously got the wrong end of the stick – but do explain exactly what your relationship is to us, will you? And whether we may be expecting the pleasure of your company in this house again, or whether perhaps you've pissed off for good?'

'Judy, that really isn't going to help, is it? I mean, we can surely discuss this like –' (oh, God, everything I went to say sounded like a scene from a badly written romantic drama) '– like sensible adults.'

'Would you say that you've behaved like a sensible adult, though? I suppose that's something we have to look at, learned counsel. I rather think you've behaved like a bastard – and how does a bastard discuss this kind of issue with his wife – or, ex-wife, should I say? Or about-to-be ex-wife, I presume.'

I was moving around the bedroom, vaguely collecting a handful of socks here, a pile of boxer shorts there. I put them down on the bed, then opened up the wardrobe and stared hopelessly at the rail of dark suits, and sighed as I pictured the hooks of the hangers bursting through the black plastic of a bin liner. Even should I be able to retrieve such a thing from the kitchen under the relentless tirade that I could see was going to trail my every move, it would hardly be strong enough for me to be able to take away any reasonable amount of clothes, let alone books, papers and all the other bits and pieces that physically marked my existence in the house. I pulled a chair over to stand on so as to reach the top cupboards above the wardrobe, hoping I might find a holdall or something that would tide me over until my next visit, but, as I lifted one foot onto it, Judy leapt towards me at incredible speed and pulled it away. I nearly fell over.

'Don't you dare!' she yelled. 'Don't you dare go anywhere near those cupboards. That's private, you know that! All my – all my feminine stuff, as you always patronisingly call it.'

I was quite startled by the ferocity of this attack in defence of her depilatories or pessaries or whatever else I assumed she stored up there, but put it down to justifiable rage at her situation.

'Look, Jude, why don't I come back another time,' I said as gently as I could, shutting the wardrobe doors and turning towards her.

'Why?'

'Well, frankly, this is impossible. I haven't got a case; I daren't ask for one of ours in case you claim it as yours and, even if I could think of some way of transporting my things, I can't make any decisions with you following me round like this and abusing me.' I grimaced as soon as I'd said it, and resolved not to say another word, certain that I'd triggered another sarcastic reply that would spiral us further downwards into useless recriminations. I was wrong: there was a moment's silence then, to my surprise, Judy suddenly sank down on the bed and burst into tears.

I sat down beside her without thinking. I can honestly, and shamefully, say that I felt not a twinge of sympathy or even fondness at the sight of my wife desperately sobbing, so maddened and distracted was I by love. I was simply aping the behaviour patterns of a reasonable man in an instinctive attempt to smooth my path back to Stacey in whatever way I could.

'Look here, old girl,' I said, putting an arm round her shoulders and, cruelly, giving them a little squeeze as if in affection. 'I know this is totally incomprehensible, but you have to see it as me going through some sort of – what can I say? – going through a breakdown, I suppose. This isn't easy for either of us, and it's terrible that I've had to hurt you like this. I know you don't want to believe it, but it's the truth. I've explained to you that I've, quite unintentionally, fallen in love with someone else. I didn't think these things really happened, but they do – and it has. To me.'

She lifted her head at this and made the most awful sound – a kind of scream as if she was in physical pain, but with something else, something horrible, echoing behind it. I think in my pre-Stacey incarnation I'd have found it hard to bear, but in my numbed state I merely silently appraised and noted it, and moved on.

I patted her shoulder and got up, filled now with a surprising calm, and opened up the wardrobe again. I glanced along the rail and imagined myself in Stacey's living room wearing first one, then another, of my suits and jackets. I pulled out a dark-navy blazer, a black suit with a tiny grey pinstripe, a couple of pairs of cotton trousers, a plain black suit, an old beige corduroy one and a brown tweed jacket. I hesitated for a second or two over my dinner jacket, but then grabbed it in a flash of enthusiasm and smiled as I pictured myself dressed in black tie beside a glittering Stacey at some evening function. Stacey in full-length evening dress and covered in jewels was an image to treasure. I remembered the time Judy and I had been astonished when I helped her work out the amount of material she needed to make a full, circular skirt for Sally to wear in a school play. Hah! I thought, as I looked down at her still sitting on the bed, with her head in her hands. You ain't seen nothing.

'I'm taking the old trunk,' I said, 'and I'll return it to you once I've unpacked it, OK?'

She was snuffling into a tissue that she'd produced from somewhere about her person, but didn't reply.

'Excuse me,' I went on in a tone of cheerful practicality, 'I don't want to flatten you – can you just shift along a bit while I dump these on the bed? And you're sitting on the socks.'

I didn't wait for a reply, but flung the suits onto the white bedcover and went over to my shelves of shirts, from which I chose a dozen or so of the most useful. I added a handful of ties and then walked quickly out of the room and up the stairs to the tiny box room at the top that we called the attic, grabbed the old brown trunk that had belonged to Judy's father and carried it, with difficulty, down the stairs and onto the landing outside the bedroom. I was having to stop myself whistling – an overexcited optimism had overtaken me, a sense of something wonderful about to happen.

I threw open the trunk and, in a couple of journeys,

transferred the clothes into it, adding a few pairs of shoes and tutting to myself at my stupidity in not having put them and the other heavy, hard objects in first. Never mind: squashed suits and shirts could be sorted out easily enough. As I closed the trunk in readiness to carry it downstairs, I glanced at my wife, still sitting on the edge of the bed with her reddened, swollen, runny-nosed face turned towards me. Squashed people, I thought abstractedly, are another matter altogether.

Crystal

Coo-eeee!!

Sorry I didn't write last week, Stacey hon, I guess I get busy with my "new life" and don't seem to be able to find the time to write so often. I am doing real well, except for a bit of vertigo now and then. My weight loss is FANTASTIC!!! and I feel pretty good most days. Last Monday I went to a support group at the hospital where I had my WLS. We all sat around and talked about our problems and we were told to share with each other some of the difficult times we've had in the post-op. Hey!! I wanted to say – it's the pre-op that's the difficult times . . . I can take any amount of post-op pain and sickness and all that stuff. That ain't NOTHING compared to the heartache and pain and all before coming over. I remember when I was like you, Staceeeeeee, and hoping and praying that I'd be able to have the surgery so that I could find a way to stop all the pain and discomfort: my legs, back, hips, knees, etc ALL ACHED – day in and day out. I had to walk, at times, with a cane . . . and sometimes even with a walker like an old person. UGH, oh Lord, how I hate to think of that now! Not anymore!!! But there were some pre-op people there and my surgeon says he wants them to hear every side of WLS before even considering having it done. So I tried to tell them everything bad that had happened since I came over but they must have seen I was just BUSTING with the happiness of all that weight loss, so there's no way I'm putting anyone off!!

You gotta get out of that chair, hon – you should see me – I walk, and walk . . . and use exercise videos!!! Major miracle!! So, like I've said before . . . don't give up hope!! Hey – well done for ringing that hospital – I know what it's like, believe me, but you've made the first move and that's the hardest. (What does it mean, going private?) I have lost about 52 pounds and dropped 4 sizes in clothes now!! What a wonderful feeling it is to be able to go into "normal" clothing stores, buy fashionable outfits, and not ACHE ANYMORE!!! I don't have to take the meds I was taking pre-op for arthritis . . . or the pain meds . . .

So what's with this guy? He sounds kinda cute. Real British, too, the way he treats you. Is he rich? Hey – why not marry him, Stacey? He sounds cool and I guess he's crazy about you and all, so why not, and I could come over for the wedding in a new outfit and we'd have such fun. Can you get quickie divorces over there like here? It sounds like his kids are real grown up so that's OK. Just gotta get yourself over the other side first and start LIVING! And, talking of living, get your ass back into that internet café and get yourself onto Hotmail so I can get back to ya real quick – send me a message at angel4crystal@hotmail.com once you're fixed up.

Anyway, I don't need to tell you to get over here, sweetie. But I want you to know I'm still praying for ya!

Lots of love and kisses

Crystal

xxxxxxxxxxxxx

PS My friend Josh says they don't think angels are made of silk or anything no more, but they're made out of a gas. I think that kinda makes sense, don't you????

Stacey *(e-mail)*

OK Crystal! So I'm all fixed up like you said – mine's staceysalton@hotmail.com and I can get in here easy after work each day and I just LONG to get a message so pleeeeeeeease answer this as quick as you can!! Thanks for your great letter – it's just made me sooooooo jealous I could scream!!

Charlie's still around, and – yeah, you're right – he is cute. It's so weird, though, Crystal, the way he just stares at me and stuff. It freaks me out sometimes that someone can need me so much. I used to think I'd give ANYTHING just to have someone love me or fancy me like the girls at work have, but things are never how you imagine, are they?

But I ain't complaining – he keeps buying me things and my mum really likes him. Not sure about your wedding idea, though. You're stuck then, ain't ya? And don't tell me about getting split and having loads of money from the divorce 'cos he's a lawyer and guess who'd get shafted???!!

Mind you, I do have plans for him while he's so stuck on me. I ain't stupid, Crystal. I'm gonna have a word with my mum about changing my domestic arrangements, as they say. Maybe I'll be seeing ya on the Other Side sooner than we thought, eh? Geddit??

Love

your e-mail buddy

Stacey

Sally

I'm frightened about Ben. Holly rang me on my mobile last night, which was unusual in itself as we've never got on particularly well, so I suspected it was going to be something pretty serious. I even wondered for a split second if she was pregnant, but I figured even daft Ben has sense enough to be careful, especially after all the doom and gloom, terror shock lectures about Aids that Mum and Dad gave us a couple of years ago. What with that and seat belts, cigarettes and drugs, it's a wonder they can sleep at night for worrying about us. I hate to tell them that Ben and I have been 'experimenting' as they always put it, with pretty much everything in terms of stimulants – within reason – since we were twelve or so, but then try explaining to anyone over forty that you're not going to keel over from dropping the occasional tab at a party. Can't be done.

No, it was more worrying, what Holly had to say, because it confirmed something I've been half thinking for some time: that Benbo is seriously disturbed – or, at least, has the potential to be so. Ever since he began going on about quantum thingummies and parallel universes he's been a little bit weird, but I thought it was just a phase. I never paid that much attention, in any case – I've been away on my music course at weekends or out of the house so much that most of the strange goings-on have been happening without my noticing.

But since the grand exit I've had to be around a lot more. It's a good excuse, to be honest, because I was beginning to think I ought to be doing something useful with my gap year, or at least something to earn a bit more cash. Now

I've been able to put off doing anything dynamic for a little longer: no one can be expected to go and teach English to Nepalese babies or save three-eared toads in the Sahara or whatever while their parents are splitting up. It's about time we had some drama in the family, in any case. They've always been far too normal and nice, if you ask me – I must be one of the very few in my last year of school who didn't have at least one or two step-relations. Very pre-seventies.

These things are never, though, how they appear from the outside. Once I calmed down after it first happened I think I imagined I could be the hard-done-by, beautiful victim of a broken home, who'd get that lovely Winona Ryder paleness and look of noble suffering. My friends just said I looked ill. It's been rather terrible seeing Mum the way she's been, and Ben has seemed so depressed lately that I was worried even before Holly rang.

I don't know how I feel about Dad. The whole business is so surreal that I find myself looking at it all from the outside, as if it's a movie or something. It's so completely unlike him that I can't judge him as the same person: it's like his body has been taken over by someone else, and if there really is some other woman involved, which is what it appears to be from Mum's occasional hints, then that just makes it even more incredible. The idea of anyone finding Dad physically attractive, apart from it being a pretty repellent thought as far as I'm concerned, is so totally unreal that I just can't get my head round it. They say kids can never imagine their parents making love: well, Ben and I used to discuss that and, although we thought it was unlikely on the evidence that they still got it together more than occasionally, we'd quite come to terms with the idea of it in principle. But the thought of Dad doing it with someone else – well, that's just so gross as not to be tenable.

Anyway, Holly said Ben was saying some stuff about this being his fault and that he should be punished or something, and I don't like the sound of it. I know just how he feels about blaming himself, but he's such a worrier that he probably thinks he has to do something about it, rather than just wallow in a bit of self-pity, or shut himself in his room, which is more my style. It's no good talking to Mum about it, because she'll just get more depressed and anxious and smother him with love and pity and all that and that's just going to convince him even more that he's screwed everyone up and that he's causing the problem. I'll try and get through to him myself, but if Holly can't help him it doesn't bode well.

I may have to get hold of Dad. Oh Christ.

Charlie

I'd forgotten what perfect happiness felt like. No — that's not right. I hadn't forgotten: I just hadn't ever experienced it before. All the times I'd thought I'd been happy were mere foretastes of what was to come, and if you'd told me that I'd ever be able to live in the moment in the way I do now — in an everlasting, exquisite moment of ecstasy — I'd have said it was impossible. My pre-Stacey life was spent looking forward or back; pleasure was always in the anticipation or the recollection. Every second of my existence now is one I would quite happily settle for as being the last of my life, as each one is a lifetime of joy. When I am with her I marvel at the love I feel for her; when I am away from her I revel in simply knowing she is in the same world as I am and that it won't be many hours before I am back with her.

I'd been in my hotel for about three weeks, when the

wonderful moment came, which I had hardly dared to hope for, when Lena suggested I move in with them. God knows what she thought of me and my obsession with her daughter – she's no fool and sensed immediately what I was after – but for some unknown and blessed reason she clearly trusted that I was not going to abuse or hurt Stacey, and could see that the potential advantages I could offer outweighed the not-inconsiderable drawbacks of my being a married man a quarter of a century or so older than Stacey.

It was a Tuesday, and I had, as usual, called in to see them after leaving the office at Lincoln's Inn. Funnily enough, I think I would have been quite content for my life to go on in just that way for some time: the novelty of every thought and emotion being bound up with the girl I knew I would see at the end of each day was enough to keep me going. But this particular evening, unplanned and unforeseen, I moved things on a stage. We were sitting on the settee ('World of Leather sale, last year,' as Lena had proudly informed me) and my arm was draped along the back, hovering above Stacey's shoulder, bare where her blouse had slipped down on one side. A game show was on the television, and Lena was either engrossed or effectively pretending to be, and, almost without thinking, I let the tips of my fingers drop down onto Stacey's soft, dimpled flesh. The unexpected feel of it, warm and supremely yielding as marshmallow, made my body spasm in delight. She didn't move, so I ventured further and hooked my index finger under the deeply imbedded bra strap and eased it gently to and fro, enjoying the tautness of the fine strip of fabric against my finger and sensing the giant breast being lifted and weighed as I did so. She shifted slightly, stirring the sofa and challenging the springs with the change of enormous weight, and I glanced at her, anxious that I had gone too far.

The pink of her cheek and little smile of pleasure reassured me, and the quick look of complicity that she threw me over the top of her glasses couldn't have been clearer had she had YES flashing on her forehead in neon.

I smiled at her and she looked away and back towards the game-show contestants on the screen, who were applauding themselves in a confusion of over-excited enthusiasm. Stacey was still smiling, and, keeping a careful eye on Lena, who was nibbling on a cereal bar and apparently still engrossed in the game, I very slowly bent my head and kissed the side of her neck, nuzzling into the folds of delicious flesh and breathing in the smell of cheap perfume tinged with that of sweat. She giggled a little and I snapped my head back up again, terrified that Lena would look over. I decided to take no chances and pulled my arm away from her and stood up, stretching my back and sighing at the same time to cover my awkwardness.

'Well,' I yawned, 'it's about time I made my way home. Or what I laughingly call home, that is.'

That was, in all honesty, meant as a joke, but it patently struck some maternal chord in Stacey's mother that was to be the catalyst in moving my life yet again into a new and terrifyingly wonderful phase. Or maybe she had been planning her invitation for some time, and simply felt that I had at last given her the obvious cue that would justify it without her appearing to be too forward.

'I was thinking, Charlie,' she said, not looking at me, and still apparently concentrating on the screen, 'why don't you come and stay with Stace and me for a bit? Seems silly, you spending money on that hotel every night, don't it? We could do with a man about the house, and Stace and I are very fond of you, aren't we, love?'

Stacey looked up at me and the wry smile I so adored grew

wider. 'Sure we are, Ma.' She grinned. 'Me and Ma are right fond of you, Charlie. Come and stay, if you like.'

The sheer pleasure of that moment was almost too much to take, and I swayed on my feet as a wave of dizziness overtook me. With a huge effort I managed to control my voice and produce a semblance of normal speech: 'How very kind of you, Lena. It does seem a bit foolish, doesn't it? Since I – since I, er – had to move out of my home, I'm like you, Lena – I mean, without a partner, so to speak, and it certainly does get a bit lonely, doesn't it? As we're both in the same boat, as it were, it might seem sensible to –' I glanced across at her, and saw an echo of Stacey's knowing expression in the eyes that were now turned towards me. 'I mean, we could sort of pool resources, couldn't we? I absolutely insist that I pay my way. We must work out a fair rent and then you must let me contribute to the food and so on.'

'You'll have to share a room, of course.'

They were as near to openly laughing at me as you could get, but I was too drunk with excitement to care, or to wonder exactly which room Lena meant – what the hell: nothing was too much to contemplate – I'd fuck the mother, like Lolita's lover, if that would get me to Stacey.

'Of course.'

I kept looking at them; both women's eyes were pinned on me like jurors' on a defendant, watching and waiting for a sign that would betray my guilt. With an effort I stopped myself adding anything further, letting the game-show host fill the silence with his maniacally positive whoops and cries.

Finally, after a dramatically timed pause that would have done credit to one of my best summing-ups, Lena spoke.

'With Stacey.'

That did it: I had to sit down again. There was only so much emotion my poor old frame could take standing, and that had topped it. I wiped a hand over my face in an effort to stop my smile becoming so huge and daft that I looked insane, and cleared my throat unnecessarily.

'Great. That would be lovely, Lena — as long as Stacey doesn't mind, of course.'

Judy

I can't find Ben, and I'm beginning to worry. He was out the night before last and I didn't think anything of it when I woke yesterday and found his bed empty because I assumed he'd just stayed with one of his friends. It is still the holidays, after all, so it's not surprising if he wants to spread his wings a bit before he has to go back — it's going to be hard for him this coming term with all the work he has to do and the upheaval going on. So I didn't even bother to ring Holly's or Tim's or any of the other places he might have spent the night. But when I realised he hadn't slept here last night either, I thought I ought to check: it's so unlike him not to ring in. And now no one seems to know where he is — I've tried all the places I can think of and have no idea where to look next. I've left messages on his mobile, but he's often bad at switching that on, so it doesn't necessarily mean anything that he hasn't rung me back.

What's really worried me is that when I mentioned it to Sally she looked as anxious as I felt — I was so sure she'd brush it off and accuse me of being fussy like she usually does, but she didn't: she took it very seriously indeed and said what sounded like, 'I've been expecting something like this,' under her breath. When I questioned her she immediately backed off and pretended to be more casual, because, of course, she could see I was getting panicky, and I can imagine the last thing any of them want at the moment is a panicking mother. I am trying, I really am, but it's all getting on top of me and I'm not sure I can cope any more.

So I suppose I've got to get in touch with Charlie – that's the next move, I can see that. Ben may well have gone to him – I know how much he's missed him since he left – and he wouldn't want to tell me because he knows it would upset me. I know where Charlie's staying because he rang and left the number on the answering machine ('in case of emergency', he said – huh!) and I found out where it was and drove past it a couple of weeks ago. It's a horrible little private hotel in Pimlico: the sort of place we would have sneered at in the old days. I really ought to ring him and ask about Ben, but I'm not sure I can face it. So should I get Sally to do it? Or is that not fair on her? I just don't know what to do. I'm going to look so foolish at having to ask where Ben is, as if I can't keep track of my own children just because my husband's gone.

Thank God I haven't got any immediate inspections coming up, partly because I don't like the idea of leaving the children alone, but also, if I'm honest, because I'm not sure I'm in a fit state to conduct one properly. The idea of judging anything or anyone is hard to contemplate at the moment, and all this has made it utterly unimportant. I can't honestly care one jot how well or badly this wretched country is educating its young: I just want my life back.

But then I remember how Charlie looked at me the last time I saw him and I know that life can never come back, ever. I think he hates me. I wish I could hate him. But I don't. I still love him, absurdly and irrationally. It's myself I hate.

Charlie

Jesus Christ! What the hell is going on? I went to check out of the hotel this morning and my credit card wouldn't go through. I wasn't that surprised, as I knew the hotel bill had mounted up over the weeks and I've never really been aware which day of the month our card accounts are settled – Judy has always been the one to handle the financial side of things, shifting funds around as necessary to and from our joint current and deposit accounts over the years as our fortunes ebbed and flowed, shoving anonymous bits of paper under my nose for signature when necessary.

I left my bits and pieces behind at the hotel desk, together with my driving licence and so on to reassure them I wasn't going to do a runner, and told them I'd sort it out during the day and come back and collect my things and settle up later.

At about eleven o'clock I had a good half-hour or so free, so I rang the bank, intending to arrange a transfer to cover the amount owing on the card plus a good bit more to settle the hotel bill and keep me going for the foreseeable future until I could get together with Judy and seriously discuss how we were going to progress our new, separate lives. My instinct is that, since Sally's going to be away in Leeds for the next three years and hardly seems to stay at home in any case, the most efficient use of our resources would be to sell the house and divide up the profits. That place is far too big for Judy and Ben on their own (and it won't be long before he's off too, in any case), and if I could persuade them to find a little flat instead, perhaps a bit further out of town, we could all live quite well without causing any major problems. I know it may not be easy to get Judy to see it that way, but I'm hoping to approach it when she's in the right mood and make her think it's her idea.

So I rang the bank. It had been ages since I'd done so, and it took me some time to negotiate all the irritating automated choices before I finally reached a human being (and I use the term loosely). The flat-voiced, unhelpful young man to whom I eventually spoke appeared determined to block every attempt I made to communicate with him. I'd given him my name and address, which seemed to me a reasonable starting point for identifying myself and checking the amount available in my current account, but I was clearly misguided.

'Account number?'

A fall at the first fence. How the hell could I find it? In the old days, I would simply have pulled a chequebook out of my pocket and found the number at the bottom, but I hadn't carried one on my person for years, relying on cash or credit cards whenever I was out of the house, and only using the occasional cheque at home to pay for the bills not dealt with by Judy — usually those for presents for her, ironically.

'Ah,' I floundered, 'now that may be a problem. I'm afraid I don't have a chequebook on me and —'

'I'll need the account number.'

'Is Mr Benson there?'

'Who?'

'Mr Benson — the manager.'

I swear there was a snigger on the other end of the line.

'There's no Mr Benson here — this is a central communication and information facility. Where is this Mr Benson based?'

'In the bank, of course. Where I'm phoning. The manager.' I was getting irritable; it had taken me all of fourteen minutes to get through to this chap, and I could see my precious half-hour disappearing fast. 'Who else is in charge there, then? Let me speak to the new manager.'

'You're not speaking to a branch, Mr Thornton. This is a central commu—'

'Yes, yes, all right. Well, what is the number of the branch, then? And what is the name of the manager? I'm sure I dialled my bank's number, so I don't understand how I —'

'Your call has been transferred. Which branch facility do you access, Mr Thornton?'

'Ludlow Street, Victoria.'

'Just a moment.'

A click and I was back to an electronic *Für Elise*, drumming my fingers on the desk in an attempt to dissipate my annoyance and stop myself hanging up. Surprisingly quickly, he was back.

'Ludlow Street branch has been closed for some time, Mr Thornton.'

'Really? How extraordinary — I had no idea. So how can I get hold of Mr Benson?'

'And he is?'

'I told you. The manager.'

'Of?'

'The manager of my bank. Ludlow Street branch.' It was taking a supreme effort not to lose my temper.

'Oh yes, of course. Ludlow Street branch is closed.'

'Yes, I know. You told me. But I'd like to talk to him, you see, as I need to check some details of my account. Do you have any idea how I can get hold of him?'

'I'll try to find out, Mr Thornton. If you'll —'

'No! Don't bother. Just tell me — is there any way I can find details of my account without having the account number or speaking to my bank manager?'

'Wife's mother's maiden name and DOB.'

'Sorry?'

'If you can give me your wife's mother's maiden name and your wife's date of birth, Mr Thornton, I may be able to access the information you require. It tells me on my screen that these are the security inputs on your account.'

Inwardly seething at not having been given this information earlier in the conversation, I took a deep breath and glanced at my watch. Still plenty of time before I needed to get back to work.

'Milton. Judith Milton. No, sorry, of course that's her own maiden name, isn't it? You wanted her mother's. Hang on — oh, for God's sake, I'm so sorry — this is ridiculous, let me think a sec. Mrs Milton, she was — well, obviously — and her maiden name was . . . was —' Every time I tried to picture Judy's mother, absurdly, Stacey's mother Lena would come into my mind. 'Just give me a moment — let me concentrate. B. It begins with a B, I'm sure.' I paused briefly, hoping that the young man's silence could be taken as confirmation. Then, suddenly, it was there. 'No, I'm mad. Cunningham. That's it. Cunningham.'

'Date of birth?'

'Hers? Mrs — Miss Cunningham's?'

'No, Mr Thornton. Your wife's. Mrs Thornton's.'

'Oh, yes, of course — sorry. I'm being foolish. Um — now let me see — this isn't a very gallant one to ask me. I'm sure Mrs Thornton would be only too happy for me to forget this one, eh?'

God knows what I was doing putting on this embarrassingly twee all-men-together act. I surely can't have expected a response from Mr Cardboard, and Judy would have hit me had she heard me indulging in such nonsense. Mind you, I suppose she'd have hit me in any case, given the present circumstances. It did allow me a moment to cover the humiliation of forgetting my wife's birthday, a failing not that unusual, I'm sure, but in general not caused by obsessions with supermarket checkout girls.

'February the sixteenth. February the sixteenth – um – hang on ...' I did a quick calculation. 'February the sixteenth nineteen fifty-four.'

'How can I help you, Mr Thornton?'

At last.

'How much is in my current account, please, how much on deposit, and how much in my money-market reserve account? I need to transfer some funds.'

'Just a moment please, and I'll access your current balances, Mr Thornton.'

I could hear some quick tapping of keys, then, after just a second or two, he came back to me.

'Right, Mr Thornton, your balances as at close of business last night stood at a debit of seventeen pounds fifty on your current account; and a credit of two thousand two hundred and sixty pounds on your deposit account. I can't find any money-market balance here.'

'What? What do you mean? You must be accessing the wrong accounts. Just have another check, would you, please. There should be about thirty-five thousand on the money market.'

'Just a moment, please.'

As he clicked himself off the line again, a faint shadow of something unsettlingly chilly began to creep infinitesimally slowly up my back and forced me to face the unthinkable. By the time he returned, what he had to say held little surprise for me. I think in some inexplicable way I had suspected something of the sort for some time.

'No, Mr Thornton, that is correct. I've checked it against

your address details and that is definitely the right account. The levels are as given, and the history of your money-market deposit is that it was terminated on March the fourth of last year and the remaining balance transferred to your deposit account.'

'Yes, of course. You're quite right. Thank you.'

I tried to keep the shock out of my voice as I went on to instruct him to transfer enough money to cover the hotel bill, but all I could really think about was whether Stacey would still be interested in me were she to discover just how little I was worth.

Stacey

'So what's he do to you, Stace? And how can you do it – you know – with your mum there and all? It must be – well, I dunno, I just think it's a bit strange, that's all. What's he like?'

I knew Denisha had been dying to ask me. I'd tried to keep it quiet about Charlie and me, 'cos I knew none of the girls would understand, and I didn't want Warren thinking I was a right slag or anything. But Sheila had come by yesterday on her way in to work – she said it was 'cos she wanted to check which shift I was on, or something, but I knew it was just so's she could stick her nose in and find out if what they was all gossiping about was true. Fuck knows how they heard about it in the first place, but you can't keep nothing secret from them for long, not that I've never had that many secrets anyhow. I was quite enjoying that, in fact, having something going on in my life that they didn't know inside out. Having something so's I didn't have to just hang about every night with my mum hoping one of the girls might need me to tag along with them. I've been feeling right perky at work, in fact, since Charlie's been around – it's hard to say what it makes me feel like, just knowing that he thinks I'm so beautiful and all that other crap he tells me all the time, I s'pose.

Anyway, I was gobsmacked when Denisha came out with it like that in the staff canteen. 'What's he like?' and all that. Then I thought – well, that's how all the girls talk to each other all the time, ain't it? It's just that they don't usually ask you this kind of stuff because you don't usually have nothing to tell them, do you? So I felt quite proud then, and thought I'd tell her the truth and shame the devil, or whatever Ma says.

'He ain't done it – proper, I mean. He's – he's like a real gentleman, Nishe, except he likes to touch me – you know.'

'How? How does he touch you?'

'Well, you know he moved in a couple of days ago and him and me share a room, and when we're in bed he –'

She really yelled when I said that.

'So it IS true! Fuck me, Stace, why're you sharing a room with the old bugger? He's married, ain't he? You're gonna get yourself in trouble, girl, if you don't watch out. How come your ma's letting you share a room, in any case?'

'She likes him, Nishe, you don't understand. I asked her if he could stay, 'cos – well, never you mind. I have plans for him, Nishe. Anyway, there ain't nowhere else he could sleep, 'cept in my room. There's a sofa bed in my room, you see, and that's where he sleeps. He pushed it right up to my bed last night so's he could touch me and all that and then he pushed it back this morning. He treats me real well and my mum knows he's making me feel – well, you wouldn't understand, 'cos you've never understood about – you see, you're pretty and you ain't never gonna understand what it's like to be ugly like I am. He makes me feel special – like when you go with Jason and you tell me how great he makes you feel. Well, Charlie makes me feel like that all the time. He thinks I'm pretty, you see. My mum can see how different I am and that makes her happy. So we're pretending he's just sleeping on the sofa bed but Ma's not stupid.'

'You ain't ugly, Stace – we're always telling you. You've got pretty eyes, you know. And you're funny, too.'

'Yeah, yeah, sure. But I don't wanna be funny. I just wanna be like you. Like you and the others.'

'Why don't you try one of your diets again, Stace? You lost two stone that other time, remember?'

'And no one could see the difference, could they? I'm past that stage, Nishe. No diet's gonna work for me, I know that now. Shall I tell you what it's like being me? I worked it out the other day. You know about your dad being an alcoholic, right?'

'Yeah, sure.'

'You know how he is about booze, right? One drink, you said, just one drink and he's off, ain't he? He can't never have just the one, 'cos it's like an illness and if he has one he can't – absolutely fucking can't – help himself having so many that he's rat-arsed and beats up your mum and all them other things that happen to him, right?'

'Yeah.'

'And drug addicts – them's the same. Not just like when kids take a bit of speed and that, or the odd joint or shoot up just once in a while to try it I don't mean, but a real junkie. They have to stop – right out. And they don't usually manage that, neither. But – s'posing they stop, they can't never have another hit ever again, right? One hit and they're off – back on it. Finished.'

'Right.'

'I'm like that with eating, Nishe. I know that. I've known it for years, when I stop to think about it. I'm a food junkie. I can't eat normal just like an alcoholic can't drink normal – but there's a big fucking difference and I'll tell you what it is. The difference is what you do about it, that's what. Because an alcoholic goes to the doctor and the doctor says, "Right, you're an alcoholic, so there's only one cure – stop drinking. No alcohol – never. Nothing. And then you'll be OK." So I'm a food junkie and I go to the doctor and what does he say to me? "Right, you're an addict, so there's only one cure – stop eating. Everything. For ever. Then you'll be OK." Does he fuck. I'd be dead – right? So he says, "Right, just eat a little bit. Not the food you really want, neither – just a little bit of all the food that don't fill you up and don't satisfy you and don't give you that feeling you need. But just enough to keep your fucking addiction bubbling along nicely." See?'

'Yeah, I never thought of that, Stace. You're right. If my dad has just a sniff of a drink – like when he got them liqueur chocolates for Christmas and he went right back on it for weeks – well, he just can't, that's all.'

It was then I decided it, I think. It was talking to Denisha in a way I'd never talked to her before that made me face it for real. What I had to do, I mean. 'Cos the diets ain't never worked before and they ain't never gonna work again – that's what Crystal and all them others in America understand. Diets ain't no good for girls like me and Crystal.

I've known in my heart for a while now that Charlie's been sent to me by Jesus to help me (well, I don't really think that: I think it's daft, in fact, but it's like Crystal would say it and it sounds kinda nice), and it's time now for me to ask him. To be my angel.

Sally

I did try to ring Dad about Ben, and I was half relieved and half angry when they told me at the hotel that he'd checked out two days ago. I hadn't realised how wound up I still was about his leaving – I like to think I'm the one that's most in control of themselves in this family, but as I dialled the number I could feel my heartbeat going berserk and my breathing getting really fast. Once I heard that receptionist's flat little voice on the other end of the phone telling me calmly that my father no longer stayed there, all that adrenaline swishing round my system was put to more positive use, and I redialled Dad's office and practically yelled at the secretary there to give him a message to ring me urgently. Then I stormed into Ben's room and started a thorough search for anything that might give me a clue as to where he had gone. It wasn't surprising that the answer was stupidly simple: I found his address book. I started a systematic ring round of all his friends, and, after trying just a dozen or so, I tracked him down to an old school friend's.

When he came on the line I was so angry I could hardly speak: I guess I was still upset about Dad, and it suddenly seemed that everyone but me could just fuck off wherever and whenever they liked without thinking twice about all the hurt they might be causing. But poor old Benbo sounded so quiet and subdued that I soon calmed down and found myself back in the old caring big-sister routine. He tried to explain – something about 'getting away from his own head' – but I'm sure it's all part of Dad's leaving really. Bastard. I made Ben promise to come home at the weekend, and then left him alone.

I ran downstairs to Mum's bedroom and knocked on the door. She hadn't seemed to care much about Ben's disappearance, but I think I needed to go through the motions of pretending she was the caring, loving mother I wanted her to be.

I was sure she was in there, but she just wouldn't answer. I put my head down and pressed my ear against the door to see if I could hear a faint radio or anything (she often puts on Radio 4 or Classic fm very quietly when she has a headache – God knows why, as you'd think any kind of sound would be the last thing you'd want, but she says it's soothing) but it was dead silent. Or at least that's what I thought at first.

After a few seconds, I heard something. It's hard to describe exactly what it was like: it reminded me of when I came down into the kitchen once years ago and a mouse was inside the vegetable basket. I can remember the little scraping sounds it was making (they went on for ages while I stood there listening) and I didn't know what it was at first, then, once I realised there was something alive inside where all our potatoes and things were, I had to go and get Ben and he said it must have been a mouse and he showed me all the droppings. We never did catch it.

Anyway, this noise was a bit like that. Funny little scrape-scrape-scrape sounds, followed by a kind of sigh, or whisper, then a sort of quick, rustling, papery noise and then the scraping all over again. I just couldn't begin to work it out, and I stood bent over at the door for at least a minute, trying to put a picture to the sounds, like a quiz or something. Scrape-scrape-scrape-sigh-rustle. Over and over. I began to feel a bit scared, imagining there was a bird or huge insect trapped in there that might fly out at me if I opened the door, but the noise seemed too regular for that. If Mum really was in there – and I thought I'd heard her go up the stairs a while ago – then I knew it was no good trying to push open the door to look, even if I was brave enough, because she always locked it when she had a headache 'to make sure I'm left in peace', she'd say.

I called her again, but as there was still no answer I gently turned the handle and pushed the door. When it began to swing quietly open I knew she couldn't be there.

But I was wrong. I'm not sure now if I wish the door had been locked. It might have been easier if I'd never found out. If Dad had never found out.

Charlie

I could sense something was brewing, of course. Stacey's darling eyes give away more than she knows, and when we were settled into our beds and I was stroking her in the way I love to, she was looking at me very thought-fully. The night before, she giggled and closed her eyes when I felt her gorgeous skin and ran my hand over her beautiful curves, but last night she was quiet and just watching me.

'What is it, you lovely, divine light of my life?' I asked in a whisper. (Although our door was shut and Lena's room is on the other side of the landing, it's such a tiny flat that I was worried we could be heard.) Even my silly love talk didn't make her laugh this time, and I felt a tiny stab of anxiety. 'What is it, darling? Why are you so quiet? You're not ill, or hurting somewhere, are you?'

'No, Charlie — it's nothing like that. But I love it when you look all worried about me: it makes me feel like crying. No one except Ma ain't never worried about me before like you do. Denisha says you're my father figure, 'cos my dad went off when I was little and all that, but you don't seem to act much like a father to me. Well — I dunno though, come to think of it, when you read all them things in the paper — Billy Connolly's dad was feeling him up and that, you know. He said so on *Parkinson*. Disgusting. At least my dad never done that, but then he wasn't here long enough to get round to it. But he never tried it on when he was here. I'd soon have told him where to get off, I can tell you.'

I smiled at her. 'I certainly love you as much as a father would, Stacey, and you know I'll always take care of you if I'm allowed to. And of course I worry about you, darling: you know how — how completely and utterly besotted with you I am. If you're not well then I'm not well — don't you see? You are me, Stacey. I am you. You'll never be able to understand this — I know that. It's something I'd only read about in books before it happened to me, and I'm not stupid enough to think for a second that the way I feel about you is something that you can ever possibly feel for me. I realise that.'

'But I do feel —'

'Shh, it's all right, darling. I really don't want you to think you have to say all those things. You don't. It's OK. I know you're fond of me — and you probably even think you're a bit in love with me, because I make you feel good and confident and loved and beautiful. All the things you should feel — that you deserve to feel. But it doesn't matter: it's enough for me that you let me worship you and love you and be with you. Touching you like this is — it's the nearest thing I can imagine to being — well, in religions they'd call it being in a state of grace, or nirvana, or ecstasy or – Buddhahood or something. I feel nothing but love and light and peace and wonder, and if I was a religious man I'd say – I'd say when I look at you and feel what I feel, I see the face of God.'

'Fucking hell, Charlie. You're right weird, sometimes.'

'I know. Don't worry – I'm not as weird as I sound. It's just love, that's all. I had no idea. No idea.'

'Would you do anything for me?'

'Anything. Come on, darling – what do you want? What can I do? Anything I have is yours – just tell me.'

'I want to be thin.'

It nearly broke my heart when she said it – she looked so sad and so vulnerable, but at the same time so much on the defensive, as if she expected me to laugh at her.

'I haven't seen that look since our bogof days, Stacey. Relax, sweetheart. You can say anything to me – I promise you. You're lovely, Stacey. You mustn't mind what people do or say – you're –'

'Piss off, Charlie – I'm fat. I'm horribly fat and I hate it and I can't stand it no longer and you can help me.'

'I love you just as you are. You're perfect.'

'You said you'd do anything.'

'And I will – I meant it. I will. But I don't want you to make yourself more unhappy by always wanting something; always struggling with diets or pills or –'

'No, it ain't that. No more diets, Charlie. I want to go over to the other side.'

'How do you mean?'

'I want the slimming operation. I want weight-loss sur-gery – that's what it's called.'

'No, Stacey, not an operation – that's dangerous. I can't – I can't risk anything happening to you. You're my life.'

'If I go on like this, Charlie, I'm gonna die anyway. My doctor says –'

'Don't be ridiculous! You're young – you're healthy.'

'I ain't healthy, Charlie! Face it. I'm sick – I'm as sick as if I got cancer. I got arthritis and my insides is all squashed and I'll have diabetes soon and my legs is all ulcered and you've no idea what you're talking about. Anything, you said. You said I could have anything.'

'Don't cry, darling – please, please don't cry, I can't bear it. You can – you can have anything. You will have whatever you want, I promise you. But this surgery idea is just crazy, Stacey. I'd do anything to keep you well, to make you happy. I've said that and I mean it. But not surgery, darling, it's far too dangerous.'

'Oh, yeah? How do you know? What do you know about it? I know everything. I know the hospital what does it and I know what it's like and I know it works. My friend I write to had it done and she's lost masses already. I find it hard to go into work now, Charlie, and I know I'm gonna be like she got soon. All she done for months is sit in front of the TV and eat. I want more than that: I want a life and I'm gonna get it whether you help me or not. If my fucking doctor won't help me get it on the NHS and you won't help me I'm gonna find someone who –'

'Stacey – Stacey, my darling – please stop crying.' I shifted myself over onto her bed and put my arms round her and held her. 'I will help you – anything you want – I'll do it. Anything. Don't worry, my angel, I'm going to help you do whatever you want. I promise. Shh.'

She snuffled and burrowed into my shoulder like an animal and left it wet and sticky when she looked up at me. 'No, Charlie,' she said, and she was smiling now, 'no, I'm not the angel. That's you.'

'How do you mean?'

'Well, over there – in America – when they go over to the other side, they all get themselves an angel. Even before they go over, I mean. Like for support and for telling all their friends how they're doing and all that. Like the men with Aids have a buddy – you know. They get an angel. You're going to be mine, aren't you, Charlie? I can't do this all on my own.'

'I can't think of anything more wonderful, darling. I'm your angel. For ever.'

Sally

I couldn't make out what she was doing at first. I must have opened the door really quietly because she still didn't look round, although I suppose that's not surprising when you think I'd been calling her through the door and she hadn't answered. She was – distracted. By what she was doing.

I walked up behind her, with a feeling of fear – not fear of what might happen, I don't mean, but fear of what I would see when she turned round. It was like one of those films when you see the back of someone's head and you just know that when they turn round they're going to have no mouth or be covered in blood and stuff. The funny scraping noise was still going on, and of course I could see now that it was coming from her. It made me think of the mouse again, and the really strange thing was that as I got nearer I saw a little pile of mouse droppings on the dressing table top right next to where she was sitting. That was so freaky – like I was still in my memory while I was looking at the present.

But then she did turn round, and in one jolt I knew what she was doing and understood that it wasn't mouse

220

droppings at all. She was holding some sort of blade in one hand, and the other was resting on the dressing table. On top of a card. But that wasn't the only card. There were – dozens – no, hundreds – of them. In a messy pile on one side of her: all different colours, with pictures all over them. And names: Treasure Cove, I could see on one. Wizard of Odds on another. Lucky Dog, 3 Times Lucky, Raining Cats and Dosh. And then I saw there was another pile on the other side, but neatly stacked so I could only see the one on the top. Top prize £100,000 it said, in bright-yellow writing, and next to it those stupid crossed fingers with a smile on them.

'Mum, for Christ's sake – what on earth – what are you doing? What's going on?'

She looked so guilty and unsure that it scared me. She didn't look like Mum any more, she looked like one of my friends who'd been caught taking something. She was still holding one of the cards flat on the table with her left hand, and in her right was in fact a nailfile – one of those old-fashioned metal ones that people use to scrape the dirt out from under their fingernails. But that clearly wasn't what Mum was doing with hers. I knew now exactly what she was doing, but it still made no kind of sense to me. She was looking at me but not saying anything, and her mouth was slightly open and her eyes all stary – almost like she was having a fit, or as if she was one of those people who've had a stroke and can't speak; I almost expected to see some dribble come out of her mouth.

'Mum, are you OK? It's me – Sally. Do answer me, for God's sake: what's going on?'

'I'm – I'm –' she began at last, and she rested the nailfile on the glass surface and lifted her other hand off the card as she sat back slightly on the stool. I could see that card properly now: Game of Two Halves, it had on it, in red against a striped green background. 'Oh, shit. I suppose this was bound to happen one day, Sally. Sorry.'

'What on earth are you —'

'I'm just playing this one. I'll stop in a second — I —' She broke off as she saw me looking at the card and she glanced down at it.

There was silence for a moment while I tried to think what to say.

'Two Halves,' she went on, 'you get two games on this one, you see. Two on one card, but they're entirely separate — you could even win twice in the same game. It costs two pounds, of course, not like the others which are one pound, but it always seems to me that your chances are better somehow on the double one. There's another here, look —' And she reached over to the messy pile on her left and began shuffling through them. 'Somewhere here, there's a — yes, look, here it is: Millionaire. It's another two-pound one, and there are two games again. See? And there are five prizes of a million on this one, so I always think that's a good one to get, because —'

'Mum, stop — what is all this? Did you buy all these? There are hundreds here — how can you — I mean, how long have you been doing this, and why? This is crazy, Mum. You can't possibly win on these things — you know you're bound to lose, don't you?'

'No, that's not true, Sally. I knew you'd feel this way. I knew you wouldn't understand — I've won lots of times, you've no idea. I just need to get through a few more and I'm bound to hit one of the big prizes, I'm absolutely certain of that.' She was beginning to look a bit tearful, and in spite of my own feeling of misery and sadness at seeing my own mother behaving like some lunatic stranger I knew I had to keep calm and be rational enough for both of us or I, too, would start crying.

'Look, Mum – I know you've been upset lately. What with Dad going and everything, it's been so hard for you. I understand, I really do. But this is just nonsense, Mum, spending all this money on these – these con things. It's madness, you know that really, don't you? You're just finding something to worry about and get worked up about because your real worries are so difficult to sort out – I'm sure it's something like that. That's what's going on. But you've got to throw all these away and forget about them – no more, Mum – absolutely no more – do you understand?'

She bent down and picked up the small waste bin from under the dressing table and with the other hand slowly scooped the little pile of dark-grey scrapings into it as she spoke. 'No, no, Sally – that's quite impossible. I couldn't stop buying my Instants: I've won loads of times, like I said. And I'm bound to hit one of the big prizes: a really big prize. I can feel it. I couldn't stop now, not after all this time.'

'Mum, you're not thinking clearly. You must have spent hundreds of pounds on these things – and what have you got out of it? Honestly? A few pounds? You can't go on like this, you really can't. Mum, you're frightening me, please – please don't be so strange. I can't bear it.'

'Oh, darling, don't be so – insecure. It's all right. I'm still your mum – I'm still the same. It's just you didn't know about – about my hobby, that's all. It's something that keeps me going, you see. And you've no idea how many times I've bought you things, or taken you out, on my ill-gotten gains, as my mother would have called them. Other people have hobbies they spend money on, don't they? Sometimes things that are bad for them – like smoking, or doing some dangerous sport or – you know. Well, I just happen to need to do my little bit of scraping from time to time – it's not doing any harm. It gives me a chance to feel – excited, and – and on the edge of something. I like to look at them before I've uncovered them – you've no idea how lovely it is to look at a big handful of them before I've touched them, and they're so perfect and pretty, and they're holding all those secrets: all those numbers and symbols and words that are hiding underneath that nobody, nobody knows. There's nothing like that feeling, Sally. They're so much better.'

'What do you mean? Better than what?'

'The pools. That's all they had, really, in the old days. These are so much better – I can do them whenever I like and I don't have to post them or – well, you can see that, can't you? They're just so much more fun and exciting.'

'But you didn't ever used to do the pools, did you, Mum?'

'Well, yes, I did, darling. Not every week of course, or at least not at first. But yes, I did. And horses. Before they had the lottery and these Instants.'

'But I don't understand – isn't all this just since Dad left? Mum? Oh no, Mum. Please – for God's sake, please stop doing that.'

She had picked up the nailfile and was scraping on her wretched Game of Two Halves again.

'No, Sally, I won't. I'd rather you hadn't known about all this, but now that you do I'm not going to lie to you. I won't stop – and I shall go on buying them whenever I like. It's my money and if I need to spend it on a few cards to keep me happy then that's my business.'

'All right. But – if we're being honest – then tell me how long you've been buying these things. Is it since Dad left, Mum? Or were you buying them before?'

She didn't answer, but she put down the file and stood up. She pulled the stool over to the built-in wardrobe on the other side of the bed and stood on it to be able to reach up to the cupboards at the top. She opened one door and took out a small, blue, travelling vanity case, which had been at the front of the cupboard. 'Take this a moment, Sally, please,' she said, and I jumped up and took it from her. 'Put it anywhere,' she went on, 'it's unimportant. I just use it to — so that no one sees all this.' She thrust her arm deep into the cupboard and, in one strong, sweeping movement, pulled out a large cardboard box, which tipped on its side and spilled out a vast quantity of fluttering, showering little pieces of card that cascaded onto the floor all around me.

I couldn't speak for a few seconds. The sheer amount of the fucking things — there must have been thousands of them — together with all that it implied, was impossible to take in. Slowly, I began to understand: the headaches, the locked bedroom door, the radio — now that I knew, it seemed so obvious that something had been going on. How could we all have been so stupid?

'I don't understand,' I said. 'Why on earth have you kept all these?'

She smiled at me. 'For one thing I didn't want you all finding out and telling me to stop, and I couldn't be bothered to keep hiding them in the rubbish — you know how nosy our old cleaner used to be. Then it got to be a habit, and — I know it's stupid — I've got a system. I'm sure the squares and numbers and things they pick aren't really random — I mean they couldn't be — so I check back as often as I can on the old cards of the same types, so I can work out which ones are most likely to be winners. Beat the system. I don't do it often, but it's really quite fun, looking back over them. Anyway,' she went on as she climbed off the stool and began tidying the cards back into the box, 'what did you want to talk to me about?'

I felt as if I was in the middle of a particularly ludicrous dream, but I answered calmly, as if we'd been having the most normal conversation in the world. 'Ben's OK. He's at a friend's.'

'Oh, that's good.' She turned and looked straight at me for a second, then shook her head slightly, as if getting rid of a tiresome fly. 'No, that really is good. I'm not completely blind, Sally – I can see how impossible I'm being. You must think I don't care about anything at all. It's just that I've – I've switched off the part of me that feels things – if it's on, I find it very hard to bear everything that's happened. You see.'

Stacey (e-mail)

Hiya, Crystal – Wow! You're not gonna believe this!! I'm gonna do it – the surgery – and I almost got my surgery date!!! D'you remember when you wrote to me and told me that you'd got yours? I do – 'cos I was so happy for you but I was so jealous at the same time. That's when I really started thinking that maybe I should do it too. Now I'm coming over to the other side – it's just so cool I can't believe it!!

Charlie's been so great to me – it's amazing. He has been like an angel – just like you said, and he's taking care of everything and I just feel soooooooooooooooo HAPPY! We spoke to this doctor up in Manchester (that's in the north of England, not near here in London) which is one of the very few hospitals in the whole country to do this and the doctor said that once he's seen me and if all the tests go OK then I can have the op done pretty soon. It costs £7900 – I don't know what that is in dollars but it's a LOAD of money, and Charlie is gonna pay it all 'cos to get it done on the NHS – ooops, sorry, you probably don't know what that is but it's when the government pays for it – would take forever and he's not even sure if they would ever pay for it. And I don't have insurance like you do, so this is the ONLY way and I'm getting it and it's just soooooooooo cool!! If I was over 29 stone (that's over 400 pounds!!) then it would cost more, but I'm just 325 pounds (JUST – she says???) so it's only £7900 (ONLY???). Isn't that weird, that it costs more if you're bigger? Do you suppose it's 'cos it takes longer to get through all those extra inches to find your stomach??? They probably need a map for some people. Only kidding. He said it's because it's more complicated to do. More dangers and all that.

Anyway, I thought there's no harm seeing this bloke and having the tests and that. It's not like they can force me to go on with it, is it? So I'm going up in a few days to be checked out. I'm feeling a bit scared though. I know some people have died having this surgery, haven't they? That's just so strange to think about. Last night I lay in bed and Charlie was asleep next to me (he was snoring so I couldn't get back to sleep) and I started thinking about it. Is this a chance I'm willing to take? Is it worth it? What if I die? Then I think about all the things my own doctor has said to me about what's wrong with me and how I'm gonna get diabetes and the heart problems and blood pressure and all – so that makes me think about how long will I live anyway – if I go on like I am now – and I know I'm still gaining, however much I kid myself. And what will my quality of life be if I stay morbidly obese? (You see, Crystal, I'm learning all the right words now.) I kind of wish now I hadn't asked the doctor about people dying 'cos I hoped he'd say it was impossible but he didn't, although he says they've only ever had one man die in all the RNYs they've done and that was some rare complication that I can't remember. But he went on and said that all operations carry a small risk and all that, so I can't quite get that out of my mind. But I know really I'm making the right decision. You understand what I'm saying, though, don't you?

Write soon, Crystal – I'm gonna be feeling so strange now, until it's all over. Am I really gonna do this? I can't believe it – it seems so unreal.

Love and kisses

Stacey

Charlie

I thought my life had become unreal enough as it was, what with moving out of my family home and living with an obese checkout girl in Balham, but when I rang Sally back after the frantic message she left at the office I realised things were even stranger than I'd thought. She'd originally rung me about Ben – who has since turned up at a friend's, apparently. I was trying hard to express the relief I knew I ought to feel, in spite of my continuing numbness to any part of my old life, when Sally went on to tell me that it appears Judy has become addicted to gambling (of the most bizarre kind). One of the compensations, I suppose, for everything having become so peculiar lately – and I don't use the word lightly – is that nothing much surprises or shocks me. I'm in this wonderfully cushioned state of bliss (I think I appreciate the true meaning of the word for the first time in my life) and, short of anything happening to Stacey, or causing me to be separated from her, nothing can touch me. Dear God, I even found myself crossing my fingers and inwardly praying just now as I let the thought of losing her cross my mind – I think I'd carry a rabbit's foot or offer up a human sacrifice if I thought it would prevent it.

My life would have no meaning without her – no, it's more than that, because I don't feel it has a meaning anyway – it would quite simply not be a life. That's the only way I can describe it.

I didn't feel anything much talking to Sally, which you'd think I would. Even over the telephone I could hear how upset she was, by the tremble in her voice: it sounded gulpy and very nervous, either because she was trying to stop herself yelling at me, or just because speaking to me made her feel so emotional – I couldn't tell. Or, of course, maybe it was having discovered that her mother, as well as her father, appears to have flipped (although, from what she tells me, this bizarre addiction to scratch cards has been going on for some time, so the change in my life can hardly be held accountable). Poor kid – two parents going completely doolally simultaneously – I almost feel sorry for her. Unfortunately, though, all my feelings are already spoken for, so I can only sympathise intellectually, rather than actually experience anything first hand.

It does explain the bank account. It threw me into a state of panic initially, but once I got used to the idea that our savings had disappeared I found it almost liberating. A new life should be founded on new money – the pitiful amount remaining in the old account is part of my old life, and I shall not take any more of it.

It was surprisingly easy to borrow money: with my apparently impeccable professional and personal credentials the new bank was only too happy to advance me ten thousand pounds, albeit at an excruciatingly high rate of interest. No matter – if all goes well with Stacey's tests I shall hand over seven thousand odd within the next few weeks, leaving me a couple of thousand for our living expenses. I have no wish to look much further into the future. Judy earns good money, and if she can just pull herself together I'm sure she'll manage — it's not as if anything has really changed in any important way for her as it has for me, and there's nothing outstanding on the house or the car. I've absolutely no desire for her to suffer because of my good fortune and I'll keep paying a proportion of my earnings into her account, what there are of them.

I can't, of course, foretell how much longer I'm going to be able to work — there's no question it's been affected and I know I've messed up a couple of times recently by not taking on some of the cases my clerk had promised I would, but I'm afraid I just can't worry myself about that at the moment. I must be available for Stacey at all times just now, particularly once she starts this round of tests and evaluations and so on. And — dear God, don't let me think of it as it frightens me so — I have to be there all the while she's in the hospital and on the — under the — Christ help me, let her be all right. I hope this surgeon knows what he's doing, that's all. It sounds logical enough what they propose to do, and he assures me that, in their unit, they haven't had a single serious problem since they've been doing this operation, but it still terrifies me.

I know I shall have to go round to the house and talk to Judy and the kids, so I'd better do that soon, before I have to go up to Manchester.

Chipstead

This has to be a first. I've been asked many strange things in my career in the retail food business, but I don't think I've ever been asked before to grant leave for a girl to have a cosmetic operation. I like to think I keep myself pretty up to date with what goes on in the world around me and that I'm tolerant and fair in my dealings with the staff – in spite of some not inconsiderable provocation – but I have to say that today's request did take even me by surprise.

Let's face it – people are fat because they overeat. There's simply no two ways about it. And nowadays there is no possible excuse for being unaware of that basic fact, just as smoking gives you cancer and too much alcohol damages your liver. I've always felt the need to take responsibility for the state of my own body and I do find it hard to sympathise when people cause their own problems.

But let that be for the moment. We've all had times when we've overindulged and not behaved as we should have, and I'm the first to join in the party spirit on the right occasion and relax a little. My job is extremely stressful at times and I need to let my hair down and have an evening out every now and then. I like a drink as much as the next man, and I'm also very into a bit of Salsa at the moment: great for letting off steam. No, I don't think I'm being unreasonable when I say that there is a certain point – an invisible line, if you will – which needs to be drawn between a spot of overindulgence and plain greed. And in my book Stacey is a greedy cow. Now I wouldn't say that to anyone else, but it's my personal opinion and no one is going to change it. So when she came into my office today and asked for sick leave to go and have an operation to make her thinner I had to bite my tongue to stop myself giving her a good talking to. I'm almost ten years older than the girl and I do feel responsible for her in some way, but it's not my place, I had to remind myself: this isn't in your brief. My friends are always telling me I take too much of my work home with me – 'You'll wear yourself out, Warren,' they say to me. 'You've got to stop taking the whole world on your shoulders.' I know they're right, but I'm just a people sort of person, that's the problem. I'm oversensitive to the needs of my staff, that's always been my downfall – too much sensitivity in every way.

So I had to hold back from giving Stacey a good old lecture. It's the parents I blame, you see. I thank God – frequently – for my own upbringing, where I was taught old-fashioned values and good plain common sense.

'Quite apart from whether I can sanction the necessary time off, Stacey,' I said to her, 'are you sure this is a good idea? Doesn't it seem a little drastic to be cutting yourself about and messing with your body when it may be just a simple matter of a healthy diet?' (I thought it my responsibility to at least make an attempt to put her right.)

'It's the only way, Mr Chipstead,' she answered, looking back at me across the desk. I was pleased to see that she was, at least, managing to look me in the eye. I've long been aware that she fancies me, of course – heaven knows, there are enough jokes about it in the canteen – but she does seem to be less nervous these days when I need to talk directly to her. There's no doubt she's acquired a bit more confidence since she began the curious liaison with Mr What's-his-name.

'And does it really work, Stacey? I mean, you certainly don't want to put yourself through all this unless it's going to be effective, do you? And maybe it's dangerous – there are generally all sorts of horror stories behind these kind of miracle cures.'

'It does work. It really does – and it ain't half as risky as it used to be. It's three-pronged, you see. That's what the surgeon told us.'

'How do you mean?'

'They staple up your stomach so that it's really small.

About the size of – I'm sorry – you probably don't want to hear none of this, do ya? You don't wanna hear about what goes on in –'

'That's all right, Stacey. You won't find me squeamish – it's very important to keep ourselves abreast of what is going on in the world, you see – without knowledge we –'

'Yeah, OK – whatever. Anyway, if you're sure? They make your stomach about the size of a lemon, so you can't eat much. By stapling it across the middle – or across part of it somewhere – I'm not sure if it's exactly the middle, 'cos I don't know how big it would be normally, come to think of it. Anyway, it ends up much smaller, so you feel full really quickly. But then there's more to it than that: they bypass part of the tube – you know, the intestine – so whatever food you do manage to eat gets absorbed less.'

'Really? How clever.'

'Yeah, it is. And then there's a third thing that happens – which I don't quite understand, although he did explain it to us, but if you eat the kind of food what you shouldn't it makes you feel really horrible. Fatty stuff, I mean. If you eat that then you feel terrible, so you soon learn to eat the right kind of vegetables and that. So you lose weight in three different ways.'

I must admit I was quite impressed by the way Stacey described it to me. She's quite on the ball really, when she can drag herself out of her usual lazy attitude to life.

'Well, Stacey.' I smiled. 'Rather you than me. I find it hard to believe nature intended you to have staples in your stomach, but if you really do feel it's the only way forward then I shall do my best to sanction your sick leave with head office. You're a valued member of the SavaMart team here in Victoria, and you know the company policy on staff care and wellbeing. I'm sure we all wish you the best and you must let me know as soon as you have a date. Hopefully you'll be back at the checkout in next to no time. Perhaps even see a little less of you once you're back, eh?'

I gave her a tiny wink to show I had made the joke intentionally — just in case she thought I might have been unaware of what I had said. I stood up and moved around the desk to let her know the session was over, then hesitated at the door as I saw her struggling to prise herself out of the chair.

'Do you need some —'

'No, no. I'm fine.'

She glanced up at me and I noticed she had turned bright red with the effort — or with the embarrassment — of heaving herself up. Stacey has very unusual eyes — one might almost say they were attractive in a smaller setting — but on this occasion their rather pretty colour was entirely lost amid the shiny redness of her large, sweaty face. I am ashamed to say that as I stood waiting for the poor girl to manoeuvre herself out of the chair, I found myself not entirely sorry that she was going to be absent for a while at some point in the next few weeks.

Judy

I'm feeling quite proud of myself the last few days that I'm managing without slipping up to the bedroom for a quick flutter. It's not easy — if I tried to describe it to someone it would sound so silly — but I do miss it dreadfully. The temptation is so strong, especially at the moment: with Sally out most of the time and Ben staying with a friend it would have been so easy to spend time up there. And doing my cards was something I always kept in the corner of my mind as a possibility – a sort of escape route, something I could always turn to for a bit of excitement, and that I could get an answer to straight away. I think that was part of it: the fact that so many of my worries and problems, however small they were, seemed insoluble and permanent. My tickets gave me an instant answer – even though it was usually a bad one. At least there was always another chance.

I've taken to watching a lot of television. I never used to watch much in the evenings, especially if Charlie and the children were out and I was on my own; I would read or work on a report, or maybe do a bit of tapestry while I listened to the radio – or, of course, slip upstairs for a while. But since Charlie left – and especially since Sally caught me in the bedroom and I've been trying to cut down on my cards – I've found it a great comfort. I can absolutely understand now why elderly people see it as a friend in the corner of the sitting room. It certainly does help to fight the loneliness that I feel creeping up into my head if I stop too often to think. Who'd have thought how terribly I would miss him? It's completely unexpected.

So when I became aware of the banging earlier on I didn't feel frightened – merely curious. At first I thought it was part of the background noise to the programme I was watching, and when it became clear it wasn't, I assumed it was coming from another, distant, television set or radio. A kind of muffled thumping, but not like when there are builders next door or someone is playing a record upstairs: this was too dense and regular for that, and it went on far longer than the two or three minutes one might expect from the average music track. I thought it must be either some background music to a thriller or perhaps someone beating a drum on a march a few streets away. As it went on, though, I began to feel uneasy, and I turned down the television to try and isolate it.

Once I'd turned off the loud chatter the noise changed character – or at least my perception of it did. Although it was still a slow, drumming beat, I noticed now that it was less regular than I had thought and was no longer a background accompaniment but seemed much closer – as if the sound was being made by someone in the house. I got up out of my chair and put my glasses down on the small table next to it, then stood still, unsure what to do next. The strange thumping continued, and at one point I thought I heard a faint cry, but it was very hard to work out from which direction it was coming. I walked over and pressed my ear to the wall that adjoins the next-door house, but was still none the wiser – the sound just seemed to be part of the fabric of the building, and when I tried listening in the same way on the opposite wall it was just as loud and just as directionless. I wished Charlie was there – well, I wished that all the time, but at that moment I needed him as a physical presence.

I pulled back a curtain and looked out of the window, vainly hoping that I was still misjudging the distance of the noise and that it could, after all, be coming from outside – perhaps from a lorry or a large piece of machinery – but the street was empty. As I turned back from the window I heard the cry again – and this time there was no mistaking it. A sound of human misery and possibly pain, without doubt coming from the same source as the thumping. I was trembling a little now, partly because I was beginning to feel frightened, but also because the unmistakable evidence of someone's desperate unhappiness, so startlingly and unavoidably close and real, was shockingly sad.

I used to think how ludicrous it was in thrillers or

horror films when the heroine sets herself up to be mur-dered/raped/scared out of her silly mind by walking back into the haunted house, or up the stairs towards the killer or by locking the back door when it's quite obvious the maniac is already inside the house. You know the kind of thing – completely unbelievable.

But I was wrong. I know now that such action is perfectly possible, and I know why. I suspect there must be some in-built genetic predisposition in all of us (for if it is in me, the most physically cowardly person I know, then it must surely be in everyone) to seek out possible sources of danger. One is drawn towards it, in the same way one is drawn to scratch at a sore that would be better left alone, or to ask of a loved one, relentlessly, the question one doesn't want answered. I walked out of the sitting room, opened the door in the hall at the top of our cellar stairs and slowly walked down them, in spite of the obvious increase in the volume of the noise as I did so. There could be no doubt that the origin of the sound was somewhere down there, yet I didn't hesitate to make my way towards it.

I could see clearly, because the single bulb that lights our small cellar was already switched on, and the varying brown shades of the familiar mess of boxes, old lamp standards and other accumulated clutter were outlined by sharp shadows like a cubist painting. I realised I was holding my breath as I neared the bottom of the steps: the thumping still went on, and, as I looked around to try and identify its source, suddenly and awfully came another of those devastating cries.

It was then I saw him, as I walked into the small storeroom to one side of the steps. He was kneeling on the floor in the far corner of the wretched little room, his back towards me, his head pulling back rhythmically and regularly before it snapped forward and hit the wall in front of him with a loud, dull thud. Even from where I stood I could see the blood running down the side of his face, and when his cry came again it was the more terrible for seeing the miserable creature that made it. Ben, my darling son, my baby, my little boy.

The shock of seeing him made me release the breath I had been holding in a noisy spasm, and he turned and looked at me. His hair was dark and wet at the front from the blood and his eyes were red from crying, and I moved towards him and knelt beside him. He felt cold through his shirt and I rubbed him vigorously without thinking as I kissed him and whispered to him.

He was still half-heartedly trying to bang his head against the wall, and I kept one hand pressed firmly against his forehead and tensed each time I felt the muscles of his neck pulling against my shoulder. After a minute or two the movements slowed until they eventually stopped completely, and he relaxed back against me like a broken toy. I stroked his forehead, avoiding the patch of grazed, mashed skin, and murmured a few loving, calming words into his ear.

'Why darling?' I said at last. 'Sweet, dearest Ben, in God's name, why?'

'I just thought – oh Mum, Mum!' he said, and he bent his head down into his chest and his shoulders began to shake against me. I shushed him gently until he was calm again and I was able to wipe his eyes and the worst of the blood from his face with the edge of my sleeve. 'I just thought,' he went on, 'that I could help things – change things – if I just – no, it's no good – I can't explain. It's too difficult.'

Charlie

'But don't you feel any responsibility?' she asked, quite reasonably, I thought. It was hard to explain that I didn't feel anything at all, apart from the obvious, so I kept quiet, which I could see infuriated her even more. 'They're still your children, Charlie,' she went on, 'and it's just not on to abandon them like this.'

'Oh, come on, Judy,' I answered, 'they're virtually adults, you know. You really can't use words like "abandon" in this context – it's not like you to be so melodramatic.'

'It's not like me to be in this melodramatic situation! You have a son who is seriously disturbed – and even when we had no idea where he was you took absolutely no interest – and you've walked out on your family with no warning whatsoever and shacked up with some grotesque tart from the corner shop. I think I have every right to be as melodramatic as I like, as you charmingly put it.

'I freely admit I still love you desperately, Charlie – God knows why – but it doesn't mean I'm blind and stupid. I can still see what a bastard you're being. I just can't believe it – you were always so wonderful to the children – and to me – and now you're behaving like a complete stranger; no, worse than a stranger. A stranger wouldn't let us suffer like this – any normal, humane person would have to do something to stop all this pain. It's not as if it's difficult; it's terribly simple, Charlie: just come back home and we'll talk about all this. I'm not saying I'll ever be able to forgive you – only a saint could promise that – but I do know we can work things out and maybe even get together again if we can just talk. But this silence and this – this – disappearance are cruel and unworthy of you. Christ, don't you remember how you always used to talk about the terrible effect that people splitting up had on their families? When you and I used to compare notes about the children we both came across in our work and how stupid and selfish and cruel their parents were being? And now you're doing it yourself – don't you see that? I just can't believe it of you, Charlie, I really can't.'

She was crying now, and I tried hard to make myself feel as I knew I should on watching my wife in tears, but it was impossible. If I took an objective view of the situation I could see that, of course, she was absolutely right, but the fact that my heart was now disengaged from the rest of me and belonged to someone else was having a fascinating effect. I suppose I can understand now why murderers and rapists are able to behave in the way they do: if I, a supposedly humane person, could stand back and calmly evaluate the harm being done to the family I had always loved and protected, and yet experience no pangs of guilt or unhappiness, then anything was possible. I tried to look suitably sympathetic, but knew I was failing.

'And why the hell didn't you tell us you'd moved out of that wretched hotel? Where are you staying? No, don't tell me, I don't want to know. But you could at least have had the decency to let us know you weren't at that number any more, and given us some means of contacting you. You bastard.'

I hadn't thought to tell them I wasn't at the hotel any more: I suppose I should have, but there were all kinds of things I 'should' have done that I hadn't. (In any case, I certainly wasn't about to give them Stacey's home phone number – I could imagine that leading to all sorts of unwanted conversations.) When Judy had phoned me at work she'd been, understandably, furious and upset – she'd clearly had the most terrible shock on finding Ben in that way, and not being able to get hold of me till the next morning must have just about put the lid on it. I'd reluctantly agreed to come round and see her, supposedly to talk about Ben and Sally, and this one-sidedly hysterical meeting was the result. I still wasn't quite sure it was going to achieve anything, but felt I had to stay for a while longer to at least go through the motions of taking an interest.

'Did he – was he able to say what he was doing?'

'It was perfectly clear what he was doing. He was banging his head repeatedly against a brick wall until he made it bleed. He was crying. He was –'

'Yes, I know that, Judy – you know perfectly well I mean "why". Why he was doing it.'

'I'm sure I don't have to tell you it's a classic symptom of extreme distress and frustration.'

'No, indeed you don't, Judy. But Ben is a level-headed boy – are you really telling me that because of my leaving he has suddenly flipped and become a neurotic?'

'Don't say that! Don't sound so casual about your own son – I can't stand it! No, he hasn't suddenly "flipped", as you put it. He's been – unsure – about things for some time, although you obviously haven't noticed. His work at school has been getting on top of him and he's always been sensitive. Don't flatter yourself that your action has been the only cause of all this. It's just been the – the wonderful icing on the cake, I suppose.'

'Sarcasm really doesn't suit you, Judy. And I can hardly be accused of being the only parent to behave oddly – enjoyed spending our savings on all that gambling, did you?'

God knows why I said that – just the truth popping out, I suppose. I thought she'd explode, but, much to her credit, I must concede, she controlled herself and closed her eyes for a moment, before taking a deep breath and continuing, ignoring my unhelpful interjection.

'What are we going to do? He was talking some nonsense about getting into a parallel universe or something. I'm really frightened for him, Charlie — he's just at the age when something like schizophrenia could be starting, and I don't like the way he is at all. What shall we do — how shall we help him?'

Just then something happened that could be seen in the context as being extremely unfortunate, but that for me, in my particular parallel universe, was unexpected and wonderful. We were interrupted by Mozart's Fortieth. Heaven knows why that's what she'd chosen for me — I'd have guessed that Oasis or whoever it is now was more her style, but then the darling girl never fails to surprise me. Scrolling through the choices on the phone and making me laugh as easily as she always can, she'd said something about it being 'a pretty tune' and had insisted that it was right for me.

Judy looked quite startled. 'What on earth is that?' she said.

'Excuse me,' I answered, taking the phone out of my pocket and standing up.

'But you don't have a mobile — you've always said you wouldn't be seen dead with a — Charlie! Don't walk away from me! Listen to me!'

But I had already disappeared back into my real world. I pressed the little phone to my ear and smiled to myself as I walked into the hall. On hearing her sweet voice I immediately forgot everything else and concentrated on her news.

'All the tests were OK, Charlie — isn't it brilliant? I have a date! I need you, Charlie — come home. Come home as quick as you can!'

Stacey

Oh, Crystal — I just can't believe it! I'm over!! I'm on the other fucking side (excuse my language but I'm just soooooooooooooooooooo excited that I gotta tell someone how I feel and you're my bestest friend and I wanna be able to say ANYTHING to you). I had the surgery last week and I'm OK, although it was pretty awful and I've been through a kind of hell and back. But I don't have to tell you!!

My angel Charlie took me to the hospital for registering or whatever they call it and I felt sooo nervous I can't tell you. I had to sleep the night there and they kept weighing me and I had to give samples in jars and all that stuff and they was taking my blood pressure and I kept thinking they was going to say, 'No! You can't have it done after all,' but they didn't and I kept kinda half wishing they would so's I could just go back home and have some chocolate and forget it. Can you believe that? I was actually wanting to go and eat some chocolate when I'd come so far!! Fucking weird I am, I tell you. Anyway, in the morning I had to put on one of those gowns that do up at the back and then they checked everything again and weighed me again (like I needed that like a hole in the head, as my mum says) and then I had a few minutes back in the room so I rang my mum to say goodbye just in case. (I've got a phone next to my bed and a telly of my own and it's really like a hotel here 'cos I'm private!! Cool!) That made me really upset 'cos I couldn't bear the thought of leaving her all on her own. I didn't care about me — I really didn't, 'cos I'd kinda made up my mind I didn't wanna go on living the way I was in any case, but I knew she was so worried and scared and that made me feel really bad.

But I did it, and I managed not to cry too much and then I had to say goodbye to Charlie. Well, that was OK. I mean, he's really sweet and all that, and he's been good to me over all this and paying for it and that, but it's not like he's family – d'you know what I mean? So I didn't feel anything much, except a bit sorry for myself when I saw how frightened he was at the thought of me maybe not coming through it. I suppose he felt about me not coming back like my ma did, but I couldn't really get so worked up about that. I mean he's only known me for a few months or whatever it is, for fuck's sake, so he can't really care about me in the same way she does, however much he likes to feel me up and all that. D'you know what I mean? But I kinda pretended to be all sad and stuff, 'cos the poor cunt's paying for it and he's left his wife and all so it was the least I could do, I thought.

They took me down into this little room and the guy who was going to put me to sleep (whooops! Not like my old dog, I mean!!) had to search for somewhere to put the needle in and in the end he managed on the inside of my arm where my elbow bends. He asked me to start counting and I really thought I'd get to ten but I think at about four I was OUT!!! Weird!! After that I don't remember anything. Not even in the recovery room, where they told me I was talking away like anything. Hope I didn't say nothing embarrassing, like the way I talk in the pub when I've had a few drinks.

It all went OK anyway – or so they tell me. I remember being wheeled back into my room and I saw Charlie there so I gave him the thumbs-up sign. I didn't feel nothing – they'd given me loads of morphine. They made me walk that same night which was awful but I was still a bit woozy from all the drugs so I just went along with it, but I couldn't piss for anything, so in the morning they put a tube in me and that was such a RELIEF!! Whew!! So many tubes then, 'cos I had one for oxygen and the one in my arm still – which kept beeping on the machine if I bent my arm so's I had to keep it straight all the time which was real annoying – and tubes into my tummy and fuck knows what else. Wired for sound I was, I can tell you. They made me keep trying on the loo, even after I'd been through the tube, and it was so small to squeeze onto it in the space next to the wall that it didn't help. Can you believe that?? A place that does surgery on fat people and the loo is normal size?

Most of the doctors and nurses was great and really funny, except one called Angela, who was a bitch. Anyway, on the third day they told me I could go home, and that's where I'm writing from now. Well, not really home, of course, 'cos we're too far from the hospital to stay at Mum's, so we're in a bedsit hotel thing which is OK. But it was really hard not eating anything and just having all the liquid stuff. I got Charlie to bring back a tub of Kentucky Fried Chicken just so's I could watch him eat it – that sounds crazy but you know what I mean, don't ya? And I grabbed one piece of it and stuffed it in my mouth and chewed it and chewed it and I spat it out in the rubbish bin. It was so good just to feel something I could chew, and getting the taste really helped although I felt a bit sick for a while.

I went back to the hospital for my first check-up yesterday and I've lost 12 pounds since the op one week ago!! In one week!!! I'm so excited, Crys, it's unbelievable. I knew I was feeling different and have even been imagining that my chin rolls was smaller . . . but maybe they are!!

The surgeon was really pleased and said I can add soft mushy foods to my diet as well as a little crispy food – YIPPEE! I came straight home and ate some cream crackers – just two of them with some mushed-up sardine on them. It took me over half an hour to eat them, 'cos I chewed each bite twenty-five times like they told me – I felt really full!!

Is my life really changing? Am I going to have a life after all? I can't believe it.

Love and kisses

Stace

xxxxxxx

Charlie

I wasn't that surprised when the letter came. In fact I'd been expecting it for some time but hadn't realised that, of course, it would have difficulty finding me — I assume enough gossip had got through to chambers for them to know I wasn't living at home any more, but I hadn't given them a new address so it must have been a bit awkward. Having failed to reach me by phone — I'd been ringing in every day up to a week or so before to avoid giving them my mobile or Stacey's home numbers — they clearly decided that to send it to the house was the only option. Amazing that Judy bothered to do anything with it, though I presume that, seeing the headed envelope, she guessed it was bad news and took a delight in making sure I got it. Particularly in the way that she did it — very inventive, I must say, and guaranteed to cause as much embarrassment and humiliation as possible.

She'd left my name, but had crossed out our address and written next to it in red felt tip: NOT KNOWN AT THIS ADDRESS — TRY C/O THE FAT CHECKOUT GIRL AT SAVAMART, VICTORIA STREET. Clever that. Double whammy — or at least intended as such — to upset both me and Stacey in one fell swoop. Didn't work like that though as far as Stacey was concerned, as only Lena saw the original envelope, which she showed me later and in private, and she opened the letter and put it in a new envelope which she sent to me up in Manchester. The supermarket must have had a good laugh — I can just imagine old Chipstead splitting his sides over it, and showing it to all the Andys, Sheilas and Denishas. I wonder if Lena read the letter? It would have been hard not to, but she's been remarkably inscrutable about her daughter's boyfriend's disgrace if she did so. She certainly hasn't said anything to me – very restrained.

So I am out of a job. I might have been able to save it had the letter reached me sooner, but it was already past their pathetic little deadline before I got it. I'm not at all sure that I would have tried, in any case – all I felt was relief that I wouldn't have to leave Stacey any more during the daytime when we returned to London. The wretched business of paying back the mounting interest on the loan and earning a living will sort itself out somehow or other; the main thing at the moment is to make sure Stacey's recovery continues to progress and that she has everything she needs.

Her new eating regime unsettles me: I miss having meals with her, and not being able to buy her little treats of boxes of chocolates and the jam doughnuts she used to adore. I started buying her flowers instead, and I just loved the way she looked so excited when I brought them back to the bedsit we were staying in for the first couple of weeks after the op. I don't like the way she keeps measuring herself, though, and standing on the scales – it's getting obsessive. She just laughs at me when I tell her, and says she was always just as obsessive before but I didn't see it because she did it all secretly. I worry that she'll end up anorexic – she talks about eating all the time, and how much she can fit in her new tiny stomach. She even tried a mouthful of chocolate pudding the other day to see if it would do what they said it would – and it did. She was really ill with the 'dumping' syndrome that they warned us about from the sugar and had to lie down. She was thrilled – says it proves it's working.

She's right – she does seem a little thinner. She's even looking forward to going back to work, so she can show the others. I don't care, naturally, how she looks, as long as nothing threatens her health: I think she's probably lost enough – she should stop worrying now and just eat as much as she can in the new stomach situation and concentrate on building up her strength.

I wish they hadn't been so accommodating about giving her this time off: I'd rather she didn't go back to that ghastly supermarket at all. I've offered to support her (haven't thought how the hell I'd manage, but I know I'd find a way), but she says she wants to work and that I must stop interfering. I'm feeling – how shall I put it? Very insecure about things. A sense of dread.

Chipstead

I had to pretend to be pleased when Stacey returned, because I feel very strongly about enforcing the company policy on staff morale. I first became aware of the importance of individual staff motivation when I was promoted to senior manager – I had of course received the usual training from my supervisor on becoming junior manager, but it was the spring seminar that really opened my eyes, and you're not invited to them until you're a senior. I was privileged to be invited to the seminar last March at the Dulton Hotel and Golf Club just outside Skegness, where the company line on skill-enabling and multi-tasking performance scheduling was explained in detail.

We were treated to a very nice meal on the Friday evening, then a day of meetings on the Saturday during which we were encouraged to bond with the other senior managers in informal groups of six. Each group was given a set of questions for discussion, and after a bit of a nervous start I felt I made a healthy contribution to the debate. On the Sunday morning all the delegates were re-assembled in the ballroom and the group leaders (not including myself on this particular occasion but I've been advised there's a strong possibility I might be one next year) stood up and read out the results of the previous day's deliberations. It was excellent and very motivating, and I felt quite proud of our Victoria store when results were analysed and added to the flip chart at the back of the room. (What a wonderful invention the flip chart is! I can't think how I would manage without the one I have installed in my office: a brilliant tool for staff reminders and so on.) The rest of the Sunday was spent in relaxation and colleague bonding — I found the whole experience A1.

So I felt obliged to express my satisfaction at Stacey's safe return from her operation, although, between you and me, the average till speeds have been noticeably faster since her departure four weeks ago. She told me the procedure had gone well, and, I must say, she did look considerably brighter on her return yesterday.

Her obesity has never really been a problem for me as regards her work (although I do sometimes wonder whether customers fill their trolleys less fully when confronted by the sight of Stacey waiting for them at the checkout. Bit of a startling reminder of the effects of overindulgence.) It's more her attitude which has been the stumbling block to her progression: we all understand feeling a bit down in the dumps from time to time, but Stacey's glum expression and lack of conversational skills do put off some of our regulars no end. So if this new, brighter outlook is going to continue I shall be well pleased — I noticed she was attempting the occasional smile at the customers, and she'd put some mascara or eye shadow round those unusual eyes of hers. She even appears to be working a little faster — will wonders never cease?!

I thought Sheila looked absolutely stunning when she

came in this morning: that short skirt really shows off her legs and as for the tight, stretch top with 'Baby' on it in glitter – well! What can I say? It was all I could do to stop myself taking a good, long look straight at those fabulous breasts of hers. All the girls know the next spring seminar is not that far away, of course – I'm not stupid! We're allowed to invite a guest to join us for the Sunday afternoon and evening – preferably another SavaMart colleague – and Denisha and Sheila are both hoping I'll ask one of them. I may well do so, in fact. The company gives us tea in the afternoon and the dinner dance in the evening is out of this world. I felt quite lonely last year being on my own – I didn't like to invite anyone along until I had seen what the others were doing. I'd hate to have brought one of the juniors, for instance, and then found everyone else had one of the management team as their guest – would that have been embarrassing or what? I did have a couple of dances with one of the secretaries from head office accounts whom I'd come across during one of my training days, but as she was there as a guest of my regional manager I certainly wasn't going to monopolise her – even though she'd been at the wine quite heavily and made it clear she'd have been happy to have a one-to-one finance meeting in my bedroom, if you get my meaning! But now that I know a considerable number of the invited guests were at junior level, I shall feel quite at home with whichever of my girls I invite. Still a few weeks to go, though, so I'm not going to rush into asking one of them – I'd like to be absolutely sure they'll be suitable before I mention it. Sheila does tend to wear rather revealing clothes (I'll never forget her outfit at last year's Christmas staff pub quiz at the Bear) and she might be a bit out of her depth at the Dulton. Class will out, as my mother always says. Now there's a woman who knows about style.

Crystal

Hiyaaaaa, Staceeeeeeee!!

I told ya you could do it, didn't I? Welcome, welcome, welcome, gal, over to this side. You're gonna love it here, hon, and it just gets better, I can tell ya. I'm doing just great – I have a beautiful new guy in my life and I'm still losing and everything's just wonderful and God is being so good to me. My mom says she feels so happy for me that she thanks the Lord every day and lights candles for me and stuff – isn't that just so cute? And I say a special thank you to my personal angel, 'cos not many people know that they have the day-to-day running of our lives and all. Makes sense, don't it, that God don't have time for all the itty-bitty things that need sorting every day – that's where angels come in.

No, I still say I won't send you a picture – you've been asking all these months and I still say no way, no how! I know I sure look prettier now than I did last semester (even though there's surely a lot less of me to admire!) but I guess I've just got used to you knowing me as a friend and not judging me on the way I look, Stacey honey, so I'm just gonna keep it that way for now. I love you sending the photos, though – don't stop, will ya? Yes, I can definitely see the weight loss – for sure I can. Your chin is coming out of those rolls and your arms are looking real pretty – keep it up, Stacey.

Hey – I might be coming over next month. My gorgeous new man is trying to arrange a visit – we've never been to Europe before and we want so much to see the Louvre and the Tower of London and all, so if he can get the MONEY sorted (!!) we might be over in your part of the world before too long and then we could meet up??!! Wouldn't that be just amazing? Soooooooooo cool!!

I know you said your part of London is on the south side,

right? – are you anywhere near Maidstone? That's in a part
called Kent. My cousin Randy Brotwen lives at Maidstone –
do you know him? We might be staying with him for a few
days when we visit London so that's when we could all get
together.

Are you still with Charlie? How's he doing? Still crazy
about ya?

Love and kisses, and may your angel watch over you

Crystal

xxxxx

Judy

'Ben, do you want to talk about it? Would it make you feel
better? I can't bear to think of you being unhappy, darling,
and I'm sure there are things I could do to help if you'd just
talk to me.'

We hadn't really ever properly discussed the terrible night
I'd found him. By the time I'd calmed him down and
dropped him off at the Chelsea and Westminster to have
his head looked at (he refused to let me go in with him) we
were simply making small talk. I could tell he didn't want
me to start questioning him, and I thought the priority was
to get him thinking about other things – mundane, practical
things that might take his mind off whatever awful thoughts
had been besieging him in the cellar. The hospital said that
his forehead was fine – simply superficial damage – but that
he had to check with our GP, who sent him on to some kind
of therapist, but Ben has consistently refused to be drawn on
exactly what went on during the two sessions he had with
him. Over a month since I'd found him, with the tiny scars
on his forehead the only outward reminder of that horrible
night, we still hadn't talked about it, and, although he'd

been considerably calmer and more his old self than I'd seen him since Charlie left, I'd been feeling guilty about not having tried harder to get through to him.

'Come on, darling,' I said. 'I'm sure you'll feel better if you can bring it out into the open, whatever it is – or was. We've all been very affected by Dad's going, and I know you and Sally finding out about my – my addiction, or whatever we call it, hasn't helped anything. Let me help you now though, darling – you always feel better when you talk to me about things, don't you?'

We were sitting either side of the kitchen table. I'd been making a real effort for a while to cook some decent meals and insist that the three of us sat down at the table to eat them: it had been only too easy, since Charlie left, to get into the habit of picking at things, or eating at separate times in front of the television. We were finishing off a spaghetti Bolognese – Sally was out at the pub with some friends – and Ben looked across at me and smiled slightly, before reaching over and taking my hand. 'Sorry, Mum. I know I haven't really talked much about it. But I'm OK – the therapy guy helped, and I've been talking to Holly, so I haven't been bottling things up, I promise.'

I tried not to feel jealous, and merely smiled encouragingly.

'I'm not trying to make you talk about things you don't want to, Ben. But there's no one quite like your own family, you know; don't shut us out too much. It's amazing how much it helps just to let things out. I've been trying for years to end my ridiculous gambling habits, and I was always so terrified of any of you finding out. Now you have, it doesn't seem so shameful, and the odd thing is that, because it's no longer so shameful, it seems easier to stop. I'm really trying, you know. Maybe it's the dark secret I needed, rather than

253

the vice itself.' I laughed a little, in an attempt to lighten the words which were sounding stupid even to myself. 'You'll probably find me indulging in something really outrageous next time! When Dad gets home tonight we'll —' I broke off and shook my head. 'What am I thinking of? How silly. Sorry, darling. I — I just forgot for a moment.'

There was a pause, then Ben said, very softly, 'You really miss him, Mum, don't you? Sally and I love him and miss him loads, of course — in spite of what he's done — but I'm just beginning to realise how much you need him. You've always seemed so independent and capable — I suppose Sal and I took the two of you for granted. Your relationship. Now I look back it's extraordinary how happy you both were in each other's company — Sally was saying just that the other day. Isn't there some way — do you think you might ever — I just can't believe Dad's going to go on like this always. I think he's having some sort of middle-aged breakdown and that he'll come out of it. Would you — do you think you could take him back if he ever —'

'I don't know, Ben. You're right. I miss him all the time — more than I would ever have thought possible. There's no one else — and I mean no one — I can talk to like I can to Dad. Because there's not one single person who's lived through the years that Dad and I had together. When we were first going out and on into our early married years — learning so much together, and then those years of you two growing up and of us loving you both so much: who else can ever understand that? Share in those memories and love you both in the way we do? All that private family language: the silly words and expressions. Who can I turn to when something reminds me of one of you, or of an argument from long ago, or a boring evening that we have a shorthand code for? I hate what he's done and I thought I'd learn to hate him too. I keep trying to be strong and not react like the jealous, wronged woman — it seems so feeble to admit I want him to come back. But I don't really hate him, Ben. If I'm honest, I almost feel sorry for him — it's as if he's in a strange state that isn't really him. That's what's so surreal — he and I would have joked together about this kind of situation: the fat, stupid checkout girl and the man making a fool of himself over her, I mean — and now the one person I want to talk to about it is the problem himself. Unbelievable, it really is. Then there's money, of course. I always handled that side of things, but at least I always knew he was there to back me up. Now I'm going to have to face it on my own at some point and sort out the future. Financially, I mean.'

'Oh, Mum — you really shouldn't think about that now. We'll manage. I mean, we're OK, aren't we?'

'It isn't quite that simple, I'm afraid, darling. Our savings have — well, frankly, Ben, I've more or less gambled them away over the years, and I don't know just how your father thinks he's going to support himself and his — how shall I put it? His mistress? Is that a grown-up way of putting it? I'm sure you can imagine how I'd really like to describe her — anyway, there's us to consider, isn't there? My earnings aren't that good. Certainly not enough to pay your school fees and support the three of us while Sally's at Leeds. I'm going to have to sit down with him at some point and talk about it. If he thinks he's going to persuade me to sell this house he can think again, I can tell you.'

Ben looked rather shocked and it made me realise how sheltered they'd always been. Charlie and I used to think it was a good thing, the way we made them feel secure about money: now I wasn't so sure.

'But Dad earns loads, doesn't he?'

I smiled and shook my head.

'I'd hardly have called it loads, at the best of times. But, however you describe it, it may not be for long, I suspect. I didn't tell you about the letter I forwarded, did I? It was from the office, so I thought I ought to do something about it, rather than chuck it on that pile in the cellar like I have all the others. I was sure he hadn't been turning up for work and I assumed it was about that – I'd been having calls from them asking where he was and so on – so I thought the letter ought to reach him, and I put "c/o the fat girl on the till" or something on the envelope and sent it to the supermarket.'

'Mum, you didn't! That's pretty cool in fact,' said Ben, and I could see he was tempted to laugh.

'Now that's exactly what I mean, you see – yes, it is funny. Don't worry, I can see that. I don't mind your laughing – not a bit. And Dad would have laughed too – a lot. It's just the sort of little thing we'd find funny. That's one of the things that makes me feel so very lonely, Ben – my best friend has disappeared, and changed into someone I don't know any more.'

Ben

'I'm OK, Hol, I really am. I understand why they think I'm not, but what they don't see is that I'm just operating on a different level. It's like that children's story about the ugly duckling – it's only because he was different that he had a problem: if he'd been brought up among the swans then of course he'd have been accepted from the word go, in spite of being a revolting colour and all "scrubby" or whatever it was.'

'Bit of an obvious analogy, Benbo, even for you.'

'It may be obvious but it's spot on. Not that I see myself as a swan – in fact, I know I'm more of a – a – what kind of creature grows up ungainly and unattractive as well as starting off like that?'

'You're not unattractive, you know that perfectly well. You're just fishing.'

'No, I'm not – all right, not unattractive then, but certainly on a level with the ducks. I'm just saying – that – that I'm different, but not better.'

'Salamander.'

'What?'

'How about a salamander? I've always thought they were rather interesting, but not particularly attractive – or unattractive. Just different.'

'From ducks.'

'Yeah. And from lots of other things.'

'Absolutely. OK – well, I'm just a salamander, and if the ducks can see me like that and accept that, for instance, I don't happen to have little webbed feet that paddle about in ponds, but use my – oh shit, what do salamanders use? Tails? Fins? Anyway, whatever, you get the point. It's a question of accepting the differences and not trying to change.'

'All very well, but your behaviour hasn't been exactly salamander-like. We ducks get a bit upset when our fishy friends bash themselves to bits in the cause of difference.'

'Yeah, well, I know. I was just trying something, that's all.'

Holly looked so worried when I said that that I wished I hadn't. I wouldn't really be able to explain to her what it was like, or what I'd been trying, so it was just opening up something complicated when there was no point.

'Are you really upset, Ben? About him going? Your dad, I mean?'

'Now who's being obvious? No, I don't think so. It isn't only that. But it does make everything a bit more — meaningless, I suppose. They're not fish, by the way.'

'What?'

'Salamanders aren't fish. They're —'

'I love you, Ben.'

It was so amazing when she said that. It was like an electric shock went up my legs and zapped through my balls and right on up into my head. Quite scary, but fucking brilliant at the same time.

'Say that again.'

'Why, are you deaf or something? You heard. I don't have to —'

'No, really, Hol. I mean it. I have to see what happens. Say it again.'

'I love you.'

It happened again, exactly the same. So it wasn't just the surprise of it — of her saying something so definite and so unexpected. It was much more than that. I wouldn't have believed it possible if I hadn't experienced it myself. I waited, staring at her, hoping she'd be forced to say it yet again by my silence. And she was.

'I love you.'

I laughed — it was so exciting and so wonderful what this was doing to me. 'Fucking brilliant,' I said at last, still laughing. 'Fucking brilliant!'

Stacey

Charlie took me out to the Angus Steak House last week — I was so scared to go but it was absolutely wicked! I sat there and didn't make a pig of myself — I just couldn't believe it. Six weeks ago when I was still on the wrong side I'd have had two or three Cokes, a starter of something like onion rings or chicken pâté, loads of bread and butter all through the meal and a huge steak with baked potato (more lovely butter!) or chips (and sometimes I could get away with having both by making Denisha order them). And finally of course dessert. Usually chocolate cake or ice cream with butterscotch sauce. Last week I ordered just . . . a baked potato! That was it! Not even anything to drink except some water! I ate most of my potato with a tiny bit of Flora and had about two bites of Charlie's rump steak. I felt so proud of myself, and best of all I felt full and satisfied. I'm really enjoying my little tiny tummy so far!

I'm back at work now and I feel so different about everything. I've lost about 38 pounds so far and I'm four sizes smaller in trousers – it's so exciting to go shopping but I'm trying to stop myself buying too many clothes 'cos I just know they're going to be too big any minute now – fantastic!

The girls at work have been brilliant. I was worried they'd all look at me funny 'cos I knew Warren would've told them about the surgery even though I only told Denisha and she promised not to tell the others. I thought they'd be whispering and that, the way they do, but they was OK. At first they didn't say nothing, but I made a joke about it in my morning break 'cos they just couldn't BELIEVE that I never had a chocolate biscuit or nothing with my coffee (in fact, now I never even have coffee with my coffee, if you get me, 'cos I just have one of them cartons of apple juice!!) I felt like them health freaks – it was really cool. I'll be at the gym next! I might be, in fact, even though I was joking just then. I might go and have a look – Sheila says there's lots of big girls go and it ain't too bad for staring and that.

I felt quite smiley once I was back on my checkout. It's amazing knowing I'm shrinking while I'm sitting there; it's good being back in the same old place 'cos I can feel the difference from when I was sat there just feeling depressed and wondering when I'd be able to put a sweetie in my mouth without Warren or daft Mrs Peters noticing. Today I was being all cheerful like, saying good morning to our customers and all. Some of them looked quite shocked 'cos I never used to say nothing. Made me laugh that.

Mind you, Charlie's looking a bit bleeding miserable these days. He says he don't mind that they've sacked him, but it don't seem right for a man like him to sit around with me mum all day just watching the telly and waiting for me to come home. Right weird, if you ask me. And I went out for a drink (water, if you don't mind!) with the girls last night after work and he looked right grumpy when I come back. Said I shouldn't waste money by going out spending after work! Fucking cheek. I'm the only one what's earning, I said to him – if I want to buy a few drinks that's my business. And if you must know, I said, it was Sheila what bought us all a drink to celebrate me losing over two stone so fast.

I've decided I'm gonna let Charlie fuck me, in fact. I just get this feeling he thinks I owe him something (and I know I do, though he never said he was paying for my operation for me to pay him back something – he said over and over again that it was just 'cos he loved me and wanted me to be happy. Oh yeah?). And I don't want to never be in someone's debt, you see – it makes me feel right awkward when I think he's waiting for me at home and all. If I let him have his end away then we'll be all square, that's my point. Fair's fair. I'll have to let him do it before Crystal comes over, 'cos she and her friend are going to stay in the house for a week or so and I think it'd be embarrassing to try and do it with Charlie while them two was asleep on the settee or whatever.

I just can't wait for her to come. Only two weeks to go now and she'll be here on her visit with her new fella. I bet she's gorgeous — and he is too! I wouldn't never have been brave enough to do what I did without Crystal — and I ain't never gonna forget it. She's my real angel, that's how I see it anyhow. I'm gonna give her a really brilliant time in London while she's here. Dunno what she'll think of Charlie, though, even though I've told her all about him in my letters. He's a bit pompous for going out with — he can be a right wet blanket. I'll have to tell him it's a girls-only outing when I take her out, that's what.

Chipstead

I must say, I continue to be amazed just how much Stacey has perked up since coming back. We've all noticed it. Her weight loss is quite obvious now, and she's still smiling and even beginning to chat a little to the customers. You could knock me down with the proverbial. Whether it's due simply to the controversial operation (my cousin saw an item about a similar procedure on *Oprah* and said she was by no means convinced it worked) or whether it's due to the old boyfriend, who I note is still hanging around, it's hard to say. There's no doubt she's got a bit of a sparkle in her eyes these days, and I noticed she came in this morning positively reeking of perfume and looking very flushed and pleased with herself.

I wonder if they actually do it? I heard the girls discussing it in the canteen the other day and I pretended not to hear so

I could discreetly listen (I see it as part of my job to monitor the social wellbeing of my staff, and I considered this particular piece of managerial eavesdropping was justified in this instance). They were giggling like anything, in the facile way they do, but I have to own that some of it was quite funny – particularly when they were speculating about positioning: who would be 'on top' for instance. Sheila was hilarious about poor old Thornton getting squashed flat if Stacey ever took it into her head to take the upper hand, so to speak. I wonder.

Charlie

What a darling girl she is! She knew I was feeling blue and she gave herself to me at just the right time: she has an instinctive goodness and generosity that is quite overwhelming. I was getting so worried that she was losing interest in me, and now it's clear that she loves me as much as I love her. What a lucky, lucky man I am. She's adorable; glorious. We had nearly made love so many times that I hadn't realised how much more it would mean to me to consummate our relationship in the fullest physical sense, and it was everything I could have dreamed of. It was a wonderful gesture of love and – and cherishing of me. In her own sweet way she's made it quite clear that it doesn't mean she's going to allow me that divine pleasure all the time – she's really quite moralistic, I think, underneath all her bad language and apparent vulgarity. I can see it meant something very special to her and not just a random act to be undertaken whenever one of us happens to feel like it. Never mind, I am content simply to be with her, sleep next to her and adore her. I only wish her pen friend wasn't coming to stay — I hate having to share my darling with anyone.

Judy

I have to face the fact that he is probably never coming back.

Stacey

Bugger me. I'm gobsmacked. I really am. Gobsmacked. I was so excited this morning about Crystal coming that I just couldn't wait for eleven o'clock. I didn't go into work, 'cos I certainly didn't want her met by Charlie at the door and Crystal having to sit and think of things to say to him until I got back, and even if I said I wanted Mum to be the one to look after them I know Charlie wouldn't have allowed it — he don't want to be left out of anything. Anything that's to do with me, I mean. He's been a bit better since the other night (it wasn't too bad, in fact, although it was all over a bit quick) but he's still too bleeding nosy and jealous about everything for my liking. And he has this stupid smirk on his face now when he looks at me since we done it — like we're in on some special secret together or something. Look, mate, I feel like saying, you've had your payment, right? So don't make a big thing out of it, 'cos it's not like Brad and Jennifer or nothing — it was just a quick fuck 'cos I owed you. But I can't do it to him, not right now, anyway, 'cos I feel kinda sorry for him at the same time.

Anyway, I stayed back from work so I could be the one to welcome Crystal and Wayne. (I told lovely Warren that I had to have a check-up and he was OK about it – he's been ever so friendly to me lately and he even jokes with me like he does with the others. He made a really funny joke when I said about my check-up – something about the checkout – only I can't remember it now but it was fucking clever.) Mum had the living room all ready – we'd put a sheet and that on the settee and Mum said she'd make up a nice bed there after we'd had our tea and then Wayne could have Mum's armchair what pulls out into a lying thing. Mum had bought a box of chocolates and put it by the settee and then she was so guilty 'cos she hadn't even thought that it might be difficult for me and I felt so proud when I said, 'Mum, it's fine. You can offer those chocolates to Crystal and Wayne and Charlie and take one yourself and it don't bother me one bit.' Brilliant!

Anyway, the doorbell rang and I felt quite nervous as I got out of my chair to go and answer it. Fucking hell! I'd have been nervous if I'd known what was coming, wouldn't I? Mum pulled back the curtains and took a peep outside and she looked – what's the word? – kinda surprised and puzzled at the same time. 'Oh no, love,' she says, 'it's not your friends. I think they must have got the wrong house – see what they want, will you, Charlie?'

'No, I'll go, Mum,' I says. 'It's our house, Ma, not Charlie's.' He looked buggered when I said that, so I went straight on and says, 'It's not fair on poor old Charlie to make him do all our running about. He does quite enough for us as it is.' That cheered him up – I didn't want him sitting there with a miserable face when Crystal come.

I went out to the hall and I could hear voices from the other side of the front door. I felt just a bit scared for a second – I should've asked Mum what these people looked like, I thought, before being so smart and saying I'd answer them – s'posing they're muggers or something? We don't get many people ringing our bell, 'cos it's quite a quiet street, really, and except for the odd Jehovah's whatnot there ain't that many what come along it. It's probably some of them, I thought, or those foreign students what try to sell you tea towels and that (I always tell them to fuck off – I can't stand students).

But it wasn't. I could tell that straight off. They was far too well dressed and – and glamorous, for religious nutters or students. Kinda beautiful, although it sounds funny to say that about guys. One was a tall, plump black guy, with his hair in a ponytail and a lovely long leather coat on, and the other one was blond and a bit thinner. The black guy smiled at me, and his eyes was all sparkly and bright – he had eyeliner round them like the singers do and I could see he had blusher on his cheeks too.

He put a hand out to me, but I moved back in the doorway a bit and half shut the door in case he was gonna grab me and try and get in and take stuff or something. His fingers was long and kinda girly-looking – for a second I couldn't think why they seemed that way, but then I realised with a bit of a jump that he had nail polish on too. Fuck me, I thought, that's going a bit far. He just smiled even more, and pulled his hand back and clasped it with the other one in front of him, really gently and delicately, like a dancer.

'Hello, darling,' he said, and his voice was velvety and very low. Husky, I s'pose you'd call it. 'Don't be frightened, sweetheart – I'm Crystal.'

Chipstead

I couldn't be more pleased with my store. I really feel we've put ourselves on the SavaMart map lately, with our sales being so healthy and staff morale and attendance being of such high standard just now. It makes all my hard work worthwhile, when I arrive in the morning and check the sales figures and the QC sheets and go through any outstanding matters with Mrs Peters and find that everything is humming along so satisfactorily. It's what life is all about, I say to her. Job satisfaction and enough of a healthy social side to balance the day's work and you've got your life sorted, Mrs P.

As for Stacey — well, I just wouldn't have believed it, if you'd told me a year ago how well she'd be working and what a valuable member of the team she'd become. She's still a very big girl, of course, I won't deny that — but I've never been one to discriminate, and it's not so much the change in her size that has brought her up in my estimation, but the change in her attitude. Of course the healthy heterosexual in me also recognises that in spite of her size she's fast becoming very attractive. I've never been one to fancy the anorexic look of many of the girls around these days — I've always been a bit of a tits-and-bum man. I like a bit of meat to get hold of, if you know what I mean. And our Stacey has certainly got plenty of that! Why she still hangs around with that old man I cannot imagine: still waits for her outside every evening, he does. Looking very pathetic now, though, I must say. He's unshaven, most evenings, and doesn't ever say hello any more. In fact, if I didn't know better, I'd be inclined to shoo him away from the staff entrance – he's got a funny look in his eye. She could do far better for herself.

Charlie

I knew I was right to feel trepidation about the pen friend coming to stay. It's six days now since the arrival, and I still can't believe 'she' has turned out to be a 'he'. I like to think I'm relatively liberal and broadminded, but I have to confess an instinctive uneasiness at the sight of a tall young man wearing make-up and prancing effeminately about the room. Even the way he sits is unnervingly female – he sort of pouts as he settles himself into the chair and crosses his legs while he looks up at you from under his eyelashes. Stacey tells me he sometimes even wears dresses at home, but thought we might find it a bit too shocking. Too damned right. As he was considerate enough to wear trousers to assuage our old-fashioned sensibilities, one might have thought he could have gone the whole hog and washed off the lipstick and powder and cut his hair and nails. Still, it's only what one sees in Soho every day of the week, or, indeed, on television nowadays.

Stacey and Lena, of course, simply find it amusing. They're doing their best to persuade 'Crystal' to put on his female clothing, but, so far, I'm pleased to say that he has refused. Last night he was sitting next to Stacey on the sofa, and I swear they could have been two schoolgirls, the way they were giggling and pointing out rock stars and so on in the magazine they were reading.

'Ooooh, he is simply gorgeous!' said Crystal in that strange, husky voice of his. Do I find it huskier because I still instinctively feel he is more female than male? Coming from a real man I suspect it's of a fairly average depth of tone. 'Honey,' he went on, turning towards her and stroking Stacey's hair (that irritated me, I can tell you), 'is he your type? D'you want me to fix you up now you're getting slim and gorgeous, sweetie? Pardoning your presence, of course, Charlie!'

I ignored him and continued to stare at the television. I have never in my life watched as much of the wretched thing as I have since moving in with Stacey and her mother. It is switched on first thing in the morning and remains on throughout the day and evening, and any attempt I make to put it off is met with outrage. Stacey, in particular, has a strangely personal relationship with it, and claims that, as it was her only true friend before she came over (as she will insist on calling it), she refuses to abandon it now that she's on the other side. I've come, unwillingly, to know the names of most of the characters in *EastEnders*, to shout out the answers to the pathetic quizzes that pop up throughout the day and to laugh, grudgingly, at the cheap jokes and ghastly innuendo of the comedians. But to have a real live transvestite, or transsexual or whatever he/she calls himself, sitting on the sofa was too much — I felt as if the room had been invaded by a walking, talking Lily Savage.

But as it was not my home I felt powerless to intervene, and there was no question of leaving Stacey alone with her new friend. Crystal's 'partner', Wayne (you couldn't make it up, could you?), seems perfectly happy to take off and explore London on his own, and has tried hard to persuade me to go with him and 'do' Buckingham Palace and so on, but Crystal remains obstinately at Stacey's side.

There is never any question of my leaving Stacey in any way, at any time, of course, but I was especially reluctant to leave her with someone who patently made her so happy.

Not that there is any question of sexual jealousy – Crystal is demonstrably and totally not a threat in that direction – but I am jealous of every smile that he inspires in her, and every warm word that he extracts from her. Before his arrival it was bad enough hearing her stories from work, of how amusing Denisha was, or how charming Warren had been and so on, and now I have to watch the same thing going on at home. Up to a few weeks ago I was the only person who could achieve such miracles: where were all these charming, amusing people when she really needed them? Ha! Stacey is blind to her only real friend; to the only one who truly loves her for herself, no matter what her shape.

She is remarkably transformed: I had no idea someone could lose so much weight so quickly. She's already talking about another operation to remove the sagging skin from her upper arms, the top of her thighs and across her darling tummy. I shall find the money somehow – however much she irritates me at the moment, there's nothing I can deny her.

Crystal and Stacey have their obesity experiences in common, of course, and last night, after the tiresome teasing about getting Stacey 'fixed up' with some rock star or other, their conversation turned, as it has every evening, to an endless repetitive discussion of surgery, diets, clothing, incisions, catheters and God knows what else.

'But have you tried the new low-cal Popsicles?' Crystal was asking, running a finger down each side of his mouth and rubbing the surplus lipstick away between his fingers.

'What the fuck are Popsicles?'

'You don't know what POPSICLES ARE, STACEY? My GOD, you just haven't lived, they are soooooooooo delicious!'

'He means ice lollies,' I interjected, but shrugged to myself as I realised neither of them was listening to me.

'They are just fabulous – and if you get the new low-cal ones they're almost zero calories and just give you something satisfying to put in your mouth – if you'll pardon the expression!! Ooops! Sorry, Charlie!' he giggled, and they both looked across at me.

I don't think I could have managed a smile even if I had wished to try, and I kept staring at the television, aware that they were pulling faces at me and watching my reaction carefully.

'Oh, just ignore him,' said Stacey as she realised there was no way she was going to get a rise out of me. 'He ain't got no fucking sense of humour, that's his problem, Crystal.' Out of the corner of my eye I could see that she had turned back towards the unnerving creature next to her on the sofa. She giggled. 'It's so weird, calling ya that, now I know you're a bloke. I feel like I oughta call you Peter or Gary or something a bit – well, you know, something a bit more butch.'

'Oh, sure – like I'm really butch. Like I'm mister macho, honey!' This made them both giggle some more, and Crystal put his arm round Stacey and gave her a squeeze. 'No, listen,' he went on, 'I've used the name Crystal – and no, I'm not gonna tell you my real name for nothin' 'cos it's so gross – I've used it ever since I called myself that in a show, so all my friends call me Crystal (or sometimes Crys so it's kinda boy and gal at once, which is cool). If you're embarrassed when we're out or something, then you can do that, too. Just call me Crys.'

'Oh, no, I won't be embarrassed,' answered Stacey, looking up at him and still snuggled against him. 'I think it's ever so sweet. It's just funny, that's all. And why didn't ya tell me?'

'What? My real name, you mean? Honey I just said, I'm not —'

'No, I don't mean that. I mean why the fuck didn't ya tell me that you was a boy? Why did you write to me as a girl? I bet I told you stuff I never would of to a guy.'

'I never thought. It wasn't a plan or anything, Stacey angel, I can promise you that. It just kinda happened that way: I never thought a thing about it. When I saw your ad in that slimming mag for pen friends and I wrote to you — d'you remember? All that time ago? Well, I just signed it Crystal and put that as my name with my address on the envelope 'cos — well, 'cos that's my name, I guess. I mean, that's just so much my name now that I never think it's funny or unusual or anything — so I never thought about what you'd think. I read your letters for a long time before I realised that you thought I was a gal. And then I guess I just didn't wanna spoil it. You being so kind and sweet and — and needing me so bad. That was so cool. Look, honey — if you think you've had a rough deal, just imagine what it was like for me. Black, gay AND fat? Hey — that's just winning the jackpot. I got plenty of friends, sure, but you were kinda special to me, and I just kinda left it too late to tell ya all that at once. And that's why I didn't wanna send you a picture, like you kept asking. I just thought it'd be better to let you see me and meet me and — and then I'd know how you really felt. 'Cos if I did it in a letter you'd have had time to cover all that up, wouldn't you? See? And you know how you feel when you're getting ready to go over the other side, don't ya? You don't need no problems. You just want your angels to be there for you and help you. You've been another angel for me, honey. You know that, don't ya? God's angels are shining and perfect and look after me every minute of every day from up in heaven where they walk on the edges of the Lord's kingdom, but you've been my angel here on earth.'

I wasn't sure how much more of this I could take, but I kept my attention rigidly fixed on *Fifteen to One* and resisted the temptation to run out of the room. I must have shown something on my face, because I became aware that they were both looking at me.

'I don't think Charlie believes in my angels, do you, honey?' Crystal said smilingly.

I continued to ignore him, and he turned and whispered something into Stacey's ear; she then leant against him and burst out laughing, more loudly and harshly than I'd heard her before. She whispered something back to him, and then they both laughed some more, irritatingly and relentlessly, rocking about on the sofa in childish hysterics.

After a while, and with a lot of 'oh dear's and 'dearie me's, the ludicrous laughter slowed and Crystal took a tissue from his pocket, screwed the end into a point and delicately wiped the eye make-up from beneath his eyes where it was running a little. 'Now, to be serious, honey, how's the indigestion? Is it better today? Have you stopped that burping and farting trouble?' This, of course, produced even more giggles and I couldn't take it any more.

'Oh, for Christ's sake!' I exploded, and stood up and walked out of the room, using the excuse of a visit to the upstairs lavatory to take a few minutes to pull myself together.

To my horror, when I came down again they had gone. A note on the table informed me they'd gone out for a drink and would be back later.

Judy

Ben seems like a changed boy. I'm so pleased and relieved. I have a feeling I'll never quite get to the bottom of what he was going through that awful time I found him in the cellar, but maybe that's for the best. I sense he feels embarrassed about that now, and I'm the first one to understand about wanting to put things behind you. He's still seeing the therapist, and I suppose with him – and Holly – to talk to he'd rather I just stay in the background. Just Mum.

And I'm doing well, too. At least with stopping myself buying any more cards – there are still a few up there that I haven't scratched, and it's almost unbearably tempting to pop upstairs and look at them, but so far I'm holding out. But it means, of course, that now there's nothing to distract me from the real problems. And it hurts. Makes me feel raw. I've been using Ben and Sally as excuses to avoid facing Charlie's shocking behaviour – I know I have. If someone had told me what he'd be doing, how he'd leave me in this grotesque, humiliating way, I just wouldn't have believed it. And I don't think I quite believe it even now: it's so ludicrous as to be like a bad dream.

But Ben and Sally are OK – I know that really. They see all this as just one part of their lives, but for me it's – and I know I should be bigger than to have to admit this – it IS my life. Charlie and I were such a unit – in spite of all our difficulties and irritations – and nothing can ever replace that amount of time spent together and all the experiences we had in common. That's what people don't understand until it happens to them: however much you think your marriage is unhappy, it's got to be bloody unhappy to make the alternative a better one.

There isn't an answer to it: simply time, that's all. I shall bury myself in my work, as they say, and keep my head down until the pain begins to subside. I'm an attractive woman and I certainly don't intend to shut myself down for the rest of my life, there'll come a time when I shall be ready to – to – what does one do nowadays? Go on dates?

Well, why not?

Stacey

It's ten weeks now and I just can't believe how much I've lost – I'm down by about 60 pounds. It's so weird to get on the scales and see it continually go down instead of up. I know the weight loss will slow down eventually, but at the moment it's just magic. Two pounds, three more pounds gone – it's unreal.

I know the doctors told me that to fully recover takes six months, but – for me – I'm only nearly three months out and I feel better than I have since I was a teenager. I feel great. People treat me different now I've lost weight – even though I'm still big I ain't as gross as I was. And I know it shouldn't matter what size you are but it does. Even that Vanessa, who used to look so smiley and jolly on the TV in the old days when she was big, says now that she was only pretending and that she hated it really.

It's brilliant to go into normal shops and look at the clothes; I used to do that in the old days just to imagine I could wear them and people always used to stare at me and whisper and I knew what they was thinking – what the fuck is that fat lump doing in here when there's no way she could get into any of this? And they was right. And then I'd go to one of the outsize stores, as my mum calls them (only they don't call them that now, they have all them fancy names to make you think it's OK to be fat), and I'd see all them tents (well, marquees, more like, just like the one my cousin had for her wedding) and I'd get so depressed I'd go home without buying nothing. And now I can look in Marks, or Top Shop and, although I ain't there yet, it don't seem quite so crazy any more.

Charlie says I'm 'fading away'. But he's such a depressing old git these days that it don't matter what he says. He thinks I need him 'cos I'm gonna have the op to take away all my hanging bits, but I can manage on my own, thanks all the same. I'm saving from work now, and the hospital says I may be able to pay it off in instalments, in any case, so I shan't get it done until I can pay for it myself. I know Charlie was good to me and all that, but I never asked him to fall for me, did I? It's not like he didn't want to leave his wife and come and get shacked up with me — it's not like I forced him or nothing, is it? I don't owe him nothing, in fact. He's had his fun out of me — I never said no to all his fiddling and stuff that he used to get off on.

Course I ain't never told him what Crystal and I got up to that night we went out. No point in causing aggro — he's touchy enough as it is, so I think it's best to leave well alone.

Crystal

Hi, hon!
How're ya doin??? Wow — I miss ya lots! And didn't we have fun???? You wicked girl!

Well, I'm back at work now, and the show's goin' great. I've been telling all the other guys and girls about my British trip and they are soooooooo jealous!! I wore my cute outfit that you made me get from British Home Shops (is that right?) to a party that my friend Gavin gave the other day and everyone just drooled.

I have great news. Me and my darling friend Wayne are gonna go through a ceremony of commitment next month!! Is that cool or what? Do you have them over there? It's so cute – you promise to love each other and share all your stuff and that and it's gonna be so beautiful. My ma and pa are coming over – they're really supportive, like I told you – and Wayne's brother's coming from Arkansas. His parents aren't too cool about it but that's OK. I'm gonna wear an all-white suit with a cute frilled pink shirt and Wayne's gonna be in his leather jacket and tight jeans. Way to go!!

I guess my angel's been working full time for me up there. Life is just so good I can't believe it. It seems such a short time since the op and today I've lost over 97 pounds. I almost crapped myself when my big butt measured a demure 42 inches!!! I wish I'd kept some measurements before I came over to the other side – I kind of remember my hips being 54 inches but I wish I knew exactly.

God bless and keep you, Stacey darlin', and don't stop writing!!

LOL (which reminds me – still not get LYLMS? Love You Like My Sister, of course!) and kisses

Crystal

PS did ya ever tell Charlie???!!!

Stacey

It was really funny when I told him. I ain't never seen someone so — what's the fucking word? — that stupid one he uses. Discombobulated. That's what he was.

I'd known I had to tell him for days. It's just he'd been looking so piss-miserable that I kept putting it off. Well, he's always miserable these days, as I've said before, but somehow lately it's been making me feel a bit — what? — scared, I s'pose. Specially with Crystal gone, it's just me and my mum up against this old guy who's cracking up. That's what he is — cracking up. I thought once Crystal had gone he'd cheer up — having me back to himself again and all that stuff — but he never. I know what it is, of course, I'm not stupid. He knows I'm having a really good time, now that everything's going so well for me and the weight's still coming off and all that. He always said he wanted me to be happy, but I know that's not fucking true, is it? It's what they say in all the stories and that — I just want you to be happy, my darling — all that crap. What they mean is, I want you to be happy with me — and no one but me. Or else.

So I'd been putting it off a bit, although my mum kept telling me to get on with it. She was right, and I knew it. I just didn't know how to bring it up really, and I wasn't sure how he'd take it. Although I had a pretty good guess. In the end I just come right out with it: I'd been practising it in my head all day at work, like what they do in comedy films in front of a mirror — you know, they practise over and over how to say something like 'I love you', and then when they meet the person they're gonna say it to, it just comes right out without all the clever stuff they've been doing in

277

the mirror. And it's always right funny. Only it wasn't so funny in real life — well, not after, anyway.

I come in from work about eight — lately I've managed to stop him waiting outside for me every night and looking a prat — and he was sitting in front of the telly with my ma, and she looked at me when I come in and made one of her faces — when her eyes look up and down quickly and her eyebrows go up at the same time — like she's going 'tch!' but without saying anything. I knew it meant he was in a bad mood, so I decided not to tell him. I sat down next to him on the sofa and I leant over and gave him a kiss on the cheek, but even that didn't seem to get through much. He looked at me and his face was right sad. Hello, I thought, this means a moody evening.

'Where've you been?' he says. This is my regular greeting every time I come in now.

'I been at work, Charlie, where d'you think I been?' I says back.

'You finished over an hour ago,' he says.

'I know,' I says. I'm buggered if I'm gonna tell him every single move I make. As it happens I had a quick sip of black coffee with Denisha in the canteen, 'cos I was right dry after shelf-stacking, but I wasn't gonna tell him that. He could mind his own fucking business, that's my attitude. He takes a liberty the way he's always nosing about.

'How'd you know what time I finished?' I says.

'I asked you this morning which shift you were on, Stacey,' he says, all quiet like. 'Don't you remember?'

'Oh yes. Well, I was late finishing.' I dunno why he makes me wanna tell lies, but there's something in the way he questions me that gets me making things up when I don't need to. I dunno why. I ain't got nothing to be ashamed of.

'Oh, by the way,' I says, just coming out with it after all my practising, 'I'm pregnant.'

There was such a silence you coulda heard a whatnot drop — pin — as my mum says. She looked as if she was gonna laugh — I guess it was the way I come out with it after all them talks she and I had about how to tell him. *EastEnders* was on, of course, and I couldn't believe my mum was looking away from it, but she was. She was watching Charlie, and, once she'd stopped herself smirking and pulled herself together, her eyes went all starey and big and she was ever so still. I couldn't look at him for a while — I didn't dare, somehow, but then I turned and faced him and I was ever so surprised.

He was looking — joyous. And gobsmacked. Like them pictures of saints and whatnot that Crystal's always sending me — he had that same kinda shining, amazed happiness all over his face. Like he'd found something that had been lost a long long time before. Made me feel quite embarrassed for him, in fact: it was so kind of — revealing, if you know what I mean; made him look real stupid, like my cousin who's special needs. So I thought I'd better say something, 'cos the atmosphere in that room was getting a bit spooky.

'Well, I hoped you'd be happy for me, Charlie,' I says. 'I was very surprised, 'cos I never thought I'd be able to have a baby, you know — not with all my problems and that. But there you are. Goes to show you never know, don't it?'

'But of course I'm happy, my darling,' he said. 'Of course I — this is the happiest moment of my life. Don't you see? This is so — so wonderful, Stacey. So truly wonderful.'

'Hang on a minute, Charlie — don't go mad, mate,' I says. It was getting even more embarrassing now, what with me mum there and all — I wished he'd just be a bit more normal.

I'd rather he was grumpy again than all this over-the-top joy stuff.

'I just couldn't have wished for anything more beautiful in my life. It's so perfect. I never dreamt – you see, I never knew I could love in the way I love you, my darling. And now – to have you bear my child, it's –'

So that was when I twigged, you see. I know it seems right stupid, looking back on it and all. You'd think it woulda been obvious what he thought – what he just assumed without so much as thinking twice. I can see it now. But I suppose I'd kinda forgotten that one time I let him stick his thing up me – I'd got to think of him as more like a friend than anything else over the last few weeks. Or more like family really, 'cos friends you don't usually get so fed up with, but family can get on your nerves, can't they? And Charlie was doing that all right. Especially since he'd been so grumpy and miserable and that. But – looking at it now – there was just as much chance of it having been his as – but it wasn't of course. I knew that for sure, 'cos of my dates.

Now I knew why he was looking so happy and that – proud and all. It seemed really funny when I realised my mistake – well, his mistake more like it. Talk about getting the wrong end of the stick. '*What?*' I says, and I was laughing as loud as anything as I says it, and I could see my mum was holding her hand over her mouth so's not to giggle too. 'Bear your child? Pull the other one, Charlie – you're having me on, ain't ya?' I says. 'Are you joking, or what? I'm not having your child, you daft bugger – it's Warren's, of course.'

Did you ever do that game when you was little when you have to put your hand up and down over your face and make it go from happy to sad as quick as you can? So you're all smiley as it goes up and then fucking depressed with your mouth turned down when your hand goes down again? Well, I swear that was how Charlie's face went. It was like he was turned off somewhere at the main power switch. His whole face kinda collapsed and his mouth drooped downwards and even his eyes seemed to sink a couple of centimetres down his face. Like a melting clay model. And he changed colour and all – he went a horrible dark purply grey. I thought he was dying or something, God's truth. I stopped laughing then, anyhow, and tried to look serious and sad for him. 'Cos I could see he was disappointed, you see.

'Come on, Charlie,' I says, 'you didn't really think it was yours, did ya? Be serious. We only ever done it the once – ooh, sorry, Ma!'

'Don't mind me, Stacey,' she says. 'You carry on, love, I'm a woman of the world. You don't have to mind me, love.'

That sounded so funny, but I managed not to laugh and I looked back at Charlie. He still looked like he might pop his clogs any second so I kept talking, 'cos I could see he was in no state to say nothing just at the moment.

'Not that I done it more than that with Warren, as it happens,' I went on. 'I don't want ya to think I been having an affair or nothing. I just done it the once with Warren. The night I went out with Crystal, d'you remember? When you was getting the hump because we was mucking about on the sofa and going on about our ops and that. D'you remember? Well, we went out for a drink and I took Crys to the Rat and Carrot, and Warren and a couple of the girls was there 'cos it was his birthday and he'd had a skinful and we just got chatting and, of course, I was only sipping some water and me and Crystal was the only ones sober, as it happens. So we took Warren back to his place in a cab and – and we undressed him and that. And – well, you don't wanna know all this, really, do you, Charlie? It happened anyhow. Fuck knows how, but it did. And they say at the hospital it's not unusual, you see. 'Cos my system's just getting going again and that, and I'm very fertile. So they say.'

Charlie

I've read about love turning, on an instant, to hate. I never believed it could be possible. It is. A great passion contains its own opposite, you see: very simple really. It's a conjuring trick – no, an optical illusion: like one I was shown as a child. It was a black and white picture – when you looked at it quickly you saw a little black rabbit against a snowy white field. If you kept on looking the cute bunny disappeared, and only then did you see the face of a devil in the whiteness and the black teeth and evil eyes outlined at its centre. Positive and negative. Which was true, and which was really there? One, both or neither? Just depended which way you looked, of course, but once you'd seen the devil that's what stayed with you.

I saw the devil in that moment with Stacey. With merely a tiny shift in my brain I saw the other side of her and of my heart. And in my case there was no going back – I don't think I could have seen the rabbit again if I'd tried – it had been cast into a dusty pile of false memories on the floor as the scales had fallen from my eyes.

It was surprising how quickly I was able to extricate myself from that ghastly house and the enveloping torpor of its inhabitants. I'd been steadily selling my clothes and possessions over the previous weeks so had very little left in any case and, within the space of three minutes or so, I had thrown it all into a plastic bin bag I found in the kitchen. I managed to avoid saying anything: I knew I had to contain my new-found rage or it was in danger of spilling over.

It didn't occur to me to wonder where I was going to stay; as long as I could find a quiet corner to myself where I could calm down and indulge in some quiet, cold exploration of my growing hatred, I should be happy. This proved easier said than done: I had no money at all and no prospects of getting any. I was already way behind with the interest payments on the loan, and, with no job or address, hardly in a position to secure another one. London is a hard place to hide away in, especially without cash, and it was only after several days of walking about the city, sleeping rough and damn near freezing to death that I came across a travellers' shelter in one of the less salubrious corners of Victoria where I could spend a few days in relative obscurity.

On my first night there I shared a table with four others, among them a foul-smelling female, dressed in several layers of impossibly greasy coats. It was when, fascinated, I watched her pull a large jar of apple sauce from the grimy depths of her clothes, unscrew it and spoon the contents into her mouth with two hooked fingers that my plan was born. God knows where the idea came from – whether it was something I'd been harbouring deep in the murkier recesses of my soul or whether I dreamt it up on the spot I shall never know. All I do know is that the plan was in my head and decided upon in a single flash of inspiration and certainty. And I never wavered: from that moment I knew what I had to do and how to do it.

Getting hold of the razor blades was easy: in spite of my shabby, unwashed clothes, my appearance was still respectable enough to convince the warden that I could be trusted with them. I claimed, among other things, that I needed a daily shave in order to look for work. Buying the jar would be more difficult: I had no money of my own at all now, and I had no wish to expose myself to the powers of authority by registering for the dole, or claiming social security or any other of the handouts available to me. For the first time I understood the ferocious desire for privacy and independence of the natural traveller; to disappear into the background and move around without being counted, itemised, assessed and generally clocked in is the ultimate desire of those of us who have seen the other side of civilisation and attempt to flee its embracing tentacles.

On the third day of walking about my local patch, turned out of my temporary home until the evening, I was beginning to panic. I wasn't sure how long Stacey would be kept on shelf-stacking – if she was returned to the checkout the whole plan could fall to pieces, but, just as I was considering more drastic measures to obtain cash, it – literally – fell into my lap. I had been on my feet all morning and, beginning to tire, sat down on the ground at the fringe of the paved precinct of Westminster Cathedral, just outside McDonald's. I knew it wouldn't take long before I was moved on – the previous two days had quickly taught me the rudiments of living rough in London – but I leant my head back against the glass window and closed my eyes, happy to snatch a few moments of rest. I didn't see who chucked the coins at me: whether it was out of genuine compassion, or whether perhaps a guilty soul on the way to or from confession felt a small gesture might ensure a better reception from the Almighty I shall never know. In any case, the £1.60 scattered on the stone in front of me would be ample for my needs. I silently thanked whatever angel or devil had brought it to me and stood up quickly, ready to make a move.

I glanced across the road at SavaMart, but knew it would

be impossible to make my purchase there: it would be hard enough to carry out the second part of the plan as it was, but to risk two excursions would be pushing my luck. I turned and began to walk along the main road towards the Army & Navy, keeping my head down and my eyes on the ground in the way I had become used to since wanting to avoid all contact with other people. I had a life quite full enough inside my own head: to allow anyone else in – even in the form of a split second's eye contact or a muttered 'excuse me' would overcrowd it to the point of danger.

After a few minutes' walk I came across a perfect anonymous Asian convenience store and, after a little deliberation, chose a jar of baby rice as being the most suitable. I added a loaf of bread to keep up my strength, and was able to pay for them and stuff them into the proffered small plastic bag without having to meet the eyes of the indifferent man at the checkout. I carried my precious ammunition out of the store and into the back streets. I found a quiet spot and, after checking for any evidence of one of the ubiquitous, infernal cameras that are proliferating in the city, prised open the lid of the jar as carefully as I could, avoiding, as far as possible, bending it or marking the surface. I had my other pieces of equipment at the ready: I reached into my pocket for the broken pieces of razor blade and for the earring, which was dirty and a little fluffy from its journeying in my well-worn jacket over the last few days, but still clearly identifiable as Stacey's. With my middle finger I carefully plunged my booty into the jar, the cheap earring glinting on the surface for a second before I pushed it deep to the bottom, the oily grime ingrained on my skin leaving a tiny dark ring where it penetrated the creamy white of the rice. The sharp shards of steel came next, the rice oozing out of the top of the jar as I again pushed my finger into it, leaving the pieces of blade hidden just beneath the surface. I replaced the lid, snapped it back in place and wiped the jar with the edge of my sleeve before putting it in my pocket.

Stacey

Well, that's a relief! I never thought he'd go so quick and without a fuss. Just goes to show you never can tell. I almost felt sorry for the silly old bugger, in fact, but, as my mum says, I never asked him for nothing and he had his kicks out of me, didn't he? Well, I know he paid for the op and that, but it ain't much to him — he's got loads of money. Sheila says anyone what lives in them houses where he and his wife do must have got plenty of cash. So I bet he's gone back there to her now and realised what a daft thing he done in coming to me. Still, I give him a good time, didn't I? It's not like he didn't get nothing out of the relationship, as it says in *Cosmo*. Anyway, I don't need to worry about him no more — that's over as far as I'm concerned, and as far as he's concerned too, I expect. Well out of it, both of us.

Warren took it all right when I tell him. He looked a bit shocked, of course, 'cos, to be honest, I'm not sure just how much he remembers about that night. I mean — he was sober enough to get it up, so it's not like he didn't want to do it or nothing (I never could see how that girl in America got done for rape, like Denisha told me. That's just plain stupid.) But it's not like he was begging me to let him do it neither. I mean, it's only fair that I should be the one to take care of it. I can't wait in fact. And I told him he don't need to worry — I'm having this baby whatever happens, but I don't need him to look after it: me and my mum can manage all

286

that. If he wants to see it then that's fine – I'm not gonna stop him, am I? But he don't have to feel obliged.

And I'm getting on great at work. I'm gonna stay right to the last minute of my pregnancy, then I'll take my maternity leave and go back after, and my mum can look after the baby. It's all gonna work out really well, I can just feel it. They say I'm OK when I go for my checks – they're gonna make me go in extra on account of the op and that, and 'cos I'm still bigger than the ideal for a first, they say. But I know it's gonna be fine – I'm still losing every time I weigh myself, and when you think there's something growing at the same time inside and getting bigger while I'm getting smaller it's kind of miraculous. Maybe I really do have an angel.

I'm on shelf-stacking again all this week. I feel right proud when customers ask me where they can find something and I take them over to the correct aisle and stuff – I never coulda done that in the old days. Not that they'd've let me loose in the store in any case – just kept me prisoner behind the checkout. That was all I was good for. I was in ever so early this morning doing the refilling and checking. Me and Sheila was having ever such a laugh and trying to get through it quick so we could go and have a bit of a break in the canteen and she could have a quick ciggie out the back. She let me do all the baby stuff, 'cos she knows I love doing that: it makes me so excited when I put all the lovely shiny packs of nappies out, and the little cotton buds and stuff.

Some fucking idiot had dumped an old jar of baby rice right at the front of the baby-food shelf – I could see it wasn't right straight away, 'cos the pop-up seal had gone. I couldn't be arsed to fill in a docket for it so I just chucked it (I'm not really a docket person, if truth be told). You find all sorts at the shop: people open packets and try stuff, or damage the goods on purpose to try and get them cheap. But we're wise to them, you see. I get quite proud of keeping an eye out for that kinda stuff in fact.

Warren's asked me out for a drink tonight so we can talk about the baby. Sometimes I think I'm dreaming, the way everything's going. You shoulda seen the way he looked at me this morning when he thought I didn't know he was watching me: it was amazing. Sort of pride mixed with — well, I dunno, what shall I call it? Lust, I suppose. Fucking amazing.

Charlie

Oh, God — what have I done? I'm a reasonable man, I'm not a monster. What came over me — how can I have done such a dreadful, dreadful thing? It's been weeks now and I can't think of anything else.

I went back to the shop within hours and the wretched thing had gone. For a few minutes I didn't care who saw me — even the terrible Chipstead or — or she herself. I swear to God I just wanted to make it right: I walked in without looking about me and went straight up to the baby aisle — I was going to take it away again, I really was. I was, dear God — I was. But it had gone. I went over to the checkouts, hoping in some mad way that I might see it in a basket, or piled on a conveyor belt, but there were only two in use and I could quickly see it wasn't there. I walked out again and rushed up and down the street in a frenzy — I knew people were looking at me and I must have made a strange figure, but I didn't care. I just needed to do something, find someone to tell.

I did grab one woman with a pram and tried to ask her if she had just bought some baby rice, but the poor thing looked frightened half to death, so I moved quickly away, having satisfied myself that her pram held no evidence of any SavaMart shopping.

No wonder she was scared: it's only when I see myself reflected in a shop window or in the back of a spoon at the shelter that I understand how peculiar-looking I've become. It astonishes me just how quickly I've reverted to something from an ancient, untamed past. I'm like a street reclaimed by nature: the paving stones shifting and tipping under the barrage of growth from below; the road, covered in moss and filthy debris, cracking and splitting to reveal the sprouting grasses beneath until it's no longer passable. That's me. My face is surrounded by a mass of wild, greying hair, unwashed and unbrushed, and the long stubble of my beard and moustache, never shaved now more frequently than every three or four days, is striped dark and white like a badger, springing from the grimy background of my filthy face. The expensive cut of my suit, shiny now with spilt food and dirt, only adds to the oddness of the effect: a well-dressed tramp.

But up to now at least the animal appearance was no reflection of the man within: in spite of everything that has taken place, in spite of the cruel way I've treated my family I have at least remained reasonably human in my actions. Now I can say that no longer: I may be a baby killer. I see blood pouring from tiny innocent lips, I see a mother sobbing over a limp little body. I know now I should have gone straight to the police and told them what I had done, but in my half-mad state I still wanted her to get the blame. I still do. But I never wanted anyone hurt. Now it's too late. God help me – where can I go? Who can ever help me?

Now

Judy

Once I'd bought the disks I was reluctant to go home again, in spite of the cold. I toyed with the idea of taking the long route back to avoid any chance of seeing the hateful girl, but, as so often, I was drawn, as if by a malevolent magnet, to risk spotting her by going the quick way past the shop. I'd seen her several times over the past months: first looking far less fat and surprisingly well-groomed – thanks to the obsessive attentions of MY husband, as I bitterly told myself over and over in the middle of the night – and then, slowly, growing again in size until her pregnancy was obvious. I had no way of knowing whether this child was Charlie's of course, and the uncertainty helped to inflict on me another, peculiarly effective form of torture.

When she first started appearing at the shop with the pram, it was always the oily manager who greeted her and picked up and kissed the baby. And now she's back at work, she arrives and leaves with him, while the wretched baby is presumably farmed out somewhere to be cared for by a minder. What their relationship is I can only guess at: I'd love to believe it's his baby – he doesn't look the type to take on another man's leftovers – but I can't tell. I've never seen Charlie there, much as I can't help myself looking. I dread it and long for it – I so much want to know he's OK, but I think if I saw them together I just wouldn't be able to take it.

So I started on the direct route towards home and, as I neared the brightly lit window of the shop, steeled myself for a glimpse of her, if I should find the urge to glance through it irresistible. But she wasn't there, and I felt the usual mix of relief and disappointment wash over me as I turned and walked on towards the post office.

Something was niggling at me as I continued along the street, and I knew there was a thought at the back of my mind that had to be resolved before I reached home, although I couldn't pinpoint what it was. As I once more approached the huddled figures in the doorway next to the post office, I idly wondered whether they would recognise me as the woman who had given them the fifty pence only half an hour or so before, and whether they'd leave me alone or try again, seeing me as a soft touch.

Then it hit me. It was my wondering about recognition that had triggered it, and I stopped, startled and confused, as something unbelievable and frightening occurred to me. It was I who had done the recognising. And not now, but on my journey out. Without being aware of it, I had seen the separate parts and fitted the picture together, only to have it dismissed by my conscious mind as being – presumably – too preposterous to take seriously.

One of the desperate, huddled figures was Charlie.

Once I'd looked at him for the second time, directly and for several seconds, it was so obvious I couldn't think how I could have made the journey all the way to Dixons and back without acknowledging it. What did I feel? It's impossible to know: even as I was going through the rush of sensations and emotions a part of me was standing back and trying to judge my own reactions, but I couldn't make any sense of them. All I know is that I didn't hesitate to squat down beside him and take his hand. A hand so well known to me and at the same time so alien with its long, filthy fingernails and fine covering of dirt. He was looking at me but I wasn't sure if he knew who I was: there was so much sadness and hopelessness in the eyes that it took my breath away and I found it hard to speak for a second or two.

'Charlie?' I said at last. 'Charlie, it's me. Judy.'

'I know.'

It was startling to hear the firm clarity of his voice — it was the only obvious remnant of the old Charlie and it sounded unchanged: if I'd closed my eyes he could have been the man of just over a year ago.

'Are you here to see her? Are you watching for her?' God knows how I found the strength to ask him. I sounded as calm as if I were discussing a business meeting, or a visit to the dentist, not enquiring about the relationship of my husband with his lover.

The effect of the question was far from calm, however. To my horror, I saw his face crumple up and tears appear in the eyes that were still fixed on mine. 'No, no!' he said loudly, and moved his hand up my arm to grip my elbow. 'Oh, God in heaven, no, Judy! It's you. I sit here hoping to see you. And every so often I do — when I'm not moved on, that is. It's all that keeps me going.'

I was as surprised by the threatened appearance of my own tears as I'd been horrified by his. I took a deep breath and stood up, pulling my arm away from his hand. Briskness was my defence against sentiment.

'Is that true, Charlie? Or are you still hoping to catch a glimpse of your tart? How the hell did you get like this?'

To my amazement, one of the other anonymous bundles came to life and looked up at me. It was one of the younger ones, a boy whose uncared-for appearance always particularly upset me. 'It is you,' he said, and managed a small smile as he nudged Charlie hard in the ribs. 'It's Judy this and Judy that and why was I such a fool and on and on he goes. Take him away, for Christ's sake — he's boring us all to death.'

So I did. I've never thought of myself as especially moral or conscientious — certainly not more than the average person

– but I have to admit I felt a huge sense of self-righteousness as I scrubbed, changed, warmed and fed the wretched creature that had been my husband. My personal Lazarus.

We've a long way to go. We don't talk about it much, but it's always there, as an uninvited, unwelcome guest in our home: a shadowy, threatening presence that never quite lets us forget it's there. Charlie is coming back – slowly – but he's coming back to a different world, one where his wife is more wary and cynical, and where trust is going to be a long time coming. And there's a little haunted corner of him that I can't reach: it's not surprising that he is filled with guilt and remorse – and I can't say I'm altogether sorry that he is – but I can feel that something happened over the past year that has left him with a terrible burden I can never quite penetrate. In many ways his behaviour is almost like the old Charlie, but there are certain things that betray him: I often wake in the night and find his bed empty (yes, we do share a room, if not the same bed) and when I try to question him he just shakes his head and says something about never being able to forgive himself, or that he'll never know for sure. Words to that effect, in any case. About what, I can't make him say, and I'm not at all sure I want to.

When we take one of our regular afternoon walks (it seems so much easier, somehow, to feel real when we're outside the house) I've noticed how he watches young children with a look of terrible sadness. Ben and Sally are both away now, of course, but I swear I see more than simply nostalgia for our children in the way he glances into prams or gazes at toddlers strapped into their buggies. Almost as if they make him feel especially guilty. And that's why I don't want to know for sure what he did – if he was the father of that child, if he instinctively looks for it in every baby we see, then I don't want to know that. The only way for us is forward – if we look back we shall fall and never rise again.